I0542463

Summer's End
(Once Times Thrice)

DIANNA HARDY

Summer's End
(Once Times Thrice)

Published by Satin Smoke Press, June, 2016
First Edition | ISBN 978-0957540453
This print version updated August, 2023

This book is set in 11.5 pt Cormorant Garamond Medium by the Cormorant
Project Authors, licensed under the SIL Open Font License, Version 1.1

Written in British English.

Satin Smoke Press
(an imprint of Bitten Fruit Books)
Hampshire, United Kingdom

www.satinsmoke.com

Acknowledgements

I've not been online very much at all since November last year, and I would like to thank my readers and the Satin Smoke team for their patience, because writing has been 'testing' for me in 2016. It's been a challenge and a struggle in many respects, and hasn't quite eased yet. It will though.

Big thanks to Amanda Pederick, my editor, for her work and for answering my many questions (read: putting up with me) about grammar and sentence structure, and my British English, in-house "Dianna" ways.

Thank you to Elizabeth Morgan, talented author and good friend, who offers an undying amount of unconditional support. You are so valued!

Lastly, a huge thanks to Alastair, my fiancé. This year (and the past three years) has been a real juggle of work, home and family, without enough leisure and play. The winds of change are coming ... for the better. xxx

Dianna
June, 2016

Once times thrice,
unbind thine heart from mine
so we may finally...

~*~

Summer's End

Prologue

*H*er hands shook; the candle flickered. "Once times thrice..."

The shadows on the walls moved like ghosts.

But why was it dark? Wasn't it supposed to be morning?

"...unbind thine heart..."

Wind whistled through the open window. Distracted by a loose wisp of hair covering her eyes, she shook her head to be rid of it, then found herself looking around her, at her bedroom – their bedroom – at the bed.

There she lay, asleep.

Oh. This was a dream – she was dreaming. Why?

She looked back down at the piece of paper in her hands. Because you never finished the spell.

The stupid spell. That's right – she'd lost it. This was her second chance to get it right.

"...from mine, so we may finally—" The wind blew out the candle, plunging her into darkness. "No."

It wasn't pitch black – she could make out some shapes. She looked down at the paper. Despite the faint light, she couldn't decipher the last word. What was it? What was it?

"It's okay, you can say it."

She jumped, startled, and turned towards the voice – the one that came from her bed. It was no longer she who lay on it, but a man that sat upon it, his silhouette enticingly familiar; his voice she knew too well.

She took a step to the left to try and see him better. "David?"

"You can say it, Pip."

"Say what?"

"The last word."

"No. I can't." Even from here, in this light, she could see the blood covering his head; staining his shirt.

"Why not?"

"You're not dead."

"I'm not living."

"You're alive."

"But not living."

"Stop saying that."

"It's true."

She shook her head in denial.

"Don't you remember?"

"Remember what?"

"This." He held up a small, red envelope.

She shook her head again, this time in confusion. "What is that?"

He smiled a sad smile. "You didn't want me to write it, but I had to."

"What are you talking about?"

"The tree."

The tree ... Oh – that tree. Their tree. "You went back to the tree?"

"I felt it was important. They were things I wanted to say. I want you to open the envelope. But first, you have to say the last word."

She shook her head, vigorously; stubbornly. "I don't want to."

The window was flung fully open, and wind rushed around the room. She let out a cry as everything went flying, the spell torn right out of her hand. Again. "No!"

She might not be ready to say it, but neither was she ready to give it up. Had she blown her second chance? She wasn't sure she'd get a third. "Stop!"

The paper flew right out the window, just as it had before, but this time, she chased it – swung her leg out of the window, paying no mind to the drop as she landed on her front lawn, expecting to feel pain shooting through her ankles; feeling nothing instead, such was the way of dreams.

The wind took the paper speeding through the air. She ran after it, not really knowing where she was going. All the streets looked strange, and they shouldn't because this was her home – this was where she'd grown up. But nothing looked like home.

She sprinted like a deer escaping the lion's claws; or perhaps she was the hunter running down her only meal. She ran so fast, she almost didn't stop in time, and yelled in alarm when the road ended right in front of her – gave way to a cavernous drop of which she could see no bottom, only unending darkness.

The wind teased the paper above her, directly over the massive hole, far too high for her to reach; then, the wind became a breeze, dropping the spell – her only way out – onto the other side of the ominous canyon. With a soft rustle, it tumbled along the ground, rolling even further away, down two monstrously high walls that formed an alleyway, until she could no longer see it.

Her face threatening to crumple, she swallowed back tears.

"What are you going to do now?"

She turned around, and there David was, still bloody and pale, but standing now, his hands in his pockets as he looked beyond the rip in the road to where the paper had *disappeared.*

"I don't know." A drop of blood fell from his head to the cement under their feet, in time with her first drop of tears. "David, you're hurt."

He stared at her, strangely. "I'm okay."

"You're not okay. You're bleeding. Let me clean you up."

"You can't. This is as good as I get now. But you can get better." He pointed at her chest.

She looked down, shocked to see blood staining her own top, spreading outwards from the centre of her breast. Every time her heart beat, more blood pooled, and the stain got bigger. "I ... I don't know how to fix it."

"It certainly is a puzzle." He turned back to the broken road. "But sometimes to find the answer, you have to take a leap of faith."

Her eyes widened, not sure if he was insinuating what she thought he was.

"You need to jump."

Fear clawed at her. "I can't jump that. That's huge. I'll never make it."

"That's why it's a leap of faith."

"No. It's suicide. That gap's got to be at least twelve feet wide."

"But they made it across." He now pointed to the other side of the canyon.

She strained to see as far as she could down that dark alleyway that looked like it swallowed all living things. She heard the sounds before she saw the glimmer of light: laughter.

Children laughing.

The glimmer of light grew, until the alleyway looked a little less foreboding, and she could now see the source of the light was the sun, shining on a patch of grass. Three figures bound gleefully around in it, playing.

Her breath caught. "Becca ... Liam..."

"And Sammy. There they are."

"Why aren't they in bed?"

"Because it's morning, Pip."

She turned back to him, confused.

"You're just standing in the dark."

Something cold landed on her nose. She looked up. "Snow."

"And you're standing in the cold."

It was cold, and getting colder with every snowflake that fell. She wrapped her arms around herself. She was wearing summer clothes. "Come with me. Jump with me."

He smiled, eyes glistening with tears. "I have to stay here."

She broke, a sudden sob escaping her. "I can't do it alone."

"You won't be alone. As long as you take that leap."

She looked back at her kids – her world – they were her world now. And they needed her. She had to try for them.

Shaking uncontrollably – or perhaps the shivering had set in from the cold snow, now falling thick and fast – she stepped back, and back again, taking step after step until she was sure she had a long enough run for the jump. Never gonna make it...

"You're going to make it," David said. "I love you." His voice cracked. "You're going to make it because I love you."

"I love you, too."

A gun fired.

The starting pistol! RUN.

Oh, god... Quick! She wasn't prepared for this sudden urgency that dominated everything. With the blood on her shirt blooming with the pounding of her heart, and snow *swirling up a blizzard, she took off against it all, the soles of her bare feet burning as they hammered against the cement of the road. She ran faster than she ever had before, because she had to make it. Had to make it for her kids.*

The edge was there before she knew it, and ready or not, she took the leap, felt her feet leave the safety of everything she'd known, no matter how unfamiliar it all seemed now. Only in mid-air did it occur to her she might actually live. She might actually make it, though it was too soon to tell. The edge was so far away.

She threw her weight forward; pushed air with her feet. She could see the landing, but ... God, no! *She wasn't near enough!*

A scream pierced the air.

It was Sammy, staring up at her.

No! They aren't supposed to see this! They aren't sup-posed to see me fail!

He opened his mouth, and screamed again.

Pippa woke up, heart thudding, sweating, eyes wide open, trying to grasp at what was happening.

Screaming...

"Sammy." She leapt out of bed, opened her door, and half-ran to his room, almost stumbling – she felt so disori-entated.

He was having another nightmare. It was the same most mornings – they always seemed to wake him at about six-thirty.

She rushed into his room, a disturbing sense of her own bad dream pressing on the edges of her consciousness, but anything she might have remembered was obliterated by her son's need. "Sammy..."

He was tucked into a ball under his covers, eyes still closed, crying.

"Sammy, wake up. Mummy's here." She gathered him into her arms, and held him against her as he came out of his terror.

Finally awake, he flung his arms around her, and buried his head into her neck, shaking and sobbing.

"I've got you. You're okay. Everything's okay."

You're going to make it.

She frowned, trying to get at the abstract memory as she pressed Sammy closer to her. Had David been in her dream? She couldn't recall, and it frustrated her more than she'd like. What she remembered most now, was that last day they'd shared. It haunted her persistently. He'd been in the garden, laying down the new patio just a few hours before the accident. It had begun to snow. She'd told him he was mad for laying it now – wait 'til the spring, or summer. He'd replied, if it didn't get done now, it would never get done at all.

He'd been right. That square patio tile still lay there, untouched from where he'd left it after they'd wisely decided there were better things to do in the house on a weekday when the kids were at school, and he had a rare morning off work.

They'd made love instead.

She'd squealed and thrilled at his winter-chilled hands from his labour in the garden. The moment had been bliss. He'd wanted to stay home all day after that – make love again. He'd boyishly teased he'd throw a sickie – something he hadn't done since he was seventeen – but the meeting he'd had that afternoon at his architectural company was far too important; the very last of the year before being handed his big partnership.

"Sod them. They don't have you for a wife – they don't understand."

She laughed. "Don't you dare – you have to go. You've been waiting for this since forever."

She brought her mind out of the past, and kissed the top of Sammy's head. His crying had eased; turned into sniffles rather than sobs. "You okay, my man?"

He nodded against her, but didn't let her go.

She sighed to herself, and sat there, cradling him. She had nowhere to be in a hurry, anyway – not at six-thirty in the morning. And it seemed like Becca hadn't been woken this time by Sammy's screaming. If Liam had, he'd stayed in his room.

What day was it?

Thursday. That's right – yesterday, they'd gone on the boat trip for Merri's birthday, sans Merri. *Might as well return the boat keys to the shop first thing, since you're up.*

Unbidden, an image of an ominous tunnel (or was it a long, narrow path?) came to mind, a field at the end of it, lit with sunshine.

Had she dreamt something like that? She racked her brain to no avail. It shouldn't make a difference, but she had that 'uneasy' feeling that always followed a disturbing dream. Remembering would be helpful so she could put it behind her.

She went back to planning the day out in her mind. She'd take the kids to her parents' house first, then drop the keys off at The Boat Shop, be back before ten, then the rest of the morning and afternoon would be theirs to do what they liked. There weren't many free days left; she'd have to go back to work soon, and the kids would be at school.

The house fell silent now Sammy had quietened down.

Loneliness pulled at her heart. It always seemed silent now.

She glanced at the doorway, imagining a dishevelled, just-woken-up David standing there with a smile and a cup of tea for her, asking how Sammy was; asking if she'd like him to take over.

Emptiness filled the space instead.

And silence reigned.

I
The Alley

With moments like the fabulous day they'd had yesterday, Pippa could almost forget.

They'd still gone out in the boat they'd hired for Merri's birthday, despite Merri not being able to be there: Liam, Sammy, Becca and herself. And Candy had come along, despite her looking as tired as Pippa felt, and she'd been so damn grateful because Candy was a laugh – *so* much fun to be around.

Jamie had been sorely missed. Having her brother home again was like a breath of fresh air for her – she hadn't told him how much so – but it was important he stayed up in London with Merri right now, helping her to arrange her mother's funeral and everything else there was to do.

A pang of envy sneaked its way into her heart as she strolled up the road towards The Boat Shop. *Merri can move forward – what about you?*

She pushed the thought right out, not wanting to diminish the memory of yesterday's glorious sunset across the waves, and how much fun her kids had had. So much fun, that Becca and Liam had both woken refreshed and revitalised, just fifteen minutes after Sammy had screamed the place down. Amazingly, neither of them had heard him.

Liam had wanted to go to Gran's for breakfast, and although Pippa inwardly cringed at the advantage she'd been taking of her parents' support, she'd wanted to do the same – had wanted the bustle of home, and the smell of eggs and bacon she didn't have to cook. She'd hauled her two bouncy kids, and a grumpy, crusty-eyed Sammy out of the house and driven the ten minutes to her mum and dad's house.

She'd left Liam learning chess with his grandfather, Becca trying to do cartwheels in the garden, and Sammy in front of the TV, still not quite awake.

Paper cup of coffee in hand, she wondered why she'd thought it would be a good idea to swing by first thing and drop the boat keys off at the hire shop. She glanced at her watch. Eight-thirty in the morning. Shit. It probably wasn't even open yet. What had possessed her to rush over here?

For something to do? To get away, get away, get away, get away...

Standing still was a curse. There was far too much time to think when she stood still, and yet 'still' was all there was. She didn't know how to move in any direction, so she didn't move. The world rushed onwards. She didn't.

Only, the past few days, it had been different. Meeting Merri and Candy, and having Jamie home... Some gear had shifted, but she wasn't familiar with the vehicle, and she didn't feel like the driver.

She grimaced, wryly, at her ironic analogy.

She found herself standing still, once more, on the path in front of The Boat Shop. Its shutters were down. Great. She didn't fancy going back though, without having accomplished something, so she wandered up towards the shack-like building. She guessed the front door to the residential part of the property was situated down the side of the shop. No doubt it would have a letterbox, or she couldn't see how the postman would deliver anything out of opening hours.

Just pop the keys through it.

She glanced at the two sets in her hand, pulled a face and took another sip of coffee. She should have stuck them in an envelope with a note or something. She hadn't thought this through.

Never mind. He'd know which boat they belonged to.

Half of her feeling determined, and half of her feeling like she shouldn't really be here, she gingerly walked up towards the shop, and then skirted around the closed shutters to the side access. It formed a long alleyway, with a dumpster flush against the wall, three black bin bags – full and tied – opposite the dumpster, and bits of litter on the ground. *Nice, Jimmy. Ever tidy?* She couldn't recall him having been scruffy or unkempt as a kid.

Jimmy, who owned The Boat Shop, had been her brother's best friend since early childhood. Both of them named James had caused far too much confusion for everyone, so her brother had become 'Jamie', his new-found friend had become 'Jimmy', and the nicknames had stuck. Problem solved. Jamie and Jimmy – a double act of their own, and often inseparable. Two years younger than she, they'd kind of annoyed the crap out of her when they were together, though she'd always gotten on fine with her brother on his own. In fact, Jamie had always seemed more mature and grown-up when it was just him. When with Jimmy, everything had descended into very basic humour and frivolities.

When she was sixteen, it had become apparent Jimmy was crushing on her big time, although he'd said nothing to her about it directly.

As if! had been her teenaged inner-response. Not that she'd told him she knew he fancied her, because he'd been strangely shy as a child in some respects. The bravado he'd often demonstrated when with Jamie, she had noticed was not commonplace when on his own. Jimmy had been a little podgy back then, and his blond hair had had a hint of ginger in it. It probably hadn't helped that his surname was Darling. Stupid things kids picked on, and he *had* gotten picked on at school, although she only knew about it because Jamie had told her so. He'd also told her off for being hard on him. It had gotten under her skin at the time – how protective Jamie had been of him. Probably because he'd been as protective of Jimmy, as she was of Jamie.

A sharp clatter came from inside the building. Someone yelped.

Pippa froze.

Two shadows lunged towards the single pane of frosted glass that made up the small window by the front door (or was it the side door?), until they were smacked up against it.

"The mug!"

"Leave it. Didn't break."

"Fuck! Jimmy..."

Panting...

"Holy shit."

Grunting...

And just in case the rhythmic movements of the shadows against the window weren't clear enough, there was an "Oooooh, god – *god*! Jimmy ... don't stop."

Right. So ... she had to leave. Like – *now*.

Her face felt aflame. This was way too much info – in HD and stereo. This was like walking in on her brother and Merri while they were ... *Eeeew!*

Too bad the alleyway was narrower than a narrow boat.

Too bad she forgot there were three large rubbish bags behind her.

Too bad the coffee in her left hand, and keys in the right hand, crippled her of any balance she might have had when she stepped right on top of one of the bags, and the bulk under her foot rolled.

She slipped.

Oh, no.

And try as she might to make no noise at all, a small cry left her lungs when she fell hard onto the rubbish, any gratitude that it had cushioned her fall completely extinguished by the fact that the bag directly under her burst. Something cold and wet (and possibly squishy) spread along the seat of her jeans. *Gross, gross, gross!* And she must have squeezed her coffee, because the lid flew off and warm wet splashed all over her light jumper, across her chest. *Shit.*

"What the fuck is that?"

"Ssshhhh – don't move."

She could hear a scramble for what she assumed was clothes. She wondered if she could scramble the hell out of there before the door opened, but no sooner had she wondered it than the fucking door opened, and a thunderous-looking, naked-except-for-jeans Jimmy pummelled out of it, ready to attack whatever intruder might be lurking.

His expression morphed from furious to surprised when his eyes landed on her. His eyebrows went up slowly. Bemusement lit the blue of his eyes, somehow bringing the point home that he stood there in nothing but denim.

So fucking what? You've seen him in piddly swimwear in your paddling pool.

"Pip?"

She might be covered in coffee and dubious bits of ... *things* ... but she was never one to show signs of incompetence when confronted. "So," she began, in an authoritative tone that sounded like she knew exactly what she was doing and was totally meant to fall onto bins, "I've got a really busy day, Jimmy, so I came to drop the boat keys off first thing, and lost my footing in your *hazardous* alleyway. What the hell? You're lucky the council hasn't stopped by."

Jimmy grinned.

It dazzled her for all of two seconds, confusing her, but that was only because her heart was pounding in her ears and she was trying her damnedest to come out of this with a shred of dignity intact.

So it was annoying that she knew he saw through her act. Of course he bloody did. He knew her almost as well as her brother did. "You should have seen it yesterday. I've cleaned it since then. Not my fault this alley's a wind trap. Every bit of crap comes rolling down here."

Miss whoever-he-was-shagging chose that moment to appear in the doorway, wearing an oversized shirt she assumed wasn't hers. She looked down at Pippa and pulled a face. "Yuck! Eeeew. It *does* look like every bit of crap comes rolling down here."

What the... Was that a reference to *her*?

A flutter of irritation crossed Jimmy's face – at least she thought it did – then he was all smiles again, winked at Pippa, and turned to— "Emma, best call it a day. I've got to open the shop soon anyway."

She stared at him, not looking like she really believed him. "Call it a day? We've only just got up. Can't we ... you know."

Pippa forced herself not to smile. *Sorry, love, didn't meant to spoil your orgasm.* She caught herself and shook her head. What the hell was she thinking? She was nearly thirty-three, not fifteen!

And this girl's ... what? No more than twenty, surely?

Whatever – not her business. Refusing to think any more catty thoughts (she gave herself reprieve for being covered in trash), she tried to get up.

Jimmy bounced down the porch steps. "Seriously, Emma – we'll catch up another day. I'm gonna help Pip get cleaned up." He held out his hand for Pippa to take.

Reluctantly, she did.

He hauled her up, and whatever had soaked into the seat of her jeans now ran down the back of her leg. "Ugh."

"You can say that again," he teased, as he pulled something from her hair. Lettuce.

Nice.

"I think I ate the rest of this two days ago."

She threw him a murderous look.

He laughed. "Come on. There's a shower in here you can use."

"Jimmy," squeaked Emma, still protesting.

What was her deal? Selfish much? Anyone else would let the woman wearing two-day-old lettuce have a bloody shower. But Pippa put her own claws away, not wanting to get into it, and addressed Jimmy directly. "I'm sorry I ruined your morning."

"Oh, come on – morning's only just begun. And you look more ruined than me."

She smirked, wryly. "Thanks."

"You're welcome." He led her into the building, and Emma finally seemed to understand she wasn't going to change Jimmy's mind. She huffed before turning back into the room, not bothering to shut the door, and angrily hunted for her clothes. Pippa glanced at Jimmy. He didn't appear bothered about her reaction as he went to close the door himself. Maybe she was always like this.

The wind whipped two leaves onto the doormat, and brushed against her bare toes in her sandalled feet, just before it pushed the door shut, with a bang, a little harder than Jimmy had intended. "See?" he gestured at the frame.

"Wind trap."

She threw him a lop-sided smile of appeasement, and tried not to think about the fact that he was having sex *right here* just two minutes ago. Some uneasy sensation stirred in her belly.

Jealousy? Really?

Wonderful. *Because you miss David. Because you miss sex. Because you miss love.*

Yeah, she shouldn't be too hard on his girlfriend. *Make the most of it, sweetheart, 'cause it can be taken from you in the blink of an eye.*

He led her away from the kitchen-lounge area, and down a ... it wasn't really a hall – just a small space around a corner, barely big enough for two. When she was out of Emma's line of vision, she stopped him with a hand on his arm. "Wait – look, say sorry to your girlfriend from me, okay? Really, I just came to drop the keys off. I was going to post them through the letterbox then leave, and then... Well, I fell."

He looked at her knowingly. "I'm sorry we surprised you."

Her face might have just burst into flames.

"And she's not my girlfriend. Here..." He leant forward, almost right in to her, and opened a door directly behind her.

She found her eyes level with his chest. When the hell had he filled out so ... perfectly? Okay, stupid question. Of course he'd filled out, he wasn't a kid anymore. He was – what – thirty? Thirty-one? She couldn't recall when his birthday was exactly, but he was the same age as Jamie, give or take a few months. And both her brother and Jimmy had loved water sports and surfing. Jamie had told her Jimmy surfed a lot now, and something about being a surfing instructor, or setting up to be one. He wasn't unfit, and he hadn't been podgy for a damn long time. She'd just never had a reason to *look* before.

I'm not looking. It's not my fault his bare chest is in my face. "Not your girlfriend?"

He raised an eyebrow at her, but gave no response. "Shower's in here."

She took a step into the wet room behind her. "You know, I could just go home and shower."

"You want to sit on that dark patch on your trousers while you're driving? Not to mention that unique aroma clinging to you."

She grimaced.

"Soap's in the shower; so's the shampoo, although it's man shampoo."

"I'm not fussed."

"This blue towel on the railing's mine. It's the only one I've got washed, but I only used it once last night, so it's clean."

She waved him off. "That's fine." She wondered if his not-girlfriend had used it. Then wondered why it mattered.

He stared at her a beat.

Was her question obvious on her face or something? *Maybe you have ketchup on your face.*

A door slammed.

Pippa jumped, then looked at Jimmy, surprised. "Was that Emma leaving? Without saying goodbye?"

He shrugged. "Yeah, she can be—"

"Young?"

This time, his eyebrows almost hit his hairline.

She inwardly cursed her quick tongue. What was wrong with her mouth today?

"Moody." There was a pause. "I seem to attract moody

women." He smiled again. "Don't worry, big sis – she's old enough."

Automatically, she rolled her eyes at him. Internally, she bristled at that 'big sis' reference. It made her feel bloody ancient.

"When you've finished, you can go into the bedroom – it's the next door along. I've got clothes in the shop – mainly beach stuff – but I'll put some of it out on the bed and you can take your pick, okay?"

"That's great. Thanks so much for this."

He looked at her as if she was a little daft. "You're family."

Jimmy left the shower room, leaving her feeling a little perplexed at everything – also at the warmth that had ignited at his mention of 'family'. Yeah, she supposed they were like family, or had been once upon a time. It must have been over ten years since he'd last been round to one of their family gatherings though. Maybe she'd have to change that now Jamie was back. Throw a barbecue for them all before the end of summer, at her parents' house, just like they used to.

Closing and locking the door behind her, she stepped further into the tiled room, then stopped, unsure. Unsure of what, exactly, she couldn't say. She put it down to everything having already gone tits up only two hours into the day.

It only takes seconds for everything to change.

She tensed at the familiar churning in her stomach whenever *that* night came to the forefront of her mind. This morning was nothing like that – not at all – but the suddenness and unexpectedness of it felt startlingly similar, and equally unbalancing.

Pushing every single last thought she could manage out

of her head, she dropped the boat keys, still in her hand, onto the floor in the far corner of the wet room, peeked at the door again to make sure she'd locked it, then shed her ruined clothes.

He hadn't been lying; at least five different outfits lay across his haphazardly made bed.

She hadn't intended to spend long in the shower, but honestly – when you had bits of mouldy food on you, no amount of scrubbing seemed enough. When she'd finally come out, she'd strained her ears and had heard Jimmy out on the shop front. It sounded like he'd opened up, and she guessed that he received a decent daily footfall over the summer with this being the only shop of its kind nearby.

The residential part of the building was well-hidden from the commercial part, but she hadn't wanted to take any risks, so she'd tip-toed whilst holding her breath to his bedroom next door. Letting herself in, she'd then shut the door, groaned at the lack of lock, and had slid a chair up against the door handle instead.

Because that always works.

Only then had she let her breath out, to have it hitch again when she'd spied all the clothes on the bed.

He'd left the curtains still drawn.

He'd also left a small pot of coconut oil amongst the clothes – moisturiser. *Thank you!*

And here she was. In a bedroom that wasn't hers.

Looking around, she noted the sparseness of the room. Did he live here, or just use it occasionally? She actually had no idea, but if he did live here, he was a minimalist, because it seemed he only owned the basic necessities for day-to-day existence. She hadn't spotted a toothbrush in the shower room, though.

Again, she fleetingly wondered why she was giving Jimmy's habitat so much thought as she unwrapped the towel from her body and dried the ends of her hair. Her eye caught her reflection in the mirror on the wardrobe door. An image of Emma flashed into her mind quick as lightning, and almost as quick came the inward comparison before she could stop it. From what she could tell wearing an oversized shirt, the younger woman had looked ... well – much more magazine-ready than Pippa ever had. Even in her twenties, she hadn't been a slim size eight, but more a curvy size ten, and now... Her eyes fixed on her stretch marks, and she became entranced by them, every one carved into a frame that was perhaps a dress size larger than it had been ten years ago, but still curvy in what she, at least, thought was all the right places. Truth be told, she hadn't given her appearance too much thought in so many years. Enough to be happy with it, yes, but not enough to obsess about how she looked compared to every other mother in town.

Her body had borne three children, and she'd never had a problem with that. Right at this moment, though, she suddenly realised David had been a big part of her ease of mind. He'd loved her 'tiger marks' – that's what he'd called her stretch marks – her 'warrior's body' that had given them a family; three lives to love. He'd never given her reason to doubt her attractiveness, and she felt irritated that a sliver of doubt invaded her now. It was hardly the first insecurity she'd had about life since the accident, though.

Since he was taken from you.

Rapping shook the door.

She brought the towel tight to her chest with a start, forgetting for a second that she'd rammed a chair up against the door. "I'm ... just getting changed!"

"Okay, no rush. Just wanted to make sure you had all you need."

Her gaze flickered to the mirror, then back to the door. "I do. It's all great. Thanks so much."

"No problem. Shop's open now, just so you know when you walk out."

"Okay."

"Cool – see you in a bit. Oh, and I've put the kettle on."

She heard him walk away, and she rolled her eyes again. That was just like Jimmy to leave a sentence on a statement like that with no follow-up. *I've put the kettle on.* Did he mean, 'Would you like a cup of tea?' Did he mean, 'Help yourself to a hot drink.'? She didn't feel comfortable with the idea of helping herself. Even though she knew him well enough, she didn't know his lifestyle. And she didn't really know grown-up Jimmy, just kid Jimmy. They'd all lost touch a bit after her brother had left the country to go study in Australia. Strange really, when Jimmy and some of her school friends still lived so close by. None of them had much contact with each other now. The years had a tendency to do that. Time ensnared you in its web, and it became difficult to fly. She'd never minded too much – David her been her point of contact for most things. She'd had no back-up plan for losing that; for losing so much.

Something peppered across the window pane, and she snapped her head in that direction. Grit pulled along by a strong breeze? She couldn't tell for the curtain covering the glass. She had the urge to yank the drapes and window open; challenge the wind; yell out at nature's cruel games.

Fate's cruel games.

She also felt jittery; limbs and joints rusty against the morning, as if she was finally rousing from a hundred-year slumber. *Shouldn't get up so bloody early; you need more sleep.*

Shaking herself out of her crazy thoughts, she placed the towel on the bed post, and reached for the coconut oil. *Oil the rust away...*

Pippa eyed the selection of clothes, all with their tags still on, looking shiny and wonderful, a couple of tops still in their packaging. They even looked like the right fit.

The feeling that slithered through her next was probably more unexpected than anything that had happened that morning, because she hadn't felt it for so long. It almost felt new: *Excitement.*

Only a fraction of it, but it was there, and over such a simple thing, too: clothes. It had been a damn long time since she'd put on new clothes.

II
Her

It didn't matter; it didn't at all. That the woman he'd admired, and secretly (and not-so-secretly) cherished for most of his lifetime was getting changed in his poor excuse for a bedroom, having just stepped out of his poor excuse for a shower.

Nope. It didn't matter. Just like it hadn't mattered with any other woman he'd had over.

Who the fuck am I kidding?

This was Pippa, and he'd always cared what she'd thought. Above all others, Jimmy had hoped for her recognition; her approval. Lord knew why. When he was very young, he'd put his crush down to her protective nature. Something of a tigress whenever a loved one was challenged, she'd never failed to place a metaphorical shield around her little brother, Jamie, whenever he'd been in need. He'd seen it time and time again. None of his own four older siblings had ever done that for him, and he'd been in perpetual awe of it.

As he'd gotten older though, and understood that that's what most families did, and his own was just a little fucked up, his attraction for her hadn't diminished. Every girl was held next to Pippa in his mind, and none of them had compared. Jamie had teased him no end, albeit with an underlying sensitiveness that was simply his nature, and the reason they'd become the best of friends. Jamie, Pippa, and the whole Corbin family had been his lifeline; his buoyancy aid when he hadn't known he'd needed one, and he was pretty sure only Jamie knew the extent to which their friendship had saved his life. He'd never wanted Pippa to know about the great fail of a gene pool he'd come from, and because Jamie was Jamie – as loyal as Pippa – he'd promised not to say a word to his sister unless she outright asked him (he hadn't wanted to lie to her face, because *families don't do that to each other*). To his knowledge, she'd never asked.

Jimmy had played his parallel life out in his mind many times: he was pretty sure he'd have ended up in jail or something. That's where his eldest brother was now. With a dickhead for a dad, a mother who didn't give a shit, and two brothers and two sisters who seemed to take after them with no remorse, he'd often wondered if he'd have gone down the same route had nothing deterred him from it.

Jamie had deterred him. Pippa had. Their accepting, loving parents had. And Jimmy had understood, for the first time at the age of ten, that his life could be different. *He* could be different.

So, it mattered. It mattered more than was comfortable that Jamie's older sister – the girl, the woman, who had always been just out of reach – was in this shoddy, cheap-looking shack of a shop that reflected everything he'd never accomplished.

But also everything you have. Don't forget that.

He swore he sensed her before he saw her; *smelled* her, too – coconut smoothed over a subtle, earthy aroma that was just her, and always had been. Jesus, that went straight to his gut; warmed him from the inside out. Not a lot made him tremble nowadays, but she came close – still.

Tremble and collapse. She'll ruin you. That's what wo-

men do – cheap sluts, the lot of them.

He frowned; beat back a rising tide of anger. That was his dad's voice, not his. Why the crap he still heard it occasionally when he hadn't seen him for pushing on five years was a debilitating mystery he wished he could solve. He wanted rid of it. All of it. "Here's your change," he handed coins and a receipt to the teen over the counter, "and your bag."

He mumbled something before leaving. Jimmy assumed it was a thanks.

It was Thursday, and Thursdays weren't too busy, even over the summer, although it was a damn site better than when the season ended. Friday was when things kicked off, and stayed crazy for the whole weekend. He turned to greet Pip the second his customer left; tried not to look like he was the least bit affected by how fucking gorgeous she looked with her dark, wet hair tousled. "It all fits?"

He could have sworn she blushed, which threw him a little as she wasn't the least bit shy. But he might have imagined it, because she looked down, smoothed out a couple of wrinkles, then straightened her whole body when she came back up, head held high. He had it bad – real fucking bad, *still*, after twenty years – because that did it for him over pretty much everyone and everything else in the world: her committed refusal to take anything lying down. And hell ... she'd been through the wringer.

"It does. You should be a personal shopper."

He grinned. She'd chosen the knee-length, leaf print, pink and white skirt, and the loose, three-quarter-length sleeve, bohemian floral top in turquoise. Yep. If he was a betting man, that's what he'd have bet she'd pick: feminine and unrestrained. "I'll consider it if a career change is ever due. But you have no shoes."

They both looked down at her bare feet.

"Right. My left sandal had some weird sticky goo on it. I've washed it, but it's wet, and I didn't want to get your floor all covered in—"

He cut her off, walking past her to the flip-flops hanging up to the right of the front window display.

"No ... Jimmy."

"No? I'm not letting you go back to your mum, all the way across town, in bare feet." He pulled down a pair of size sixes.

"How do you know I'm going back to Mum's?" she asked, defensiveness creeping into her tone.

"It's a guess, based on you not having your kids with you." And he probably shouldn't have said anything – although he wasn't sure *exactly* what he'd said wrong – because the defensiveness expanded from her tone to her frame; became almost a physical thing. He ignored it. Pippa was often defensive – it came with the warrior territory. "Wherever you're going, you're going with sole." He grinned again. "Get it?"

Her lips twitched despite the tightness of her mouth. She caved in and rolled her eyes at him.

He considered that a win. Hidden message: *I accept you, even if you're an idiot.* He could deal with that. It was another wall down, at least temporarily, and he'd gotten a *lot* of eye rolls from her over the years. And had delighted in every one. Jamie was the only other person he'd seen her give eye rolls to, and he'd come to terms with the fact, a long time ago, that sisterly love was all he'd ever get from her. It was better than nothing. It was closeness. It would do.

He was pretty sure she knew he used to crush on her, even though he'd never told her directly. He'd sort of turned it into a bit of a joke – flirted a lot – to both hide it a little, and put her at ease and not scare her off; to let her know it was no big deal.

After she'd met David, the flirting thing wasn't appropriate anymore, so he'd made a conscious effort to withdraw from her life. David was 'the one', that had been clear, and the guy was decent – he liked him a lot. He couldn't say that about all the guys she'd gone out with before meeting David. None of them had got her; none of them had appreciated her strength and what she was capable of.

"Please bill me for the clothes and shoes."

"Nope. Consider them—"

"Jimmy—"

"—a bribe."

She looked at him in question. "A bribe? You're bribing me?"

"Yes. I give you nice clothes, you don't call the council on me."

Another eye roll – yes! He was on *fire* this morning.

"I'm not going to call the council on you!"

"See? The bribe is working already."

She yanked the flip-flops out of his hand. "Dork."

"A dork with no fines from the local government, yes?"

"Jimmy," she admonished, with a lectured look. That would be the school teacher in her. *Lucky seven-year-olds.*

But she dropped the shoes on the floor, and placed her feet in them anyway. He risked staring at her feet for a second longer than was necessary. Those were very cute toes for someone with a raging temper. (Oh yeah – he'd seen her temper a few times the last two decades, the height of them when she was a hormonal teen. Around about the same time he'd been a horny teen.)

He brought his eyes back up to find her staring at him

accusingly.

"What?"

"These fit, too," she said, as if that were a crime.

He didn't get it. That was a good thing. She was a puzzle. *Must solve...*

She turned around and walked back towards the counter. He followed.

"I still have your boat keys." She waved her hand at him, the keys in them, then turned back 'round. It was like some weird dance. The Pippa dance.

"Thanks," he held out his hand for them. "Did she treat you well?"

She stalled when her hand, fist around the keys, fell into his, and he was glad, because the hairs on his arm all rose, and that beautiful warm 'glow' bloomed in his gut again. Her touch was golden. Her skin *radiated* warmth.

From her shower.

He didn't care if it was from Mars. It was all bloody beautiful. When was the last time she'd touched him? Years ago, no doubt – over ten years ago – and probably by accident. *Okay, back up, Jimmy. Coming off kinda 'creepy, needy, weirdo', here.*

He closed his hand around the keys she'd dropped, and pulled it back, only she hadn't moved a muscle, so he sort of pulled her hand back with him.

CREEPY WEIRDO ALERT.

He looked up to apologise, but found his concern rising instead. She looked peaky. "Are you all right?"

"Of course." The words were out of her mouth right on the tail of his question in that convincing, yet completely unconvincing fashion he always saw through. He hoped she hadn't caught some sick bug amongst all the rubbish she fell on.

"You gonna puke?"

"What?" she snapped, then finally snapped out of her strange state. "No!" And her hand was gone from his.

Ah, ripped like plaster from a wound. Never mind. Some wounds were worth bearing for the healing they brought. "'Cause it wouldn't be the first time a woman's puked in my presence."

"Jimmy..."

Good. Another eye roll. They were back on familiar ground.

"Shit."

"What is it?" He followed her gaze to one of the underwater watches he sold, sitting in a cabinet amongst a bunch of them.

"Is that the real time?"

"On the watch? Yeah, I set them all before I put them out on display."

"Crap, I thought it was only just gone nine."

"Nope – gone ten."

She let out a long, burdened sigh he couldn't quite translate.

"I've only just kitted you out, don't tell me you're due to become a pumpkin already."

She threw him the mother of all looks. "Are you the fairy godmother in this scenario?"

"Yep." He smiled. "I'm your bonafide lucky charm."

"Can't you be serious for more than two minutes?"

"I was. And you said nothing was wrong."

Her scowl deepened.

The shop bell clanged and they both turned and stared at the customer who'd just walked in.

He gave them both an odd look – probably 'cause they were gawping at him – then stuffed his hands in his pockets and went to look at the wetsuits.

Pippa huffed. "I have to go. I promised Mum I'd be back by nine thirty."

"I can't imagine your mum minding you being late."

"That's not the point. I've completely taken advantage of her and Dad being there to look after the kids for months."

"Surely you could use the help. Have they said no to taking them?"

"Of course not, but they're not going to say no, are they?"

"Your dad would."

She harrumphed.

She'd inherited her dad's grumpy gene. He'd told her that once. It was supposed to have been a compliment. He could still feel the sting of the slap she'd placed on his arm.

"Bring them here."

She looked at him, blankly. "What?"

"I'll look after them."

Maybe he'd sprouted feathers from his head, the way she was staring at him. She laughed. "Right."

"I'm being serious – just like you asked me to be."

"*You*, look after my kids," she said, her tone unbelieving.

"I teach kids to surf. I look after them all the time."

"You teach kids to surf?"

"Yeah, and it's way more fun than teaching adults, I'll tell you that for nothing."

"Well, if I'm ever in need of an emergency babysitter, I'll let you know."

"Make sure you do. Or surfing lessons for them. That would be cool. Get Becca on a little board..."

She looked thoughtful for a second. "Liam might be into that."

He held his tongue; let the idea sink into her mind in silence, then she took in a breath and looked back towards the rooms behind the shop. "I left my handbag in your bedroom. Back in a sec." She wandered off.

He wished his bedroom looked like a room at the Ritz. He wondered if he should tell her he only used it occasionally; that this wasn't really his home, but that would lead to questions, with answers that would lead to more questions... *The apple never falls far from the tree, does it, son?*

He tensed, irritated at the shadow that suddenly veiled the unexpected ray of sunshine this morning had been. He turned and headed back behind the counter, the safe zone – *his* space – and absentmindedly straightened the tissue paper, the cellotape, the pens, the loose receipts and papers. That strange, half-burnt poem he'd found in the alley yesterday, fell forward from the pile of sheets by the side of the till.

"Okay," called out Pip, re-entering the shop, handbag over her shoulder and her dirty clothes in a plastic bag.

He shoved everything back into place, and glanced at the customer who was now looking at sunglasses, before resting his eyes on Pippa.

"I've got everything. Thanks again for," she gestured at her clothes, "this – everything. And I'm sorry again if I messed up your morning."

"I've already said you didn't."

She returned his smile, with a question in her eyes. Whatever it was, she didn't ask it, but gave him a final wave, and headed out the door.

It was a nonsensical urge that overtook him in that second, to run out the door after her. While urges to chase her in various situations had not been uncommon in his life, this one felt a little too ... *real*. Like he might actually catch her this time. It left him feeling off-balance

He caught a final whiff of earthy coconut on the breeze that squeezed through the door as it closed behind her.

Never going to happen, Jimmy. And not just because she's way out of your league.

Nope. He shoved his hands in his pockets. Never going to happen. Because he owned a world of shit he'd never drop her in, in a million years. And that's the way it was going to stay.

III
Still

Pulling up outside her parents' house always brought her sense of guilt to the forefront. She shouldn't be here; shouldn't need them as much; should be able to deal with her life on her own, no matter how downhill it had gone. Only this time, the guilt was a little less than usual, because her head was filled with crap that was just as irritating, in a totally different way.

She hoped she hadn't caught a bug – that would be the *last* thing she needed. But she'd had a huge dizzy spell when she'd handed Jimmy the keys; thought she was going to fall over. Her stomach had turned; her breath had caught and she'd suddenly flushed hot. What in god's name that had been about was anyone's guess, but falling ill was out of the question. No way – not with three kids to look after. It simply wasn't happening.

And who was Emma if she wasn't Jimmy's girlfriend? Was she his bit on the side? His booty call? He certainly let her go like she didn't matter that much. Did she like it that way? Did he have more than one woman on the go? Was he a player?

Body like that? Teaching women to surf? You join up the dots.

More than a little annoyed at the circling thoughts she couldn't switch off, she switched off the car engine instead.

Who the fuck CARES?

Seriously, *why* did she care?

Okay, because he's Jimmy, and he's a friend – although more Jamie's friend than hers, really – but he was a *family* friend, so yes, okay, it mattered that he was all right, and not doing stupid things.

Like Emma.

"Oh, you are ridiculous," she mumbled to herself. "Act like a grown woman, for god's sake. And he's a grown man, not a kid anymore – he can do what he likes." *With whomever he likes.*

She steadied herself as she got out of the car, 'cause that dizzying hot flush came back for a brief second. *You've got to be kidding. Do* not *fall ill.*

The slight wind on her face felt fresh, and she breathed it in, feeling a little better. She turned her head to greet it, grateful she was feeling cooler already, and found herself looking down the road she'd just come from – back towards the beach, and The Boat Shop.

She shook away the most bizarre compulsion to get back in her car, and drive back to the shop. Instead, she shut the car door, and looked towards her parents' front door. It was only half ten in the morning. It felt like the entire day should be mostly over, but it had just begun. Usually, it was the other way around. Usually, she was glancing at the clock, cursing it was time to get dinner ready for the kids when she'd done nothing with her day, feeling numb – *needing* to feel numb at times so she could function and perform basic, daily tasks, and *just get through the hours.* This morning had been very different. It made her feel nervous; knocked her off-balance.

She reached into her bag, pulled out her phone, and on impulse, dialled Candy's number. She needed to hear a voice that wasn't the one in her head.

Or Jimmy's.

She frowned, and glared at the ground.

Candy's answering machine picked up. Fine – it would do. It was still an alternate place to focus her mind. That's what she needed: to get on and perform those daily chores.

The beep sounded. "Hi, it's me, Pippa. Just letting you know I've dropped the keys off at Jimmy's – I mean, The Boat Shop – so it's all done. Thanks again for yesterday – had a blast on the boat. Keep in touch, okay? Would be great to meet up again soon before the summer ends. I haven't heard from Jamie yet – about Merri, I mean – but I'll let you know if I do." She knew Candy held Merri, and her mother's passing, close to her heart.

There was nothing left to say, so she said goodbye and hung up, then looked warily back at the house.

She sighed. There was nothing for it. She had to get back to the thrall sooner or later. She loved her brood, but ... by god. It would be good to go away for a week somewhere, *alone*, and just...

Who are you kidding? You'd worry about them endlessly. And they needed her right now. Sammy was having nightmares; Becca *always* asked about her father, and Liam was quieter than usual. Which made him virtually mute.

This, too, shall pass. This, too, shall pass. This, too, shall pass. This, too, shall pass...

Forcing herself up the driveway, she couldn't help finding a fraction of strength in her new, fresh attire. She couldn't make sense of it, but eight months ago, she discovered that life didn't have to make sense. It owed you no explanations. It owed you nothing. So, despite how silly it seemed, she allowed herself to be wrapped in the strange protection wearing new clothes offered. *Thanks to Jimmy.*

Well, what was he going to do? Let you drive home in bin goo?

The coconut on her skin reached her nose. She wrapped that around herself, too – the scent. He'd put it out for her, knowing she'd feel better with moisturiser – he didn't *have* to do that. He probably didn't wear it himself.

The cool breeze felt nice brushing between the soles of her feet and her flip-flops, an added support to every step she took. *Maybe later*, she thought, already feeling a hint of that good old exhaustion creep in, *it'll carry me all the way home.*

~*~

The television was on low – almost too low to be heard – but that created a more soothing atmosphere, those familiar sounds of mediocre daytime programmes filtering through the living room along with the late morning sun. The natural light reflected off the mainly white décor of the larger-than-average space; made everything seem pure and fresh – a clean canvas to be drawn upon.

Lauren's hand was dry in hers.

Candy glanced at her girlfriend – far too casual a term for all they'd been through the past few years – and de-laced her fingers from hers.

After a beat, Lauren's eyes shifted from the screen and rested on her face, the whites around the irises tinged ever so slightly yellow; her voice now permanently hoarse whenever she spoke. "Everything all right?"

"Right as rain. Coffee number two keeps calling, though." She eased herself off the sofa. "Can I get you anything?"

"I still think you should go in to work."

"Why would I want to do that when I get to stay home with my favourite person?"

"Oh, Candy." Her gaze went back to the screen; a small breath left her in a sigh.

"Tim's holding the fort. Besides, I'll be there tomorrow – alone in an office fighting boredom – when he'll be here getting you all to himself. I'd rather make the most of 'us' time if that's all right with you. I hate that I've been absent the past few days."

"You've been spending time with important friends."

Candy sat back down, and placed her hand on Lauren's knee. "None of them as important as you."

Lauren gave her a reprimanding look. "I know that's not true. And if it *were* the case, it shouldn't be so. Everyone should be important to you now. And to Tim."

"You know what I mean."

Lauren reached to her left for the remote, and turned the TV off. "I don't need babysitting, Candace."

"That's not what I'm doing."

"Then go in to work."

"You know I won't, stubborn wench."

Lauren's sharp laugh became a hard cough.

Candy's smile faded, and she rubbed her lover's knee in comfort, willing the brutal spasm to fade; reality to fade...

It took a good fifteen seconds or so, until she cleared her throat, tenderly, and rested her head against the back of the sofa. Whether it was the cancer or the medication that made her so tired at this stage, Candy didn't know. She supposed it didn't matter anymore. Only everything did – everything mattered today more than yesterday, because control was slipping. In every sense. She didn't know what to do to ease Lauren's pain nowadays. Or Tim's. Or her own.

"What are you afraid of?" her girlfriend croaked out, eyes closed against the sun that filled the room.

Candy breathed in through her nostrils, flaring them as she did so in an attempt to keep the tears that tingled at bay; to keep her voice light. "Is that a serious question?"

"I'm not at death's door yet."

"Lauren—"

"I'd call you if I needed anything; if I felt worse. I can still manage to pick up a phone you know. I'm not going to suddenly melt away to nothing like the Wicked Witch of the West."

The tears surfaced, damn them. Candy blinked them away, not wanting Lauren to see them.

"Although ... when the time comes, I'd take a bucket load of witch-melting water over a bucket load of chemo any day of the year, and no mista—" Another cough caught the end of the sentence as it gripped her chest in its clutches.

Candy winced for her suffering, and blinked again, feeling the full weight of futility. When the cough had died down, she edged towards her and took her face in her palm, stroking her cheek with her thumb until Lauren opened her eyes, and settled that wry stare on her. "You *are* a stubborn wench. And if I one day stumbled across flying monkeys in the broom cupboard I wouldn't at all be surprised."

A smile.

"But I'm not here because I'm scared. I'm here because I love you. And I'd like to love you as much as I can before you become a puddle, okay?" She didn't let her answer, but leaned in, bringing herself up on one knee, and placed a kiss on her lips. Lips that were parched. "I'm going to get that caffeine fix now. Are you sure you don't want something?"

Lauren's gaze danced all over her face, conveying thoughts she kept to herself. At last, she met Candy's eyes again. "Iced water, please."

"Coming up." She kissed her once more before shifting from the sofa.

"Candy."

"Yes?"

"I love you, too – so much. That's what makes it hard. As well as easier."

Fuck.

"I know." She made her way towards the kitchen, losing her fight with her tears as soon as she entered the other room. Rapidly wiping them away, she reached for the bag of fresh, ground goodness, as well as her phone that sat on the counter, the volume turned low. She thought she'd heard it ring earlier, but Lauren hadn't seemed to, so she'd let it be, not wanting to distract her from her place of calm by moving.

There was a missed a call from Pippa. She'd left a message.

She listened to it while she put the kettle on, wondering how the hell that woman coped on a day-to-day basis. Yesterday on the boat had been a welcome break, despite Lauren being constantly on her mind. Pippa was good fun; was somehow capable of making you feel you could keep going that little bit longer when you'd thought yourself at the end of the line, and that wasn't down to any effort on her part – it was just her personality; who she was. She had no clue of Candy's situation, just a sense (without a doubt she had a sense, because Candy was getting shit at hiding it from everyone) that all might not be well.

And she had no clue how she did it. Pippa must surely be feeling exhausted herself – looked it, anyway – with her three kids, all of them a hoot in that mildly hazardous way exclusive to youth, bouncing along every second of the day at a pace that didn't seem humanly possible.

Pondering on whether to call her back, Candy's phone sang its ringtone in her hand, making her start. "Merri..." And hell if her breath didn't rush out of her in a sore combination of grief and relief at seeing her best friend's name on the screen.

She pressed to answer. "Hey, you."

"Hey." She sounded tired. Did she know anyone who wasn't right now?

Yeah – three people. Half your size. A girl, and two boys.

She snorted to herself, then walked towards the kettle as it began to bubble. "I've been hoping you'd phone."

"I know. I'm so sorry I couldn't yesterday – it was just crazy the amount of stuff to take in and papers to sign, and appointments to make... I thought about you all on the boat."

"We missed you."

"I missed you, too."

"Happy birthday, sweetie. Belated, anyway."

"Thanks."

"So, how've you been? Besides the obvious."

A long sigh. "I don't know what I'd do without you guys; without Jamie here."

"He made it then, huh?"

"Yeah," she heard her voice grow lighter with what Candy knew was a smile. Many a long night had they spent nattering away on the phone as teens – she could read every change in tone.

"Thanks for your part in that, by the way," she said. "He told me you gave him what for."

"I wanted him off my lawn."

Merri laughed.

"How are you coping?"

"Well, I'm still here." There was a pause. "I'm still anxiety free."

"Wow. What is that – 48 hours without a panic attack?"

"Almost three days."

"Double wow. Go you."

"I know. I keep thinking maybe I'm in shock; maybe the attacks will come back without any notice and it'll be back to square one."

"Not square one – more like square a hundred. You're with Jamie now; your entire life's changed."

"It has. Especially with mum gone."

One of those bloody tears slipped, her face crumpling, as she finally got that spoon of coffee in the filter. "I'm so sorry, hun."

"Don't cry. You'll set me off."

"Look at me blubbering – it should be you in pieces. I mean that in the nicest possible way."

Another laugh, this one shorter. "I know."

"How was seeing Michael?"

"It was good, surprisingly ... weirdly. He was great about everything."

"You told him about Jamie?"

"He asked."

"What? He *asked*?"

"He did. After I broke up with him."

Hot water almost spilled. "So you did it?"

"Yep. We're officially over."

"Do I need to say sorry about that, too?"

Did she just hear her shake her head? "It's all good. I think maybe ... maybe we can be friends. Further down the line, or something. He's still around at the moment, being all Mother Goose until he knows I'm okay, but he's giving me and Jamie space. He says all I have to do is call him if I need anything."

"Bloody hell. I'd never have put Michael Fortune and Mother Goose in the same sentence."

And this one was a hearty laugh, despite the gravity of everything. "You don't know him. Maybe I didn't know him that well either. Listen, I wanted to let you know the funeral is likely to be a couple of weeks from today."

"You know I'll be there."

"Right." She hesitated.

"What is it?"

"I also wanted to let you know I hadn't forgotten where we left off."

"Where we left off?"

"What you told me – about how someone you love is dying of cancer?"

Oh.

Candy stared at her coffee as she stirred the maple syrup in with one hand – she never had sugar in it anymore. "Okay," she squeaked, her stomach squeezing at Merri's words. She didn't want to talk about it now – not about Lauren dying, and certainly not about how she'd been in a polyamorous relationship for the last five years. That wasn't the kind of thing you broke to someone over the phone. Her parents hadn't taken the news of her relationship preference well face-to-face – you'd have thought she'd told them *she* was the one dying, not that they knew about Lauren's illness because they didn't really speak to her anymore – she didn't want to risk the same thing happening with Merri. If they talked about it over the phone, she wouldn't be able to gauge her reaction.

"Now's probably not the best time to talk about it, is it?"

Relieved, she shook her head, forgetting Merri couldn't actually see that.

Or maybe she could. "That's fine. I really just wanted to say that I'm here if you need to, okay? You can phone me."

"You're fucking awesome, Merri. But go spend time with Jamie, and on everything you need to do for your mum now – my stuff can wait."

"Time doesn't wait."

Whatever Candy's next words were, they caught in her throat. She lifted her still black, scorching coffee to her lips, and took a gulp of that instead.

"So, tell me all about yesterday on the boat."

And the conversation took a turn for the lighter, as it always did when fun times were mentioned. The milk finally went in the coffee as they chatted. She managed to pop ice out of the ice tray for Lauren with one hand, then fill up the glass tumbler with water from the tap. *See? Single-handedly. You're fine. You're like Wonder Woman.*

When they finally said their goodbyes, she felt balanced once more, as she needed to be to walk back into the living room.

Half way in, she slowed her pace, treading lightly on her heels until she came to a halt ten feet from the couch. Lauren was where she'd left her sitting, her head thrown back upon the backrest of the sofa, eyes closed. Still. Very still. For a moment, the world slipped away – it always teetered a little anyway, nowadays – then came back when she spotted the rise and fall of her partner's chest, slow and shallow in medicated slumber.

She closed her own eyes; silently took a deep breath. She couldn't shake it – it had been like this the past few days whenever she saw Lauren – the ever-growing possibility that this time might be the last.

On slightly shaky legs, she made her way back to the couch, and set Lauren's iced water on the side table.

She kept her hot mug in her hands.

Careful not to depress the sofa too much, she sat, and curled her legs under, to the left. She lay her right temple on the backrest, mirroring Lauren's position, and studied her face – the lined corners of her eyes; her hard mouth, only made hard by a three-year grimace at all she'd had to endure; her thin wisps of light brown hair poking through her head scarf, not yet regrown to their fullest...

Merri's mum hadn't looked like she was dying.

Lauren did.

Candy watched her in peace; let her sleep, happy she had a moment with no discomfort, even if during those rare times, *all* she did was sleep, unaware.

She watched her in peace, despite half of her wanting to jump in her arms; take her in an embrace; share with her the thousand thoughts that raced through her mind every day, and hear hers until she got to know her all over again; love her all over again. Because too soon, she and all her thoughts would be gone forever.

Because Merri was right.

Time didn't wait.

IV

Crossed Wires

"There you go, Pippa – all clean. The trousers need another hour or so to dry. You can pick them up tomorrow if you like." Her mum placed her folded clothes on the cleared dining table. The wall clock read just gone 7 p.m. Dinner had been earlier today due to the early start they'd all had.

"Thanks, Mum. You know I could have washed them at home."

"And stink my house out for the whole day? No, thank you, darling."

"I don't know if we're going to come by tomorrow."

"Well, you're always welcome, you know that."

Pippa fell silent, torn between her gratitude – her *need* – for her parents' support, and not wanting to rely on it. The truth was, she wouldn't have made it. The past eight months would have been a hundred times worse if they hadn't been there to hold her up. But almost a year had passed – for how long was she going to use them as a crutch?

But you're still broken. Take the crutch away and you'll collapse.

"You look lovely in these new clothes, by the way," she commented, her voice softening a touch. "I didn't get a chance to say so earlier."

"Do you think? Becca's certainly taken with the outfit.

You'd think I'd dressed for a ball."

"We don't often see you in a skirt."

"Ha! Try running around after three children with a skirt on."

"Oh, I have, darling."

"You had *two* exceptionally well-behaved kids."

"And Jimmy. He practically lived here at one point. He's a good boy, that one. Strong."

Pippa looked up from where she was sitting, and from the magazine that she was only half-reading to pass the time.

And to avoid going home.

'Strong' wasn't a word she'd have associated with Jimmy, although she wasn't sure why. It had just never been the first word that came to mind where he was concerned. Joker; lad; geezer; a bit of a dick. But 'strong'? "You think so?"

Her mum glanced at her, puzzled.

Puzzled at what? She suddenly felt clueless. Like she'd missed something obvious everyone else had already spotted.

"Helen, is there any of that crumble left?" her dad asked, making his way into the room.

Her mum raised an eyebrow. "If you're after dessert, there's fruit."

He made some sort of disgruntled noise.

"George, you remember Jimmy, don't you?"

"Remember him? Couldn't bloody get rid of him at one point." But he said that with a chuckle. "Good lad, that. Pulled himself out of the gutter. How is he?" he asked, looking pointedly at Pippa.

"Er ... fine, I guess." *Gutter?*

"Good," her mum added, her head in the fridge as she put the last of the dinner leftovers into it. "We haven't seen him in ages – not for at least ten years; not properly, any-way – it would be good to catch up."

"I was thinking about having a barbecue here, like we used to as kids." Then she inwardly winced, not just because the words had come out of her mouth without thought, but because she'd unwittingly invited everyone over to her par-ents' without asking permission first. "If that would be okay with you, of course."

"Goodness, yes. The more the merrier. Invite Jamie's new girlfriend, too. About time we got to know her better, since discovering she was the one to ... well, you know."

"Pop his cherry," said George.

"Dad!"

"Oh, George!"

"What? It's true."

Pippa closed the magazine – trying to read it was prov-ing a pointless exercise. "Men don't have cherries to pop."

"Well, what the hell d'you call it then? It's all the same thing. Where's the fruit, Helen?"

"Where it always is, George."

"And when Jamie comes back down for this barbecue," he continued, taking an orange from the top of the fruit bowl, "he's leaving the bloody car."

Pippa smirked. That had been quite out of character for dutiful son, Jamie, to kidnap The Beast with no coherent plan. And a testament to how much he liked Merri. "I've said you can borrow my car whenever you like in the mean-time."

Another grumble. "So, when is the barbecue?"

"I don't know. I only just thought of it today."

Her mum pulled a chair out and sat down with a sigh – one of those 'end of chores' sigh. "Saturday's good."

"That's in two days."

"Best be soon to catch the height of the summer weather. It'll turn before you know it."

"I don't know if Jamie and Merri can come down at such short notice."

"Best find out, eh? And make sure you invite Jimmy."

"Mum…" she felt exasperated. "I don't know if I'm free to go back to his shop tomorrow, and I don't have a number for him other than the shop number, and I really don't think he's going to answer his work phone at this time."

"Oh, I think I have a mobile for him." Her mum pulled away from the table again.

"You have his mobile number?"

There was that puzzled look again. "He gave it to me years ago, but most people keep the same number, don't they? Hang on, I'll go find it."

He gave her his mobile number?

She didn't know why that seemed strange. Especially since – Jimmy had said it earlier – they were as good as family.

Her dad pierced his orange with a knife. "Yes … good lad, that. Your mum and he became very fond of each other."

Had she just entered some kind of parallel universe? "When?" she blurted out. Because for the life of her, she couldn't recall this so-called 'special' Jimmy they were all referring to.

"Oh … hmmm … let's see." He paused, looking thoughtful. "It was after you went to university I think. Yes, that's right. He needed a place to stay for a few nights, and he slept in your room."

Her mouth fell open. "He slept in my room? You gave him my *room*?" *How* did she not know about this?

"Well, darling," her mum reappeared with a piece of paper in her hand, "you were gone. You weren't using it."

"All my *stuff* was still in it."

"Needs must. It was important."

Oh, Jesus fucking Christ, had he gone through her stuff? "Mum! He had a crush on me when we were kids."

Her mother laughed to herself. "I suspected he might have."

"It's not funny! He probably went through everything in my room!"

"Oh, Pip, I really doubt it. Here you go – this is his number." She handed the piece of paper over.

Pippa grabbed it with a scowl.

"Darling, it was fifteen years ago."

The scowl remained. She'd had private journals stashed away in that room; teenaged thoughts she'd written in teenaged magazines; information about guys she'd dated and how annoyed she was *she* hadn't popped her cherry yet ... not to mention all her underwear.

She could feel her face growing red, which was stupid, because her mum was right: it was fifteen years ago. Water under the bridge. It shouldn't matter anymore.

"Why don't you give him a call."

"What – now?"

"Yes. If the barbecue's to be on Saturday, then the sooner the better – everyone needs as much notice as possible."

She felt caught up in a whirlwind. She'd only suggested the barbecue sixty seconds ago. "But I don't even know if Satur—"

"Saturday's perfect," her mum carried on. "Especially since George said he's going to mow the lawn tomorrow."

He glanced at her, surprised. "I did?"

"Yes, dear, you did. Pippa, darling, give him a call." She

pushed her pile of freshly cleaned clothes towards her. "I'd love to see him again."

Fuck it. He'd given her new clothes, and her mum, who had emotionally bandaged her and been more of a mother to her kids than she felt capable of right now, wanted to see him.

She gave in and reached for her phone, on the table to her left. *Me and my big mouth.*

Jimmy tore off the till slip totalling sales over the last three months.

Shit. His heart sank straight to his stomach. It still wasn't enough to get him to Christmas – not this year, and it had been a good season. Summer was nearly over though.

His surfing lessons were an extra boon, but unless he worked 24/7, which was impossible unless someone else ran the shop full-time – someone he couldn't afford to hire – the money earned from those lessons wouldn't cut it.

His mind ran over the possibilities it had run over every month for the past two years. *Dead end.* He just had to carry on the way he was, which made him feel—

His mobile phone rang: **CAIT**

That weight in his stomach – that spot his heart had sunk to – twisted in a mild sense of revulsion that was only mild because he'd accepted the bitter pill that continued to keep him afloat. Was it nearing the end of the month already?

CAIT

He didn't want to take the call.

Swallowing reality with a drying mouth, he reached over and hit the ignore button. He'd face her tomorrow when he'd had some time to gear himself up to it.

His focus went back to the till receipt, and the accounting books that lay open across his counter. *Fuck reality.*

His phone went again. Annoyed, he reached for it: **EMMA**

He sighed, answering it this time. "Hey."

"Hi!" she replied, bright and chirpy at the other end – vastly different to how she'd left him that morning, but this was expected. This was very much like Emma, and he didn't mind, because she eased his plight when it all got too much, not that she knew the half of it.

They had a perfect arrangement. She was a final-year university student not the least bit into commitment. She wanted fun, not a boyfriend, and he needed relief from...

The life you're half way to fucking up big time.

She made it better, because she was impetuous, and frivolous and made him feel like he still had choices; still had control over the mess spread across the surface in front of him, even though she was the one who mostly called the shots where their 'friendship' was concerned. He didn't mind that so much. It wasn't love, it was lusty escapism – he had no pressing desire to be a part of her world, nor she a part of his. Their worlds just collided every now and again when it suited them both, and it usually did suit them both. He didn't mind letting her govern their arrangement for the most part – it made his life easier not having to organise the wheres, hows and whens.

Except for right now.

Right now, he minded, and nothing felt easy, although he wasn't sure why because usually Emma's buoyant voice was enough to make him feel better about five-figure digits with that *minus* sign hovering in front of them.

"You want me to come over tonight?"

He hesitated. Which was also odd, because he never hesitated with Emma – they were all about impulsive actions that draped a rose-tinted sheen over life, making every black hole sparkle.

Not tonight, though. He fidgeted with the receipt in his hand. "Not tonight, babe. I'm whacked – been a long day."

He could practically see her pout. The imagined vision didn't even muster up the urge it normally gave him to bite her lip. What had changed? What was different?

Yes, *Cait* loomed over him, but it had been that way for a while, and he was not down-hearted by nature.

"Is it because of her?"

Jesus Christ. He dropped the receipt. She *couldn't* know about that shit. "Who?" he asked, his voice tight.

"The bin woman from his morning," she snipped back.

"Ooooh..." He relaxed, letting his worry ease a little. "You mean Pippa?"

She made an irritated noise at the other end. Surely she wasn't jealous. They'd agreed not to do jealous.

Nevertheless, if she *was* jealous, there was a small part of him that felt oddly proud it was Pippa who managed to rile it up. "We're good friends – we grew up together."

Another huff. He wasn't sure why – that was supposed to have reassured her.

"Whatever. Look, I dunno if I'm free tomorrow, so I'll see you when I see you, okay?" It wasn't really a question because it was said far too abruptly.

Bemused, he leant forward and rested his elbows on the counter. "Okay."

That was clearly the wrong response. She made a noise that sounded a bit like a cat being strangled, then promptly hung up.

He chuckled. She *had* gotten his mind off the crap he

was in after all, with her emotional bull-headedness.

And there went his phone *again*. This time, the number wasn't one he recognised, but he smiled, 'cause he had Emma sussed. He'd pissed her off, so she was calling from another number – she'd done that before. About seven months ago, soon after they'd first met, he'd managed to get under her skin about something or other. She'd hung up on him, then had 'accidentally' phoned him from some other number and not left a message, knowing he'd phone back to see who had called. It had been some 'other guy', and she'd made a huge effort to sound gleeful and flirty with this other guy while Jimmy had had to listen at his end.

It hadn't fazed him at all, much to her annoyance, but it *had* amused him no end. He had a lot of time for the crazy games college kids played, perhaps because he'd ended up not going to university after all. He'd missed out on that whole era of his life, despite his best intentions, and Emma sort of made up for it with the way she was.

He answered his phone with a grin, determined to win at this before she could even get her foot in. "Honey, if my pussy was as gorgeous as yours, I'd be making the most of it, too. You know I don't mind what you do, or who with. I'm easy."

Perhaps the heavy pause at the other end should have triggered his alert, but he'd gone and made the assumption that no matter whose phone Emma was calling him from, she was right there next to them whispering instructions in their ear.

The droll, wry reply, when it finally came, gave mortification a new meaning. "A little *too* easy, don't you think? Jesus, Jimmy, your mother teach you to speak like that?"

The silence came from him this time, as the floor rose up to meet him – metaphorically. Or maybe not – he swore his stomach was down there somewhere. "Pip?" *Oh, fucking hell!*

"I think so. Although, I've never considered myself so ... bluntly appealing to anyone."

"Aaaah, shit."

"Mmm-hmm."

"No, really – shit. I'm so sorry. I thought you were—"

"I don't ever need to know, Jimmy."

"I didn't know you had my number. Did I give you my number?" That had come out more curt than he'd intended.

"I can now see why you wouldn't," was the slightly cool retort, and this was going all wrong.

"Of course I bloody would – you can call me any time, I just didn't realise you *had* it."

"Actually..." her tone became somewhat sheepish, "my mum had it. Said you gave it to her years back and hoped it was still the same. Sorry. I wasn't sure whether to use it."

He bit his curse back this time. Holding back on the potty-mouth might ease her ire considering how he'd just greeted her. "Pippa, I'm glad you've got my number. Keep it. Phone whenever you like."

The line went quiet once more.

Fuck, fuck, fuck... He never wanted Pippa to be on his 'people who hate me' list. "I really am sorry. Can we start over? Look, I'm going to hang up. Phone me again."

"What?"

"Phone me again."

"Don't be daft."

"Hanging up now. Phone me back."

"Jimmy—"

He hung up.

He waited.

His screen lit up with her number, he pressed ANSWER,

and put on his best 'automated' voice. "I'm sorry, all the lines are currently busy while James Darling washes his mouth out with bleach and reflects on the direction his life has taken." *That last part's too fucking true.* "Please hold. You will be connected shortly."

"You idiot."

"Luuuuuuuuh-la-la-luuuuuuh..."

A muffled laugh reached his ears, and he smiled.

"You call that singing?"

"That's *exactly* what 'on hold' music sounds like."

Her laugh grew louder.

He let out an internal sigh of relief, and finally eased into the conversation. "So, what may I do for you this fine night?"

That sheepishness in her voice was back, a soft sound that he knew reflected a softness within that she never let surface. It made him want to wrap his arms around her. *Yeah, but you want to wrap your arms around her even when she's throwing snark at you.*

This was true.

"Um ... there's a barbecue at my parents' house this Saturday, and we wondered if you wanted to come. I don't know if Jamie and Merri can make it," she added quickly, "it's such short notice, and you don't have to come, but I just thought ... you know ... with this morning and the clothes ... um ... it would be good to say thank you. Properly, I mean."

Pause.

Speak, Jimmy.

"Er..." He had trouble forming words; this had the feel of her asking him out, or something, which he knew she wasn't. This was just a family invite to a get-together. Nevertheless, every boyhood dream he'd dared to have surrounding Pippa was suddenly present, and tangible, and that was new – very new – and *false*, because illusion, which this clearly was, never turned into reality.

"And my mum really wants to see you."

Thank you, branch. Yep, he'd grab that. "I'd *love* to see your mum again."

"Great," she breathed out, sounding somewhat relieved. Perhaps he wasn't the only one feeling the weirdness.

It was no lie, though – he *would* love to see both of her parents again, and her mum had been more of a mum to him than his own had *ever* been – he suspected Pippa didn't really know that, 'cause all the shit at home had hit the fan after she'd left for university.

"So ... come over. On Saturday. Say ... from 2 p.m.?"

"My last surfing lesson on Saturday is at one, so that's perfect."

"Great," she said again.

"Great," he repeated.

And a final silence told him they'd run out of things to say. "So..."

"So ... I'd better go and sort the kids out."

"I think I can hear them."

"Everyone can hear them."

They both laughed, and he sort of didn't want to end the chat.

"Okay ... see you, Jimmy. Don't forget to spit that bleach out," she teased, and before he could respond, she hung up.

Jesus Christ, what had he even said to her? Something about her pussy being gorgeous? His face heated. It wasn't the only thing that heated, and he could put *that* thought right out of his head.

As if. When have you not *thought about Pippa that way?*

That wasn't fair, he argued with himself. When David

had come along, he'd known it was over. No more casual flirting; no more daydreams of—

Her pussy.

"Bloody hell," he muttered, shaking his head. "Get your head out of your arse." He slammed shut his three accounting books and decided he'd deal with it all tomorrow. A night surf was calling. The cold sea, the cool breeze, and no circling thoughts for an hour ... yeah – heaven.

Just as well, he frowned, his thoughts turning to Cait as he made his way to the back of the shop. *Because the end of the month is always hell.*

V
Goodnight

Pippa put her head around the door frame and saw Liam at his desk, bent over his homework, the light from the lamp the only light in the room. He was in his pyjamas, all ready for bed. "Hi ... you still at it?"

He looked up; barely smiled. "Nearly finished."

"All right. Need any help?"

The back of his head shook. "You wouldn't get it – it's algebra and hypotenuse triangles."

"Hey! I'd get it. I teach maths sometimes."

"You teach to seven-year-olds, like Sammy. He doesn't do this stuff yet."

"Well, I can still help. I had to learn all this when I was at school, too, you know."

"That was like a hundred years ago. And you always asked me to ask Dad about maths."

"Right – because he's the architect. It made sense. But I can help now. And it wasn't a *hundred* years ago, thank you very much."

"It's fine, Mum, I got it," he mumbled, and tucked his head lower, getting on with whatever he was aligning with his ruler.

She sighed, not wanting to push him. He was so hard to read sometimes, and lately, more and more so. "Come get me to say goodnight when you're done, okay?"

"Mmmm."

She assumed that was a yes. Holding back another sigh, she left him to it, wondering if she actually would understand the damn homework if she saw it.

She made her way to Sammy's room. He was on his games tablet, his kid's version of the iPad. "Time for bed, squirt."

"Oooooh," he moaned. "Just two more minutes..."

"You said that *ten* minutes ago. It's never two more minutes and you know it."

"I've nearly beaten my score!"

"Sammy, no."

"Muuum!"

She crossed her arms, not moving an inch, and he finally ended the game with a huff, and two red spots of rising anger to his cheeks.

"Come on now – you can play on that whenever you like."

"I'd like to play on it *now*."

"*Except* for now. There's all of tomorrow, and Gran said you were on it most of yesterday. How much of your summer homework is left, by the way?"

"Just the 'making a tower' stuff."

Arts and crafts – wonderful – I can handle that. "That's fantastic, well done." She took the tablet out of his hands and ushered him into bed. "I can help you with the tower this week, and maybe we can get you something for finishing all your homework on time."

His eyes lit up as he pulled his duvet over himself. "Like the next game in the Thieves of Baleria series?"

She frowned. "Is that for this thing?" She looked at the tablet. Why couldn't he like the games about history and science?

"Yes."

Lovely. "Sounds fun, and not at all inappropriate."

"Dad bought me the first two *ages* ago."

"We *both* bought them for you – I was there, I remember. I also remember not believing they made this stuff for six-year-olds."

"I'm seven now. And all my friends have the third one already."

"I'll see how much it costs." She picked up his old, still-cherished teddy from the floor and propped it up on the chair next to his bed. They'd bought that for him, too, the day after he was born.

She blinked away the sudden sting in her eyes. Where the hell did the time go? From teddies to Thieves of ... where? Bulgaria?

"Mum?"

"Yes, sweetie?" She tucked in the duvet around him.

"I don't want to go to sleep."

Her heart squeezed at the small tremble in his voice. "Because of your nightmares?"

Looking forlorn, he nodded.

"Oh, honey..." She dropped a kiss on his forehead. "You don't have one every night, and I'm going to leave the light on like we agreed."

He didn't look convinced.

"And I'm right next door if you need anything – just ten steps away, that's all."

"So ... I just need to be brave?" He had his dad's eyes to a tee – big, round, hazel orbs – currently in pleading mode. Christ, it was sometimes all too much. She put her own pain to one side.

"You already *are* brave. And these nightmares ... they're going to go away. One day, they'll just stop and you won't have them anymore, as long as we talk about them."

"I don't like talking about them."

"I know, but we *need* to talk about them."

"They're about Dad."

"Yes, I know. And I know it hurts to talk. But you need to try and tell me what happens in them. We need to talk the nightmares away. Can you try and do that soon? Because until I know what goes on in them, I don't know how to help."

After a few seconds, he reluctantly nodded, fear still conquering his expression.

"You want to talk about them now?"

That was a definite shake of his head.

She made a final tug on the duvet and placed a last kiss on his cheek. "All right. 'Night-night."

"'Night," he whispered back.

She hesitated. "Do you want to hold teddy next to you?" She almost hadn't asked – knew he was going through that phase where he hated being thought of as a 'baby' in any way.

Nevertheless, after another few seconds, he met her eyes and nodded again. She handed him the loved toy, and he hugged it to himself.

"'Night, Sammy."

"'Night, Mum."

She pulled the door to, leaving the night-lamp on as promised, praying he had a good night.

Last stop: Becca. She should really be the first in bed at four-years-old, but that was never the case. In her defence though, she'd never been a difficult child to get ready for bed. She happily went through the washing and changing routine at her own pace – with some help, of course – then doddled around in her room, busying herself with her toys until Pip made her way there. She was also a heavy sleeper. And an early riser. Any concept of a lie-in that had been re-gained after Liam and Sammy had finally gotten into a good sleeping routine, went straight out the window with Becca, who had *never* slept late once, as if she was somehow at-tuned to the coming of dawn.

Pippa caught sight of her through her open bedroom door, humming quietly to herself as every single toy animal she owned was neatly arranged around a tea party she'd laid out on the floor. "Wow, Becca, this looks amazing." *And crowded.*

She beamed. "It's an animal tea-party."

"At bed time?"

"It's a night party like grown-ups have."

"Aaaahh."

"Daddy once said all grown-ups turn into animals at parties."

She pulled a face. "Right. I think that might have been one of Daddy's jokes."

Becca rolled her eyes, looking far too much like herself for her liking. "Of *course* it's a joke, Mummy. People can't *actually* turn into animals."

"Hmmm ... good thing you're so clever."

"Miss Little at playschool says I'm clever."

"She's right. And all your teachers at big school are go-ing to think the same thing."

"Mummy?"

"Yes?" Pippa gingerly made her way around every care-fully and immaculately positioned toy, knowing that knock-ing any of them over would end in a mini-rant and tears.

"Do I *have* to start big school in September."

"Yes."

"But I'm going to miss playschool."

"I know, honey, but you're five in just three months, so you do have to go to big school just like all the other five-year-olds." Pippa held the duvet down for Becca, and she hopped onto her mattress. "Do you need the toilet?"

She shook her head. "I went for my last wee before I made the tea party," she stated proudly.

"Well done. And I *do* know you're going to miss playschool, but you're going to make a ton of new friends and there'll be so many fun, new things to do and so many things to learn, and I know how much you like learning things."

"So I can be as clever as Daddy is when he draws buildings."

She froze for two seconds before catching herself and pulling Becca's covers up. No matter how many times a day they mentioned David, there were moments – instances – where it still caught her off-guard.

That's because you're ON guard twenty-four hours a day.

"Yes, sweetie – just like Daddy."

"I miss Daddy more than I'll miss playschool. Are we going to see him again soon?"

She said nothing as she smoothed the duvet down over her daughter, probably a few more times than was necessary. "We can if you like." She paused, choosing her next words carefully, the image of David's 'episode' the last time she'd visited, fresh in her mind. "I was worried that maybe ... I don't want you all to be upset that he's not the same way he was before."

"Because he hurt his brain in the car accident and it can't work the same way anymore?"

She cringed at Becca's very blunt and simplistically accurate analysis. God, she hoped when she'd first explained it to the kids last year, she hadn't come across that bluntly.

She'd certainly tried not to. "Yes," she replied, her throat tightening.

Silence emphasised the glow of the night-light by Becca's bed. Her well-handled, favourite photograph of her dad – the very one that had brought Merri back into Jamie's life – was propped up against the base of the lamp.

Pippa forced her eyes away from it to see what her daughter might be thinking in her ever-turning mind, and was met with big, brown eyes – more like her own than David's – contemplating her.

Becca blinked, breaking the spell. "It's okay, Mummy. I'm not worried about Daddy, because he's like how I was when I was very little, and I didn't know how to talk, and you had to change my nappy. But I can do those things now. He just has to learn to do those things again."

Bloody hell. Her chest ached from restrained tears. Or was that a scream lodged there between her ribs. "Some-times," she took a breath in, "when the accident is really bad, and the hurt to the brain is … too big … you can't get better. Sort of like when you break something so bad that it can't be fixed." Shit. It sounded so very wrong to say that – like telling her four-year-old that Santa wasn't real, destroy-ing that sweet bubble. But letting her kids believe he was going to improve, when they now knew this was as good as it was going to get, seemed just as cruel. What the hell was the right thing to do?

Something brushed the top of her hand. She looked down to see Becca's little palm resting on it. "But the nurses will still look after Daddy, won't they? If he doesn't get fixed?"

Pippa nodded. "Yes, they will."

"That means he'll always be okay, doesn't it? Because there'll always be someone to help him do things, like there's always someone to help me do things. And when you go out and leave me and Sammy and Liam, you always tell me I don't have to worry, because there'll always be someone to look after me. So we don't have to worry about Daddy."

The wave of emotion too much, Pippa swooped in and kissed Becca on the forehead. "Sometimes, I think you're way more clever than me. You're right, we don't have to worry."

She gave her a small smile. "So can we see him again soon? I want to tell him how much I miss him."

Pippa nodded. "We'll go soon." She stood, giving her hand a final squeeze. "Time for sleep, okay?"

"Okay."

"Light on or off?"

"Off, please, Mummy. I'm nearly five now. I'm not afraid of the dark anymore."

Smiling back, she turned her lamp off, then the main light.

Becca's hushed voice reached her as she was pulling the door to. "Mummy?"

"Yes, darling?"

Then, after a pause, "I really like your new clothes."

A strange awkwardness enveloped her, as if she'd suddenly caught herself standing there, naked – exposed. "Thanks, Becca. Me too. 'Night."

"'Night."

~*~

The key in the lock of the front door turned, and Candy looked up from her book and over the back of the couch, not quite able to see through the hallway from where she was. "Tim?"

"Hi. Yes, it's me."

She heard the door shut, and she got up to greet him, dropping her book on the coffee table.

He met her halfway into the room, and dropped his bag for a hug.

"I've missed you," she said into his chest, the hairs of his light jumper making her nose tickle.

"I've missed you, too. How is she?"

How is she? That was always the first question now, whenever either of them came home. *How is she?* Selfishly, Candy missed 'how are *you*?', or 'how was your day?'. "All right. It's been a good day. She was up for most of it without much pain, and only went to bed about half an hour ago. You're back later than I thought."

He looked dishevelled, his messy, light brown hair somehow adding to the obvious exhaustion across his features. "I know, I'm sorry. It's the McCarthy piece. They decided to edit it at the last minute, then didn't like how I formatted it. Had to do it all again. Should probably have told them to sod off, but they're our longest standing clients, and I didn't want to leave it all unfinished and have to go over it again tomorrow."

"Ah. They've always been funny about their articles, haven't they? They're the same with my photographs," she smiled, trying to take the weight off his shoulders. At the moment, she and Tim were each trying to run a small publishing house single-handedly while the other looked after Lauren, and with Lauren having been the one to manage most elements of the business, they'd had to relearn a few things in the process. "I've left you some dinner."

"You're a gem. Thank you."

"I'll heat it up for you."

Tim thanked her again, and made his way to the sofa, all

but falling on it as he kicked his shoes off. Their home was a country cottage, small and cosy, yet the three of them had managed well enough the past few years, filling up the space without dominating each other's. More recently, that had been harder. Even though Lauren was a shell of herself, her illness seemed to take up the room her exuberance once had, and it had become harder to feel free among the confines of the two-bed house.

Pouring Tim a glass of water, she brought it over to him. "Here."

He took it from her.

"Dinner's chicken and rice. It'll be ready in about twenty minutes."

He smiled at her, his eyes red from fatigue, then tugged gently at her legs.

She happily took the hint, and lowered herself onto his lap for a kiss. It was a soft, tender flutter of lips that ended on a sigh from Tim, and her curling her head against his chest.

"I'm starving, but almost too tired to eat," he admitted.

"I know the feeling. Try and have some, though – keep your energy up."

She felt his mouth press into the crown of her head in a silent kiss. "What would we do without you to look after us?"

"Have take-out every night."

He laughed, quietly. "Probably."

"Luckily, you'll never have to know."

There was a momentary pause, and Candy looked up to see his face, wondering if she'd said the wrong thing. After all, they could have said the same about Lauren not too long ago – it wasn't exactly a fact she could swear on with one hundred percent certainty.

He was staring back at her, worry in his gaze. "I'm not doing a very good job of looking after you, though, am I? I'm sorry."

She placed her lips on his to shush him. "You're doing better than you think you are."

"I love you," he said.

Her heart swelled. "I love you, too." She resumed her position against his chest. This closeness was nice. They didn't get a lot of this at the moment, and Tim, of late, had been emotionally more detached than was the norm. Hardly surprising given their circumstances, but Candy did grow anxious about it – was he distancing himself from her on purpose? Did he not want a relationship with her anymore? Would Lauren leaving them be too much of a change for them to endure together? How would they go from being a threesome to a couple?

All futile questions with no answers, and she tried not to over-analyse it all, not wishing her insecurities to pull her away from Lauren's need of her, and from them as a unit.

Tim's heartbeat sounded against her ear, as did a muffled grunt.

Raising her eyebrows, she looked up once more. He'd fallen asleep.

Sighing, she nestled into him, as she had been, deciding to let him rest until the meal had heated up. When she'd phoned Pippa back a couple of hours ago, she'd mentioned a barbecue at her parents' house. She'd wanted to ask Tim if he wanted to come along; if he could bear to leave Lauren just for an hour or two, so they could have some 'them' time, too. Something close to normal for a bit. The boat trip had been so needed, and she hadn't known how much until it was over.

Guilt twinged.

She knew he'd turn the barbecue down. Going out nowadays – spending any time as just the two of them – felt like it was *just two of them*. It wasn't a comfortable feeling – as if they were somehow discarding or rejecting Lauren.

But you're going to have to face it some time. Soon, it will be just the two of you.

She peeked at the clock on the DVD player. Twelve minutes until Tim's dinner was ready.

She pressed further into him, his gentle snoring like a blanket of slumber, making her own eyes heavy.

Don't think about it now. Don't think about the future. It'll be here too soon.

VI
Saturday

Pippa stood by her car's petrol tank, pump in hand, watching the world go by as she filled it with fuel.

The kids were already at her parents', Liam having wanted to help her dad light the coal for the barbecue. *Sammy had bloody better be careful around it.*

She'd taken the opportunity to pop out for fifteen minutes to fill the car up since it was running on empty.

It was just before 1 p.m. The streets of the small town she lived in (if one could even call it a town) bustled with life as people made their way to the Saturday market, had lunch at their favourite places, and carried out their weekly shopping. A year ago, she'd been a part of that bustle, David carrying Becca half the time as she'd tried to make Sammy keep pace with the rest of them.

The door to the petrol station's convenience store opened, and a young couple came out, laughing over whatever conversation they were having. She thought she recognised the girl as the older sister of one of the pupils she taught in the next village over. The two neighbouring villages weren't big, hers being the largest with the weekly markets and the commercial High Street. When David had had his accident, it had been in, not just the local paper, but the news coverage for all of Cornwall. Such tragic incidents in such a small town were unusual. She'd been inundated with cards and flowers, and even some phone calls from people she'd barely spoken to for years, and while she'd been grateful for the care, at one point she'd found herself so overwhelmed, she'd disappeared for a weekend, leaving her kids with her mum and dad. She still felt guilty about that.

Add it to the loooong pile of things you feel guilty about.

Her kids had needed her and she'd bailed. It had helped to an extent – had allowed her to come back to this nook of the country where everyone knew everyone else's business, able to take the heat of the talk she was the focus of.

Of course, the focus had eventually shifted, as it always did.

And she'd been left to pick up the pieces of her family and their future – so fractured, she was still finding shards.

The numbers on the pump's screen slowed down, and Pippa released the trigger and shook the thing to get the last few drops of petrol out.

Her eye caught the gleam of the sun bouncing off something – someone's wristwatch. Glancing up past the watch, she found it belonged to a man she didn't recognise – tall, blond, maybe in his late thirties – standing by the far wall of the petrol station, a good fifteen metres away.

Staring at her.

He straightened as if uncomfortable at being caught, then opened the door to what she assumed was his car, got in, and started the engine.

Weird.

Or maybe the weirdness was finding herself the focus of someone's attention (*or attraction?*) after all this time.

Still, he had looked kind of ... startled. Almost alarmed.

Yeah, maybe you look shit. So tired it's scary as shit.

With a snort to herself, she shut the petrol cap and went

into the store to pay for her fill.

The man drove down the ramp towards the exit.

She made it a point not to stare back at him as he went by, but she couldn't help the almost-certainty his gaze was still locked on her.

Ugh. If *that* was what dating felt like after all this time, everyone could count her out for the foreseeable future. And ever.

The constant second-guessing, and defence of oneself in case Mr Date was a nutter. She'd had the energy for it in her teens and early twenties; she couldn't even imagine going through it all again now, with kids in tow. Because Liam, Sammy and Becca mattered the most. She wouldn't be looking for a boyfriend, she'd be looking for a father.

No way – not doing it.

So, why are you thinking about it?

Hell, why *was* she thinking about it? She hadn't thought about it before. Well, okay ... a little, over the past couple of months, at moments when the kids seemed unmanageable on her own and she'd felt herself losing the plot, but that wasn't a good enough reason to date.

She sucked on the corner of her mouth, concerned at her musings, as the person in front of her in the queue moved along. *Date? I can't date, I have a husband.*

And everyone acts like he's dead.

Fuck. That had been the worst part of everyone's care and attention with the flowers and the cards, and the sympathetic glances ... it had made her feel like he'd died.

And you never feel like he's dead – right?

She swallowed hard, blinking rapidly to keep those sneaky tears at bay. And the guilt. Always the guilt...

Do you want *to date?*

What? No!

Maybe not now, but what about next year, or the year after?

No – no, no, no. I'm married.

For how long?

For forever.

So ... you're not going to date ... ever again? Ever? Not for the rest of your fifty years, or however long you've got? You're not going to date for half a century?

"Miss?"

"Hmmm? What?" She looked up, both startled and angry at her internal argument.

"What pump number were you?"

Jesus. Now at the front of the queue, she gave the cashier the number, and herself a mental slap. *You. Have. A. Husband.*

One whose life had been ruined. One who was so much worse off than her, and here she was whinging about not being able to date for the rest of her life. So fucking what? He'd never walk, or talk, or damn near *anything* again for the rest of his life. He was trapped in his own frame; in his own mind. He was breathing, but gone.

No. He's not gone!

She handed over her bank card, her hand shaking more than she'd like.

The cashier looked at her funny.

Wonderful. Clearly, I do look like shit. And now I have the shakes. He probably thinks I'm on drugs.

Biting her tongue from snapping out a stream of inappropriate words, she reached for the sunglasses on her head, and pulled them down over her eyes, silently reciting another of her daily mantras: *just get through the day.*

It was already two o'clock by the time she made it back to her parents'. Everyone was in the garden.

"There she is," announced her dad when he spied her making her way up the side path.

"I'm sorry I'm late."

"Did you go to London for the petrol? Did you tell Jamie I want my car back?"

"Dad... The traffic was awful coming back, *and* I had to crawl behind a tractor for half the journey. And I let you know yesterday, didn't I? About how sorry Jamie is and how he's going to make it up to you?"

Her father sounded out his usual grunt, but she knew he was secretly pleased that Jamie was dealing with the car's due service, MOT, road tax, *and* insurance. The Beast was all sorted out for the next year, her dad wouldn't be paying a thing, and she knew he'd already forgiven her brother, despite the fact Jamie had decided to stay up in London until after the funeral, keeping the car away from its owner for longer. Needless to say, he and Merri wouldn't be making it today.

"Mummy!" Becca waved at her from the picnic table on the decking.

"Hey, munchkin." Pippa made her way to her, wondering if Liam and Sammy were upstairs, and if she should be worried she couldn't hear them. "Whatchya doing?"

Her daughter looked down at her colouring pens and paper. "I'm writing the boat man a letter."

"The boat man?" she asked, puzzled.

Becca looked at her like she was simple. "The *boat* man. Grandma said he was coming."

"You mean Jimmy?"

She nodded. "I'm writing a letter to say thank you for giving you new clothes because you love them so much." She went back to work with her brown felt-tip.

Pippa felt her face growing warmer. "Becca, I've already said thank you. We don't need to make a big deal of it." And now she wished she hadn't worn the same clothes today. She'd put them on this morning because she thought it would be a nice gesture since he'd refused to take any money, but Becca's letter seemed to turn it into—

"But they're pretty."

For god's sake... She looked down at the paper, trying to make out Becca's scrawl. She assumed that was supposed to be writing above the picture she was drawing, not that Becca had learnt to write anything other than a few letters of her name. That didn't stop her from forming her own version of the alphabet "What ... er ... what does this say?"

"It says, 'Dear Boat Man...'"

Pippa rolled her eyes.

"'...Thank you for giving my mummy new clothes when she fell inside your bin—'"

"Oh ... Becca, I didn't fall inside his—"

"'She loves them so much, and she looks like a princess when she wears them.'"

Now her face was burning.

Becca looked up at her, very proud with herself.

"Becca ... I don't think—"

"Mummy?" Becca suddenly frowned.

"What? What is it?"

"What colour was the bin?"

"The ... no – look, that wasn't exactly how it—"

"I'm colouring it brown, because brown is the colour of a lot of dirty things, but should it be black like the bin in our kitchen?"

Pippa stared at the messy lines and blobs on the paper. "You're drawing the bin?"

Her daughter pointed at the brown thing she was colouring in, then looked at Pippa like she should completely understand. Next, she moved her finger up an inch to what Pippa could *just* make out was a sad face. It had been obliterated by lashings of brown. "And this is you inside the bin."

The doorbell sounded.

"Boat man!"

"Er…"

Becca clambered off the table, taking the 'letter' with her before Pippa had a chance to talk her out of it.

Let her have her fun – who cares?

Right – who cared.

What *did* she care? It was no big deal. None at all.

Except her face was hot and she was feeling…

Feeling what?

Nervous.

Really? Why?

Because this is the first social gathering you've been to since David's accident.

It was hardly a social gathering though, was it? It was just family.

Nevertheless, she now recognised the awkward sensation of butterflies in her tummy, and Becca's letter hadn't helped. Here she was again, feeling exposed.

Because you're not ready…

Ready for what?

"Bloody hell! Pip!" Her dad's yell had her whipping her head around, in time to see a pile of napkins get blown off the serving table by the wind. "Get them!"

"Oh…" She chased them along the path Becca had just run down, and into the kitchen through the back door.

"Jimmy!"

Three delinquent napkins in hand, she looked up at the sound of her mum's voice, not used to hearing her so ... emotional. And exuberant.

She peered around the kitchen's door frame and peeked into the hallway.

"Mrs C!" came the equally joyful reply, and then Jimmy, with bunch of flowers in hand, was enveloping her mother in a hug as if he were her long-lost son.

What on earth did I miss when I went to university? She needed to find out more. Her dad hadn't said anything else after that little titbit two days ago, and she'd felt too weird about pressing further, as if she had no right to know – he'd been Jamie's friend, not hers.

"Jimmy, you look fantastic. This shop of yours is doing you well, I take it?"

"It looks after me well enough. Keeps me afloat, that's what counts. I can't remember the last time I saw you."

"Must be about seven years ago."

"Bumped into you in the street, didn't I?"

"I think so."

"You haven't aged a day."

"Why didn't you keep in touch?"

"Aaawwww, I meant to – I tried – and then life just sort of happened and I—"

Pippa cringed at the sound of a clatter by her feet, not understanding what had caused it until she realised her bracelet had come off her wrist. *Bloody thing – it's been falling off its catch for months. Why don't you get it fixed?*

Never mind that. Two pairs of eyes were pinned on her, and she'd just been caught red-handed, eavesdropping. "Napkins," she stated, holding up the paper things. "Blew in from outside."

Jimmy's smile grew wide, and those butterflies in her

stomach lurched. *As they do when you get caught eaves-dropping.*

He took a step towards her, and then stopped, and they both stood there, until standing there grew a little awkward. She felt a pull to greet him in a hug the same way her mum had – in comparison to that, she just seemed distant and cold – but that wasn't the way she'd ever been with Jimmy, so – yeah ... there she stood. With napkins.

"I'll take those," said her mother, collecting the napkins from her hands, and two others that she'd failed to pick up off the floor. Her mother also came back up with her bracelet, handing it to her in exchange for the napkins. "This is so pretty."

Pippa stared at the silver chain, decorated by a selection of tree charms. "Thanks," she found herself replying. "David bought it for me."

Her words seemed to hang heavy in the air, and she suddenly wished she hadn't brought up David. *That's why you refuse to fix the bracelet, isn't it? It would somehow taint it, to have it changed from how he gave it to you.*

"Well, it's beautiful," said her mum.

She walked off towards the garden, with a "speak later" to Jimmy, leaving them alone in the hallway.

A clock's second hand ticked.

"You look great," he said.

"Oh, thanks." She smoothed down her top and skirt, her face growing warm again at the memory of Becca's letter. "Becca loves this outfit so much," she laughed. Speaking of whom ... where was the little madam? She'd been scampering this way – where had she gotten to?

"Oh..." He thrust the orange, yellow and blue flowers at her. "These are for your mum, but ... well, the napkins got there before I could."

"Right, of course – I'll put them in a vase." She took them, pushing away the notion they were somehow for her, and even more so, the notion she wouldn't mind that so much. It had been quite a while since she'd received flowers – that weren't flowers of condolences, anyway.

"Is your bracelet okay?"

"Yeah, it's just a dodgy catch."

"I can probably fix it if you like."

"Really?"

"Yeah, I have a watch tool kit at the shop, and some pliers. I reckon I could give it a go."

"Thanks. Maybe I'll pop in with it next week some time."

"Do."

Aaaaaaand silence.

Where did words go when you needed them?

"Would you like—"

"Would you like a drink?"

They both laughed as they spoke over each other.

"I'd love a drink." replied Jimmy. "Beer would be great."

"Coming up. What were you going to say?"

He never got the chance to tell her, because she suddenly caught sight of Becca leaning against the staircase, near the kitchen, staring at them. She ducked her head a little once she knew she'd been spotted. Pippa knew that look. Despite her very enthusiastic mention of 'the boat man' earlier, she was now battling her shyness at having him here, in front of her.

"Hey!" exclaimed Jimmy. "There's the princess of the house."

She smiled, head still tucked under, and darted to Pippa's side, burying her face in her thigh, peeking out occasionally through her hair. *I really have to cut that hair.*

"Aaaw, you beat me to it." Jimmy got down on his knees.

Pippa raised her eyebrows in question, but he wasn't looking at her, he was focused on Becca.

"I was going to go for that spot. Good job your mum's got two legs." He *literally* rammed his face into her left thigh.

"Jimmy!"

But her exclamation was overridden by Becca's shriek of laughter at the sight of Jimmy 'hiding' behind Pippa. This quickly descended into a game of peekaboo as he and Becca took turns trying to catch each other out 'peeking'.

Becca was helpless, her giggling unmanageable.

"I'm not a totem pole!" But she couldn't hold a serious face as her protest fell on deaf ears. However, as quickly as the game had started, it finished, when Becca grabbed hold of Jimmy's hand and dragged him outside to 'see the barbecue'.

Boat man winked at her as he was pulled down the hallway, after a nattering Becca, no longer shy in the slightest. *That didn't take long.*

That strange, 'exposed' feeling came over her again. *Vulnerable.* That's what it was – she finally recognised it. She felt vulnerable.

The front door released its catch – having obviously not been shut properly – as the breeze took hold of it. With the back door also open, it created a mini-gale in the hallway. *Aaaah – so that's why all the napkins ended up down here.*

With a broken bracelet in one hand, and a bunch of flowers in the other, she caught the door with her foot and pushed it shut against the wind.

VII

Shining Armour

Candy watched Becca chase Sammy around the paddling pool, while they dodged the 'shark waves' Jimmy created with his arm as he swivelled it under the water. Her shrieks of delight were both welcoming and ear-splitting; Sammy's laughter no less so. Jimmy had been kneeling at the side of the paddling pool, creating waves for fifteen whole minutes, somehow managing to make the most repetitive game ever, one she wanted to join in on (but wouldn't for fear of puncturing a hole in the pool).

Neither of the kids had tired yet.

She put the last bit of her burger in her mouth.

"Hey." Pippa approached her from the left and sat down next to her on the low wall.

"Hey." She pointed at Jimmy and the kids. "This is quite a show."

"It makes a great change from the squabbling."

"I'll bet. Is there a lot of squabbling?"

"Mainly between the two boys. They're both quite protective of Becca, though, so they tend to have more patience with her even when she's pushing their buttons. Thanks for coming, by the way."

"I really wanted to – thanks for asking."

"Sorry Jamie and Merri couldn't make it."

"I would have been surprised if they'd been able to."

"I just hope you're not too bored. Please don't feel you can't join in with random chats and stuff. My dad comes across as a bit of a grump, but he means well."

Candy waved her off, her mouth half-full. "What? No … I had a great talk with him earlier – didn't think he was grumpy at all."

"Ha – he must have liked you."

"And I'm not bored."

"Good. I haven't had much of a chance to talk with you while sorting out the kids' food and then helping Dad with the barbecue, so he can eat, too."

"I've kept myself busy with this," she gestured at the scene in front of her again, "and it has not disappointed, let me tell you. Jimmy's really good with kids."

Pippa fell silent next to her, and she looked over to make sure she hadn't said anything wrong. She didn't look angry, just … a bit perplexed.

"You okay?"

"Hmmm?" Pip turned to her, distracted. "Yeah – I was about to ask you the same."

"Do I not look okay?"

Pippa raised an eyebrow. "You look as good as me."

"Aaaah."

Then they both laughed, and Candy put her paper plate on the grass by her feet. "I'm … going through a rough patch, that's all."

"I kind of figured. I wanted to say this a few days ago when we were on the boat… If you ever want to talk about it, I'm all ears. I know we haven't known each other for long, but … you know, a problem shared is a problem halved, and all that."

"Thanks." And hell, Candy *did* want to talk about it. She'd wanted to talk about it for years. She'd wanted to talk about all the things that brought her happiness, not just all the things that brought her sadness and pain, but she could never talk about it, because Tim and Lauren were a couple – *the* couple in everyone else's eyes. They were married. She was the 'third' one, and even though she'd never felt that way around them and they'd never treated her that way, the very few people who knew their situation had always treated her as such. And the rest of the people?

The three of them had naturally fallen into the pattern of never telling anyone unless they needed to know. A polyamorous relationship brought up too many questions, too many judgements, and too many faded friendships because of those judgements. And since Lauren had become ill, Candy and Tim had culled all affection towards each other in public, even friendly, non-couply affection – anything at all that might indicate they were intimate. She couldn't remember now, if that had been her idea, or Tim's idea, or if it was simply something that had happened of its own accord. Whichever it was, it ruined her a little. She missed affection.

Everyone knew of Lauren's illness.

No one knew about Candy.

She didn't think Pippa was the judgemental type, but people she thought she'd known well had surprised her. She *did* know that Pippa valued marriage, not so much because she'd said so, but because it was in her manner, her actions and thoughts, and in the way she spoke about her husband the few times she did speak about him.

Candy fiddled with her paper napkin, Becca's melodic giggle igniting some vague sense of both hope and loss – innocence, and innocence gone. "Someone ... erm ... someone very close to me is dying of breast cancer. She doesn't have long left now, and it's on my mind a lot."

"Oh, honey." Pippa placed her glass down. "I'm so, so sorry. Shit. And on the boat, I went on and on about David."

"No – no, no, no, don't do that. See, that's why I don't talk about it," she laughed nervously. "I don't want you to feel weird or act differently. I'm glad that you can talk about David. I'd talk about ... my friend, too, but it feels all so fresh still, you know? It's kind of raw."

"I do know."

Candy smiled, her heart beating a little faster than usual. She'd promised herself she wouldn't stay at the barbecue for more than an hour, feeling far too guilty at leaving Tim and Lauren for her selfish pleasure, and far too concerned over Lauren's deteriorating and ever-unpredictable state.

It had been an hour and a half.

The fun and laughter had kept her rooted; had her desperate to soak it all in before facing the heaviness of home again. She wished Tim had changed his mind and come, but she'd known he wouldn't, even after Lauren's very vocal disapproval at his decision.

"I know you know." Candy smiled a small smile. "Thanks."

"Any time," she replied, softly.

"And how are you?"

"Same old – nothing new to report."

"Really?" Candy teased. "Nothing about the adorable new clothes you're wearing?"

Pippa snapped her head around, staring at her, and Candy couldn't suppress a chuckle. "Becca told me all about it."

"*Becca*." Pippa let out an exasperated groan. "Honestly."

"It was a very dramatic tale about falling inside a bin

and being rescued by 'the boat man', who then dressed you up like a princess."

"Jesus..." Pippa dropped her head into her hand.

"I was waiting for the part where he rescued you from the tower you've been imprisoned in, and then turned from 'boat man' to prince once you kissed him."

"There was no kissing," she bit out. "At least not from me. And no tower. And I didn't fall *inside* a bin. God..."

Candy laughed. "I know – don't worry. I can just about decipher the code of a four-year-old's imagination. It's very sweet she's so into the story though. What do you mean, no kissing 'from you'?"

"I mean," she lowered her voice, shuffling closer to Candy, "he had company in the form of some college-aged, blonde when I was walking up by the side of his shop to drop off the keys. I was caught off-guard by their rather loud 'interactions', and I slipped on a bag of rubbish in the alleyway while trying to get the hell out of there. Then I fell on it."

Candy laughed out loud this time.

Jimmy looked up, and Pippa slapped her on the arm. "Sshhh."

"Sorry. But oh, lord ... do *not* tell Becca that version. Hers is so much more pretty."

"You're as bad as she is!"

"I *like* her version. Who doesn't like fairy tales?"

"There's no fairy tale."

"Are you sure?" She didn't really know why she'd asked that. Maybe because she so longed for her own fairy tale right now; her own happy ending. One she knew she wasn't going to get.

Pippa looked at her in bafflement, and she had no idea what she was thinking. Was her fanciful pondering so preposterous? Why was she always surrounded by realists?

Candy shrugged. "All I'm saying, is if there's even a *possibility* of a fairy tale, don't wish it away."

"What *fairy* tale? I fell on his rubbish."

"Cinderella was covered in soot."

"Am I Cinderella?"

"Do your new slippers fit?"

They both automatically looked down at Pippa's flip-flops, courtesy of Jimmy.

When Candy looked back up, Pippa was flushed pink in her cheekbones. *Interesting...* She decided it was time to put out the unexpected fuse she'd lit, although half of her wanted to know where it would lead. To dynamite? Or a dead end? "Oh, Pip, I'm only teasing." Then, she sighed. "It would be nice, though, wouldn't it?"

There was a huge roar, and everyone looked towards the pool to see Jimmy tumble into it, Sammy and Becca cheering at having won this little game.

"What would?" whispered Pippa.

"Fairy tales. Magic making everything all right." Candy felt that familiar pain pull at her heart. She'd have to pack up and go home soon.

"I had my white knight, Candy."

Candy looked at Pippa.

She was staring ahead at, or perhaps beyond, the fiasco in the pool. "He was mortally wounded by a metal beast. He's all but gone now. No kiss can save him; true love can't save him. The fairy tale ended."

She didn't miss the gleam in the corner of Pippa's eye, which she quickly blinked away. Candy gave her arm a comforting squeeze, not sure if what she was about to say was helpful or a hindrance, but needing to say it anyway, because *she* needed to believe it was true. "Endings bring new beginnings. Love has many truths. And knights come in all colours."

~*~

Pippa reached the top of the stairs, and scanned the landing. "Liam?" She didn't think she'd even seen him for a whole hour. "Liam!"

There was a creak, and her parents' bedroom door opened.

Liam emerged, looking flushed and avoiding her gaze.

What the hell is that about? "Are you all right? You're missing all the fun."

"Felt tired – fell asleep."

"In Gran's room?"

He shrugged. "Didn't mean to fall asleep. Just wanted some quiet."

Pippa bit her tongue. He'd been *far* too quiet of late. "Okay ... well, we've all finished lunch and we're going to have some tea soon. Did you want anything?"

He gave her a half-smile. "I'll go down and see what there is."

"Okay then."

He did exactly that, walking past Pippa and down the stairs.

She wondered if she should say something else, or let it go. He was becoming increasingly difficult to both talk to and decipher.

Instead, she went to shut her parents' bedroom door, and spied her handbag on their bed, where she'd left it, but ... unzipped.

She frowned. *Has he been in my bag?*

The bathroom door opened before she could think further on it, and Jimmy walked out, hair wet and messed up from where he'd just towelled it dry. And he was shirtless, his T-shirt in his hand instead of on him.

Which was fine.

Of course it's fine.

She made a conscious effort to meet his eyes instead of staring at his chest. They were blue. *Really* blue, like the deepest part of the sea, under the sun. She'd not really noticed before.

Liar. You noticed at The Boat Shop.

"Sorry," he apologised. "Didn't know anyone was out here. I'm just drying up after *that* much needed exercise," he laughed as he yanked his top over his head.

Her plan to focus on his eyes instead of his chest failed completely as he brought the top down and everything ... flexed.

She swallowed, trying to shake the slowly branding image of naked Jimmy out of her mind – *I mean, come on, eeeewww, it's Jimmy* – then finally spoke. "It's no problem." What the fuck was wrong with her?

It's been TOO LONG since you've had sex.

And now she was thinking about sex. *Bad, bad, bad.*

Eight months, eight months, eight months, eight months... "You ... um ... don't have to be the kids' entertainer, you know."

"Are you kidding?" And those far-too-blue eyes actually shone with delight.

Candy's put a spell on you, or something, with her crazy talk about fairy tales and magic. Pressed a switch in your brain, and now you're thinking the crazy things she said.

"That was the most fun I've had in *months.*"

"Seriously?"

"Definitely."

"Oh. Good. I have no doubt Sammy and Becca thought so, too."

"Candy looked suitably entertained, as well," he grinned.

Jealousy rose. Unexpectedly. Just like at the shop. *He noticed Candy looking?* "Well, I..." She stopped herself in time, realising what she was about to say would come out totally wrong. He didn't need to know she'd been looking as well. *At all.* "I think everyone was entertained."

He stared at her for longer than was necessary, as if waiting for her to say more.

He knows. 'Cause you're acting all weird and can't seem to stop. Totally knows.

Knows what? There's nothing to know.

And for the life of her, she had no idea what else to say, her ridiculous, silent argument – one she couldn't seem to shut off – distracting her from all sense and reason.

He nodded, slowly, accepting the silence, eyes still studying her. "That's never a bad thing. Well ... I promised your mum I'd help with sorting out the tea before I make tracks."

"Wait." She stepped in front of him, between him and the stairs.

He did as she asked, not that he had much of a choice with her blocking his exit.

"Curiosity has the better of me."

His eyebrows went up slightly. "Uh-oh."

"Why, exactly, are my parents so taken with you?"

He took a step back, and leaned against the bathroom door frame, crossing his arms, with a smirk. "Your disbelief in my ability to be a well-liked individual is truly inspiring."

She smiled, and crossed her own arms. "You know I didn't mean it that way. I know *something* happened after I went to university – that you stayed here for a few days – but I seem to be the only one who doesn't know *what* happened. And mum won't tell me. Said I should ask you."

"And this is you asking me?"

"Shall I ask again, emphasising syllables? Would that help?"

He chuckled. "Very dry, Mrs Fellows."

She bristled. Why did he call her that? "Don't call me that," she blurted out before she could stop herself.

And there he was, staring at her again. "Why not?" he asked, quietly.

She clenched her jaw.

The atmosphere had suddenly changed, but she wasn't sure why.

You know why...

No. Nope, nope. It was all too hard to think about – even the mere possibility of... *Too hard to go there.*

Go where?

NOT LISTENING. "I asked my question first."

He let out a slow breath, contemplating her before speaking. "I was going through a really rough time with my family, and your parents went out of their way to help me. Especially your mum."

She waited, but he said nothing more. "That's it?"

"Pip..."

"I don't get to know what happened? Even though everyone else knows?"

His sigh was more pronounced this time. "Ask me anything else. I'll give you an honest answer. I just don't want to talk about this right now."

She held herself tighter under her crossed arms. It kinda hurt that he wouldn't tell her, no matter how stupid she told herself that was. He was Jamie's friend, not hers.

Bollocks. You keep telling yourself that – that you don't know him. The hell you don't. You know him better than you allow yourself to admit.

Didn't he trust her? Fine. She'd do it his way. "Do you want kids?"

His eyes widened, clearly surprised at her question. Whether it was at the question specifically, or the fact she'd called his bluff about him answering honestly, she wasn't sure.

He averted his gaze from hers, stared at the door frame instead, and picked at a bit of it with his nail.

"You promised," she said.

"Why that question?" He was clearly uncomfortable.

"You seemed in your element downstairs with Becca and Sammy – I just wondered."

Pippa – just let it go.

But she didn't want to let it go. She wanted to ... know him better. After all, she was wearing clothes he'd given her. And if he wasn't going to tell her that important thing everyone else in her family knew, he could bloody well tell her something else important.

You're so stubborn.

She didn't budge, not willing to give in. "You *did* promise."

"I did." He exhaled sharply, still fiddling with the paint on the door frame. "I've always wanted kids. I'd love to have kids. Always had visions of a big family and ... doing it right, you know? Bringing them up well, and not the way I was."

She knew he'd come from a bit of a rough background. His family had lived on the 'wrong side of town' when they were growing up. But that was all she really knew.

"But it's never going to happen."

"It isn't?"

He stopped picking at the paint and looked back at her, sadness and acceptance evident on his face. It took her aback. "I'm pretty much infertile."

Shit. "Oh." *Well done, Pip. Well-fucking-done. Can of worms – open.* "I'm sorry. I didn't know ... I mean, I just wanted to ask something that was—"

"Don't sweat it. It's fine. I found out a long time ago."

"When?" *Can't help it, can you? Got to dig deeper.* "God, my stupid mouth. You know what? I'm way too pushy sometimes. You don't have to answe—"

"I found out when I was eighteen. My family were ... I needed to find money fast. And badly. I ended up going to a fertility clinic in Truro looking to donate sperm."

"Wow."

"Yeah. Me and my infinite teenage wisdom, eh?"

"You were eighteen?"

"And needing cash. Anyway ... that's when I was told my sperm count was close to zero. I got myself tested again about a year ago, after I met Emma."

She was bristling again... What was it about Emma that irritated her so much? She crossed her legs at her ankles as well as her arms.

"Still a low sperm count, so—"

"You want to have kids with Emma?"

"What?" He looked genuinely shocked. "No. No – it's not like that with her at all. Her and I are super-casual – it's just... Hell, Pip, it's hard to explain, but she entered my life at a time when I really needed that kind of uncommitted arrangement. It made me feel *free,* and I thought for the first time in a while about my future and what I wanted. I wondered if anything had changed – that's why I got myself tested again."

"You're right. It's hard to explain, 'cause I don't really get it. Being *un*committed and free with Emma, made you wonder if you could have kids? But not with Emma?"

He sighed again; went back to staring at her. "You still want to know what happened between me and your parents?"

"Are you changing the subject?"

"Turns out the first question's easier to answer after all."

"Okay, then. Spill."

"Oh, no. I don't want to talk about it here – memories. Tomorrow. Meet me for lunch."

"Lunch?" She'd gone and asked that as if the word was in a foreign language.

"Yes, lunch. You know – that thing that happens between breakfast and dinner."

"Now who's being dry?"

"You're clearly a bad influence."

She rolled her eyes, then caught herself. She did that way too much.

"My part-timer's in at twelve. I potentially have four hours free, as long as she can hold the fort. Bring your bracelet, too, so I can fix it."

"What do I say to my parents about needing them to babysit again?"

"That's up to you – tell them the truth. Tell them I'm going to tell you about what happened back then."

The truth. Right. Well, there was nothing wrong with that, was there? Tell them the truth. The truth was that this was *not* a 'date'. "Okay. Twelve o'clock."

Not a date. It's meeting up to learn information about someone and understand them better.

Idiot. That's what a date is.

"Great."

No one moved.

"So ... can I pass?"

"Oh! Yes." She stepped aside. "Sorry."

He didn't walk towards the stairs, but took a step towards her instead, a million questions in his eyes – unsurprisingly, since she couldn't figure herself out right now, either.

He stood about two inches away, and she could feel the heat from his skin. She finally met his eyes, and the heat became a palpable thing. *Going to get burnt!*

She tried to take a step back, but couldn't 'cause the wall was right there.

Jimmy smiled a slow smile. "Becca's right," he said, softly. "This outfit looks pretty damn amazing on you."

Embarrassment shrouded all else, as she wondered *exactly* what part of Becca's fanciful imagination she'd fed him. *Oh, god. THAT'S why he's been staring at you – he thinks ... he thinks...* She didn't know what he thought, but if Becca and her letter had had anything to do with it...

He turned and walked off down the stairs leaving Pippa alone with her butterflies, all that heat, and the uncomfortable truth she was finding more and more difficult to deny: she was thinking about Jimmy in *that* way. The way that needed to be reserved only for David.

Noooo...

Yes.

No.

Yes.

Shit.

When did that happen? Why didn't I stop it?

She closed her eyes, leaned her head against the wall, and tried to muster up the slight irritation she'd felt for him in her teenage years.

Big fail. It wasn't there. Irritation at Emma still was though.

Jealousy. Because you're attracted to him. Fucking wonderful. 'Adult Jimmy' was no longer 'kid Jimmy' in her mind – nowhere close – and the transformation had taken place literally in the last three days. She cursed herself for not noticing it happening. *Look at the mess you're making.*

She did look. At the wedding band on her finger.

Guilt consumed her.

Fuck, fuck, fuck. She'd stop it tomorrow. Whatever he might be thinking, and whatever Becca had said, she'd set him straight. That was the only decent thing to do.

Even if it's not what you want?

She ignored her inner-voice. Her voice was stupid. *She* was stupid. She'd told David to go out to his meeting that afternoon, when he'd wanted to skip it after their making love. If he hadn't gone – he wouldn't have needed to drive home that night...

She gasped, deeply, forcing air into her lungs, the regret that sat in the centre of her being almost crippling.

She'd told no one – no one knew. If her kids found out that's why he'd... Jesus, they'd never forgive her.

A tear fell onto her top. She angrily wiped at her face. At least the guilt had drowned out her inappropriate reaction to Jimmy's presence.

Just get through the day, just get through the day...

Three more deep breaths, and she pushed all the crap down to where it could stay. Then, she smoothed down her top, moved her hair slightly to hide the dark spot the tear had left, and made her way downstairs.

VIII
Dirt

He hadn't imagined it. By fuck, he hadn't, he was sure of that now, although he was still stuck on the when, why, and what-the-actual-hell.

Had he pushed a little too much? Been too intimate up-stairs?

Probably.

Jimmy leaned back and peered into the hallway while slicing cake. He was sure she hadn't come down yet.

There were a couple of times back at the shop when he'd read ... *something* ... in her eyes. Something that resembled attraction, or at the very least, interest. Whatever it was, he'd never felt it from her before, to the point where he'd convinced himself it was wishful thinking on this part. He hadn't needed much convincing – Pippa had always been a no-go zone for him. She'd always looked at him with an 'as if' in her eyes, and then not looked at him at all, for when he was fifteen, she'd been seventeen, and very uninterested in males who weren't shaving and driving.

Oh, she'd been friendly enough with him ... in the way one was with a pet, or a small child. He'd always had a bit of banter from her; the famous eye roll on a regular basis. But Jamie had constantly drilled into him *it was never going to happen.* Although a part of that might have been brotherly protectiveness, it was mostly just common sense, and, he suspected, Jamie's desire to not see Jimmy disappointed by pursuing his horny imagination down a dead-end. For twenty years he'd avoided that dead-end, and then, Thursday had happened.

She'd ended up falling down *his* dead-end instead.

And it should have meant nothing more than anything ever had with her, but he'd not been able to get her out of his thoughts for the rest of Thursday, despite his years of practice. Perhaps it didn't help that he'd kitted her out in clothes. Other than looking stunning in that turquoise colour, he couldn't shake the idea he'd *provided* for her – clothes and comfort. It was like hugging her without actually hugging her.

He'd done a damn good job of ignoring the sublime vision she'd left imprinted in his mind (as much as was possible, anyway) for ten whole hours, and then she'd phoned. He'd made the mortifying 'pussy' comment, and she'd ... flirted with him.

No, he'd told himself, *you're making it up*. And he would have believed it. She'd said nothing overt – it was all in her last comment and the way she'd hung up, so he'd *had* to be hearing something that simply wasn't there.

And finally, there was today.

From the moment he'd seen her in the hallway, to five minutes ago upstairs, he'd *felt* her gaze on him. Felt it like he felt the sun on his back when he surfed – no mistaking it – and this time, he'd gone through *every* logical argument he could to convince himself otherwise, but the sun on your back was a hard thing to convince someone they couldn't see or feel.

So he'd pushed. And he'd lied. 'Cause he *had* known she'd be standing in the hallway – he'd heard her talking to Liam. He'd walked out of that bathroom, shirtless, on purpose, because he remembered the way she'd looked at his chest back at the shop when he'd led her to the shower. He'd talked himself out of it meaning anything – not this time, though. This time, upstairs, the heat that lit her eyes had been perfectly clear. He'd also seen her struggle to hide it.

He was confused.

He was turned on.

He was playing with fire – not just because of her situation, but because of his.

He peeked down the hallway again. She wasn't in sight. Looking to the right instead, he spotted her outside in the garden. Ah – she'd sneaked right past the kitchen. Probably went through the lounge. To avoid him? Fuck.

It was too late – way too late. He knew himself too well, and now that he was sure of her attraction to him – hell, even if it was nothing more than a *trace* of attraction – he didn't know if he could back down, despite the fathoms of crap that surrounded them both. It was Pippa. *Pippa.* Pippa in her armed tower, and all he could feel was the desire to break it down and pull her out. Because hope was a bitch he couldn't turn away from. If he had, he'd never have found this beautiful family he'd always wished was his own.

Not gonna happen. His father's voice again. *You came from dirt, you'll stay in dirt.*

"How's the cake?" smiled Pippa's mum, stepping in from outside.

He looked down at his handiwork. *Bloody miracle you didn't slice your fingers off with your wandering mind.* "All done. Twelve pieces cut."

"Excellent. Thank you, Jimmy. Let's serve up. George is starting to growl."

He laughed. "Still has that sweet tooth, then?"

"Goodness, yes, seems to get sweeter with age. Here..." Using the cake knife, she passed him two slices on two plates, which he took off her hands. "Why don't you take those out to Candy and Pip, and I'll take these out to George and Becca. We can come back for the rest."

"Is Candy still here? I think she might have gone home."

"Oh, has she?" Helen looked up at him and smiled. "Why don't you eat that slice with Pippa, then," she said, before turning and stepping back outside, leaving him to wonder at that smile and look, and the tone of her voice.

Like mother, like daughter. It's all said without words.

He knew Pippa thought she was nothing like her mum, and very much like her dad. He damn well saw the similarities, though, between the two women, and always had. They were both fierce in highly different ways, but it was the same energy; the same warrior-mode gene they both had, although age and perhaps experience had Helen practice a subtlety with hers that Pippa lacked.

Warmth wrapped him in a blanket. He *still* felt very much at home here, after all this time. His own home was starting to feel cold after too many years not being able to nurture it the way he wanted to. He didn't consider any of the places he stayed at 'home'.

He put the plates down, and took his phone out of his back pocket, only just realising he hadn't checked it all afternoon. He grimaced. One text and one missed call from Emma, and *three* missed calls from Cait.

You came from dirt, you'll stay in dirt.

The cold feeling got colder. *You're not going to do this. You're not going to do this to Pippa.*

He had to tread carefully. He couldn't pursue anything with Pip, no matter how unlikely it might be, without sorting everything else out first. *How* he was going to sort it out, though... *It's easy – just end it with Cait. The way you end any relationship.*

But this one had lasted twelve years.

It's not the relationship you have to end, it's what the relationship provides you.

And that scared the living daylights out of him.

He pocketed his phone, picked the plates back up and headed into the garden, just as a cloud passed in front of the sun.

~*~

Candy unlocked the front door and stepped into the hallway, placing her handbag on the hook as she slipped off her shoes.

She slowed her movements as a muffled noise came from the living room, straining to hear what it was. And there it was again.

As ever, it was fear that gripped her first. Was it Lauren? Was she okay? Had something happened?

No – someone would have phoned you.

Her voice of reason had one hell of a battle to be heard nowadays though.

Because she wasn't sure what to expect, or if disturbing the unknown scene would be detrimental, she closed the front door as quietly as she could and made her way silently, treading softly, down the hallway towards the lounge.

Lights from what she assumed was the television flickered on the wall in the hallway through the small gap left by the door, not quite closed.

It's just noises from the TV.

She breathed out her relief, but then froze in front of that gap when she caught sight of... *Really?* She squinted.

Am I seeing what I think I'm seeing?

On the couch, the back of Tim's head covered the bottom right corner of the screen, but it was clear what he was watching: porn.

Oh.

She had no idea what to do.

The next soft moan didn't come from the TV, but from Tim on the sofa, the movements across the back of his shoulders becoming clearer – the whole picture becoming clearer: he was jacking off.

Okay then.

It was okay.

Is it okay?

She didn't know. Two women filled the screen in a mostly naked state, and everything became breasts, nipples and lips for a while, and...

But he's impotent.

Confusion warred with logic, which in turn warred with a warmth spreading across her thighs at the salacious images on the screen.

Clearly, he's not. There was the hurt – faint amid her persistent confusion, but still present. *He's only impotent with you. All these past months, he hasn't been able to...*

Every time they'd begun making love it had ended with Tim's inability to perform, although he'd been there for Candy each time, ensuring she had her satisfaction. 'Each time' though, had been few and far between. In the past six months, they'd only attempted to make love three times – yes, she'd counted – his ever-growing emotional distance from her a constant elephant in the room neither of them discussed.

Her eyes pricked with tears, which felt odd combined with the wetness against her crotch. She wasn't immune to lust, but it was love she missed – touch, affection...

The brunette was now eating out the blonde, rather vigorously, and the blonde vigorously enjoying it in return.

Despite the starkness of what she saw on the screen, it was Tim's reaction to it that sent a wave of heat through her.

He moaned a little louder, and clutched the left arm of the sofa as his movements became faster. Many a time she'd taken pleasure – thrived – on seeing Tim enjoy Lauren in similar ways. Likewise, she knew Tim took pleasure in seeing Lauren and herself enjoy each other.

Should she go in there and ... join in?

Half of her wanted to, but she somehow knew that would be the end to Tim's responsiveness, and a part of her wanted him to have this. With circumstances as they were, Lauren wasn't exactly able to give of herself in this way, and hadn't for quite a while. *Maybe this is therapeutic.*

Why didn't he involve you, then?

The blonde was practically screaming now, orgasm approaching, although the volume was too quiet to disturb Lauren's sleep.

Tim groaned; threw his head back against the top of the sofa...

Candy let out a short breath, aching, incredibly turned on, but still hurting. Too hurt to slip her own fingers inside her trousers and satisfy her need.

It wouldn't satisfy her need. Her need was him. Her need was Lauren.

Tim came. Silently. But she knew he'd come because she'd seen him come a thousand times before.

Stepping away from the living room door, she retreated to the front door she'd walked in from. Wiping tears from her cheeks, she glanced at the round mirror by the coat stand to make sure her eyes weren't red. After she had composed herself, she opened the door as quietly as possible, then let it shut with a bang and a wince, praying Lauren hadn't heard it, but knowing Tim would have.

She waited a few seconds, then made her way back down the hallway. "Hello – I'm home!"

The living room door swung open, and Tim, dishevelled, walked out with a smile, closing the door behind him, though not before she noticed the TV had been turned off. "Hi. I fell asleep on the couch. Just woke up."

She searched his face and pressed down her hurt. "Didn't mean to wake you. The door slipped out of my hand and closed louder than I expected."

"I don't think Lauren will have heard it – she took her painkillers before having a snooze."

"That bad?"

"She has been today."

She must have been to take the painkillers – she hated those bloody pills. And she tried to never go to sleep in the afternoon. Candy looked at her watch – five o'clock.

"Did you have fun at the party?"

I'd have had more fun making love to you. "Yeah. Pippa's kids are hilarious. I wish you'd been there."

"I'm sorry. I didn't want to leave Lauren and ... I guess I really needed the sleep myself."

"I guess you did."

He finally came in for a hello hug.

Candy sank herself into his chest, hugged him back, and resolved to talk to him about what she'd walked in on – not right now, but very soon. She'd give him a chance to bring it up first. Maybe she'd press a little – drop hints – see if it triggered some kind of truth from him.

And that was the problem – the mother of all elephants.

They'd always been open and honest with each other about everything – they had to be with three of them in the mix. For them to work as a unit, it had always been paramount that they talk out any concerns they had. That honesty had now been damaged, and however white the lie, Candy didn't know if the cavernous crack it had created was something that could be repaired.

~*~

"I can't believe he asked you to take the kids tomorrow," Pippa said, annoyed, shoving plates into the cupboard. Almost everything had been cleaned up, Jimmy had left half an hour ago, and she needed to shoot off home as soon as possible if she had any hope of getting the kids to bed on time. At least they might sleep well after the copious amounts of exercise they'd had earlier, courtesy of Boat Man.

She scowled as she thought of him.

"He *didn't* ask me, Pip. He mentioned you were meeting up tomorrow for a chat, and I *offered* to take the kids." Her mum passed her another dried plate.

"Thank you for taking them," she mumbled quietly, still frustrated at not having had the chance to ask her mum first if it was okay for her to take them. "It'll just be Sammy and Becca – Liam's at a friend's house tomorrow."

"That's even easier then, isn't it? You know it's never a problem. I'm not sure what you're worked up about."

"Did Jimmy tell you what the chat's about?"

"Not in so many words."

Not in so many words? That means he told her enough. "*You* could just tell me 'the big secret', you know. Save me going down there, then you'd have a day free without having to babysit."

"Goodness, Pippa, they're my grandchildren – it's hardly babysitting. And no, I'm not going to divulge something best coming from him."

"Fine," she snapped.

Her mum threw her a hard stare. "Honestly, why *are* you acting so put out by it all?"

"Something big happened in his life – big enough for him to be given my *room* to sleep in for a few days – and I'm the only one who doesn't know about it. It's like you all purposely chose to leave me out."

"You weren't living here at the time, and I think it was two or three months after it all happened that you popped home – it seemed odd to bring it up when it was all over by then. I don't even think Jamie was here when it happened – he was away on a school trip or something, and it was Jimmy that told him when he got back, I never said a word. It seems a little odd to talk about it now without him here, to be honest, and odd that you're disgruntled by it."

"I'm not disgruntled."

Her mother sighed. "You really are like your father sometimes."

Pippa snatched the next plate from her.

"I *do* think you should know, Pip, but he should be the one to tell you. Just listen to what Jimmy says tomorrow, and have a nice lunch out."

"It's not lunch *out*. I mean, yes, it's lunch, but it's … you know – lunch. It's a *normal* lunch."

Her mother now looked at her, both eyebrows raised. "What's an *abnormal* lunch?"

Pippa didn't respond as she put away the last plate. This was going nowhere and she was tired of thinking about the not-a-date lunch that loomed ahead. It was imperative

Jimmy didn't get the wrong idea, and she wasn't sure how to bring it up with him. That's why her back was up. Why the hell she'd agreed to lunch tomorrow, she now had no idea – she could do with not seeing him for a while. "I really need to leave and sort the kids out for bed."

"Thank you for helping with the clearing."

"No problem. Thanks for hosting a fabulous barbecue."

"Oh, it was great fun – I really did have fun."

"Me, too."

"Pippa."

"Yep?"

"What Jimmy's telling you tomorrow – it was a huge thing for him. And it's a huge thing for him to talk about."

Pippa stilled.

Her mum touched her arm, gently, in a bid to make sure she was listening. "Try and lower your defences a little, all right?"

"My defences?"

"You know exactly what I'm talking about."

Pippa said nothing, but folded the tea towels instead.

"If you want him to tell you what happened, don't make this hard for him to talk about."

Pippa sighed. "I'm not going to do that." Her curiosity was a demon. It would be far easier to let this go, but the niggle of not knowing something everyone else did would always be there.

"Good." Her mum took the tea towels.

"I'm going to pack the kids' bags and load some stuff in the car before I round them up."

"Okay, darling."

She left her mum filling up the kettle for coffee, wondering if she should stay for a cup before leaving.

No. You're only staying to put off the inevitable.

The inevitable was loneliness. It was the empty bedroom she walked into after she'd tucked all her kids in. She hated going to bed. She hated waking up more. At least sleep brought silence, and a temporary end to her thoughts and feelings.

Sammy's nightmares came to mind, as did her worry for him. She'd feel like shit if she had nightmares every night. Sleep was her only sanctuary the past few months. Sleep, and her parents' house.

She left the front door open as she carried bags to her car, fumbling for the right key to unlock her boot. The dusk had turned most colours to shades of pinky-grey that merged into each other. She'd wait half an hour before leaving. She never liked driving in this light when objects became hard to define.

The scene of David's crash invaded her mind, just for a second or so before she could push it to one side. But it was too late. When the vision came upon her now and then, it stayed, and was perhaps made worse because her own *imagined* vision followed of how it had all happened that night. She hadn't been there, of course. She'd only heard the details, and seen remnants of the aftermath behind a police tape.

The final ruling had come through three months after the accident: no one was to blame. It had been 'one of those things'. David's car and the truck had met on a bend made dangerous by black ice on the road. The bend had been on a dark, country lane. Both vehicles had been on the correct side of the road, only taken off course when David's car had unexpectedly slid. It was virtually impossible to see black ice at night. It had been no one's fault. It hadn't even gone to court.

When she'd received the ruling, she'd taken the kids to

her parents', returned home, locked all her doors, drawn all her curtains, and had cried for two hours, because having no one to blame meant she *was* at fault after all. The accident had happened because she'd pushed him to go to that fucking meeting. The blame was hers.

She looked up from the lid of her boot, the noise of a passing car pulling her out of her thoughts, yet managing to make her thoughts so much more real than they should be. She wondered who was driving it, and where it was going.

She brought her movements to a stop when, having followed it along the road, she caught sight of another car parked further down, on the other side of the street, momentarily lit up by the passing car's headlights.

She wasn't sure what seemed odd. She just stared at the parked car, trying to figure it out. The realisation came with the image of another scene – the one that had taken place this morning at the petrol station.

That's the car from this morning – dark blue Ford Focus – remember the guy that was looking at you?

She squinted against the growing darkness, wanting to make sure she was actually right. The car was over twenty metres away, and she'd paid more mind to the man driving it this morning than to the actual car itself. She couldn't see who was driving it now, but she was sure it was the same make and colour... She could only make out the last three letters of the number plate: EKN. Not that it mattered, because she hadn't paid a blind bit of notice to the number plate this morning, so she was no nearer to knowing if it was the same car.

Its rear lights suddenly came on, it pulled away from the curb, and drove off.

Her skin pimpled, and she had to talk herself out of the sinister thing her imagination wanted to make it. *It prob-*

ably wasn't even the same car. And if it was, why was it even here?

She drew a blank, then heard Sammy let out a shout from inside the house. *Ugh – not another squabble with Liam.* Probably was. They'd been good as gold with each other all day, it was bound to end some time.

The noise had dropped her back into reality, and she found herself shaking her head as she looked back at the spot where the car had been parked. She was being stupid, her mind creating drama because of what she'd been thinking of before she saw the car. Remembering the accident always took her to a dark place. Most likely, it was someone who just stopped to sort out their Sat Nav, or get their bearings. She did that often any time she was driving somewhere new. And there were a lot of dark blue Ford Focuses around.

Slamming the boot shut, she headed back into the house. *Time to get the brood home.*

IX
Commitments

Jimmy didn't want to be here, pulling up on the road outside his shop. He wanted to be home, getting ready for bed, 'cause he felt pretty much wiped out, and he fancied getting up at dawn to ride the morning waves.

But he'd ignored the inevitable: those fucking accounts he still hadn't looked at. And he needed to look at them; he needed a plan. He needed to know how dire the situation might get and exactly how long he had to try and find a way out of it if he wanted to end things with Cait.

'Cause that worked really well last month, didn't it?

He tightened his hands around his steering wheel, his engine still running, to quell the apprehension that rose fast in his gut. He'd been weak. It was different this time – last month, he hadn't been prepared; had no idea she'd pull what she did and have him second-guessing his own argument. He'd ended up giving her what she needed even though he really hadn't fucking wanted to. He let out the breath he'd been holding, his chest tight at the unwelcome memory.

Enough of dwelling on shit. He killed the engine and got out of the car.

He hadn't phoned Cait back yet, but he knew the drill: she'd ask him over next Monday. It was always the last Monday of the month. So, Monday it would be – that's when it would end. It gave him just over a week to face his

Achilles heel first: money. Or rather, the lack of it.

He pressed the code for the alarm as he walked in 'round the back. *Don't hang around. Just grab the books and go.* He often found himself hanging around here when he needed to be home. The shop was a sanctuary of sorts – his own space where he didn't have to worry about duty and responsibility, and the exhaustion both of those sometimes brought.

He must have thought too loudly, or something, 'cause whatever deity heard him decided this was the perfect time to prove him wrong and fuck him over. "There you are."

Shit. Fucking fantastic. "Cait." He turned towards her voice, steady and sultry combined – as always – his heart rate going up. There she was, slouched over the counter next to his till, making slouching look like an elegant pastime. "What the hell are you doing here? Breaking and entering?"

"Hardly, darling. You didn't even notice the alarm didn't trip when you walked in – I'd already turned it off. Must have been some pretty important thoughts taking all of your attention."

It wasn't the first time she'd found a way into this space. She knew a lot of people – probably knew whoever the fuck owned the alarm company, and managed to get a master code. *And the key?* He sighed. That would have been easy enough to acquire and copy last month, while he'd been asleep.

She laced her fingers together. "Are they the same thoughts that have kept you from returning my calls?"

Guess this talk's gonna happen right now then. Sod it – he didn't feel prepared. In the end, it was the memory of Pippa – the time he'd spent with her and her family today – that steeled him. This was just something he had to do, no matter where it led. It had gone on far too long; he'd crossed so many lines he'd never intended to cross – became someone he'd never wanted to be. At least in part. He wasn't so far gone he couldn't find his way back, but if he failed this time, that was it. "Your husband know where you are?"

"Of course not. That's why I've been fruitlessly trying to phone you – he's leaving early this month; tomorrow, in fact. Got an urgent call two days ago. This means I get to see you *this* Monday instead of waiting a whole week. And actually, I'd rather like it if you came over from tomorrow night."

Sunday? Tomorrow's lunch with Pippa came to mind, bringing with it a wave of guilt even though it was just lunch and nothing more.

Bollocks. You want it to be more. You're hoping for more.

End it. End it now.

Cait smiled, now lifting herself off the counter and making her way towards him.

She kept herself immaculate. The corners of her eyes and mouth belied her fifty-two years, but those were the only giveaways. She looked at least ten years younger than she was; kept her hair dyed ash blonde, right along with her eyebrows and lashes. She ate well, she exercised, she'd never been unpleasant to his eye, and this was going to be harder than he'd thought because her very presence – even her goddamned perfume – symbolised the security he craved. *You won't find that anywhere else, you dumb fuck. Think you can create that for yourself out of thin air? What about for those you love? Those who need it more than you?*

That almost swayed him. Almost. It was the monster wave ready to wipe him out.

Pippa's husband had had his accident around the same time he'd met Emma. The two women, from a distance and unbeknownst to them, had inspired him to take a bigger look at himself and his life – Emma with her frivolity, demonstrating every choice he'd denied himself, and Pippa with her unwavering bravery after the tragedy fate had brought to her door and every newspaper in town. He might not have spoken to her for years, but he still saw her. He still paid attention. He'd seen her struggle with work, parenting and caring, single-handedly. He'd seen her make the hard decision to put David into a home. He'd heard it all on the grapevine, knowing exactly how it must have played out because he knew *her*. He'd caught glimpses of her in town every now and then, or when she'd come into his shop on random occasions. She'd looked fatigued; beyond her limit; still looked exhausted today – but she still did it. She did what he hadn't had the guts to do. It had been a massive wake-up call.

Emma in turn, had bounced into his life with her uni talk and her uni ways, reflecting everything he'd given up; had him questioning the turns he'd taken in his past.

But it wasn't Emma's fun-loving, simultaneous attachment and detachment of life that had him questioning his future and what he wanted out of it, as he'd insinuated to Pip. That had all been down to Pippa. He saw Pip facing her own future and *living it* despite all the difficulties, and it had made him want in on his own future. The one he'd unwittingly said goodbye to at eighteen. "I was going to call, but ... we need to talk, and I didn't want to talk over the phone."

"Talk? How droll." Now in front of him, she reached up and rested her hands on his chest. "Especially when we can begin our special time of the month earlier than usual. There's also a fundraiser event on Tuesday. I could do with a mysterious, good-looking friend whose arm I can hang off –

get people's tongues wagging; always ensures you get invited again next time," she smiled.

He wouldn't falter this time. "You know I can't just up and leave my house without putting things in place."

"Which is exactly why I've been trying to call you for two days."

"Cait..."

"I know what you want to talk about." She removed her hands, and delved them into the purse that hung off her shoulder. They came back out holding a cheque. "This."

He closed his eyes at the figure scribbled on it.

"I'm not asking for your extra time for nothing."

"Cait, no."

"No?" She smiled. "You never mean 'no', darling."

Feelings of inadequacy surfaced at the certainty in her tone. He pushed them back so he could focus on what he had to do. "That's not what I want to talk about."

Her smile faded; became stony right along with her countenance. "Oh." She went back into the bag, and brought out a set of papers, slightly yellowed with age. "I suppose you want to talk about *this* then."

Their 'agreement'.

"I want to talk about it, too," she continued, her voice hard. "Pay special attention to the part where you agreed to give me three months' notice before calling it a day. That's the part you tried to get out of last month, is it not?"

"It's just paper, Cait."

"No – it's twelve years. A court of law might not recognise this as binding, but it *is* binding between you and me – bound by over a decade. I didn't force you to sign this all that time ago – if I remember correctly, you were chomping at the bit to get your name on the dotted line. I didn't make you do any of it over all the years. You came back for more, over and over again."

He blinked, his face hot.

"But I *did* make you who you are today. Your name might be on the lease for this place, but I own every square inch of this shop – I practically own every square inch of your life. And it's not just *your* life, is it Jimmy?"

She paused, and he swallowed, unable to form words, that familiar fear of lack flashing in his face on some metaphorical neon sign.

"You want to claim it all back, you see this through to the end. All I'm asking is for you to honour your promise. I've considered your 'notice' as being handed in last month. That's only two more months to go, and then you get your wish – you'll be free. Poor, but free."

Shit, he was shaking inside. Didn't care to admit it, but he was, and he didn't completely know why.

Because you're so close to the end, you can see it, smell it, all but touch it, and you just can't get there.

Fuck it.

What's the big deal, it's just two more months. What's two months when you've done this for twelve years?

He didn't have an answer to that either. This whole agreement with Cait had started to become hard eight months ago, but last month, it was unbearable. And this month... He couldn't. He just couldn't.

He turned his head away from her; looked anywhere else. His eyes landed on another of those tops hanging off a rail identical to the one Pippa had chosen from his selection. It gave him some sense of purpose – she'd been through worse than he. "No. I don't want to do this anymore. I'm grateful for everything you've offered me over all these years, but I can't *do* this anymore."

She completely ignored him, just like she had last

month. With a wry smile, she pressed the cheque into his chest, so hard it hurt. "I've never been disappointed in you, Jimmy, so I think you'll find you can. I don't know what's gotten under your skin, what could be *so important* it makes a dishonest person out of you, but I'm going to give you a bit of breathing space here, to think upon your actions and their consequences. I don't think you've properly thought through what a penniless future is like. Perhaps you should spend tomorrow visiting the homeless in the city; perhaps it'll be the epiphany you need, because I don't think for *one second* you want to put your grandmother through that, do you?"

Even though he'd already talked himself into accepting the risks, that final question still hit him like a fist in the gut.

"Undo *all* that good work you've done with her over *all* this time? No, Jimmy, that's not you." She rose onto her toes and dropped a kiss on his lips.

He didn't respond.

She then stepped back, letting him go. The cheque fell to the ground between them. She shrugged her shoulders. "Forget about tomorrow night since I couldn't get hold of you anyway – come over Monday instead – but keep the extra money." Her eyes were shimmering when he next looked at her. "I'll miss you when you're gone," she said.

And there he stood, feeling like shit. No matter the circumstances, it *had* been twelve years.

"Give me the two months I need to get used to the gaping hole you're going to leave in my life. Please." She bent down, picked up the cheque, and placed it on the display table to his right. "You're worth it all, Jimmy – always have been to me." She turned on her heel and strode towards the back door, letting herself out. "I'll see you Monday," she called out, before his door slammed shut.

~*~

Silence was golden.

Sometimes.

Standing with her back against her closed bedroom door – all the kids in bed and asleep – she wondered if she purposely delayed actively finding a solution to Sammy and Liam's bickering because the noise and chaos kept her busy; kept her mind off the crushing guilt, and the unbearable loneliness that silence brought.

The day had been wonderful, but it had pushed her buttons. It had unravelled her to see someone else – someone who wasn't their father – play with her kids so well; be so attentive with them. It was even more destabilising that they had responded in kind.

They need a father. They need a good future. And she couldn't *be* a father. No matter how many roles she played, how many articles she read about single parenting, or how many people she knew 'doing it alone', it wasn't working – at least, not for her – that had been bloody obvious today. She had a hell of a lot of fun with her kids (or *had* had before everything went to shit), but the fun they had wasn't ... like *that*. Like Jimmy had made it.

Like David had been.

She couldn't be a dozen people at once: mother, school teacher, disability carer, father ... *herself.* Who was she nowadays?

She pushed herself off the door, still uncomfortable with the silence for the voice it gave to all her thoughts. The beside lamp was on low. The bedroom was clean, tidy ... empty.

Pulling off her clothes, she grabbed the cotton top and shorts she slept in from where they were slung over the back of the vanity chair, and put them on.

She and David stared back at her from a framed photograph on the dressing table, smiling under a summer sun, about twelve years ago. They'd met while she'd been at university. He'd been on the grounds to discuss building plans for the new science unit, and it was in the crowded cafeteria where they'd bumped into each other – literally. Her juice had spilled all over her quiche salad, he'd apologised endlessly and bought her another, there'd been nowhere to sit in the bustling place, so they'd sneaked out with the tray and his sandwich, and had ended up under a tree on a grassy bank beside the History block. They'd fallen in love fast; became best friends just as quickly, and she'd become pregnant with Liam just two years later, right after finishing her teaching degree. That was when they'd decided to move back home to be nearer her parents. They'd married in a local church with a small ceremony on a beautiful, warm, calm day. It was the happiest day of her life, second to Liam being born.

She'd arranged for them all to visit him on Monday, after Becca's prompting the other night.

Pippa climbed into bed, and picked up the photograph. It still hurt too much; his brown eyes – aware, intelligent, responsive... There was none of that now. She didn't even know if he really knew who she was, if he understood what the kids meant to him – that they were his, that he loved them. Did he feel love in the same way as before? The brain damage he'd suffered had destroyed all of who he was to the point where...

She cursed under her breath, and wiped angrily at her cheeks, wet with tears. *No.* She didn't think that – she *didn't.* "I don't," she said out loud.

I don't wish that he'd died.

Liar.

Half-lie. It was just a *half-*lie. She didn't wish him gone from the world, but how was this fucking fair to anyone. Was he trapped somewhere in there, understanding everything, but unable to communicate? If so, that was tragic; it couldn't bear thinking about. But the alternative – that he was truly gone in all ways but on paper – was also devastating.

And that's where she stayed, stuck in the grey between the two. There was no moving on; there was no end.

She put the frame back down, more heavily than she'd intended. Her bracelet fell off her wrist with it, its clatter on the dressing table making her wince in the quiet of the room.

She stared at the four silver tree charms, glinting back at her under her lamp, and remembered their meeting for the first time – that lunch under the campus tree. She wondered if he remembered. She was the only one who held that memory now, and it was as frozen in time as everything else.

She didn't want her kids frozen too. She didn't want Becca to grow up always looking backwards, or for Liam to never have a male figure to talk to, or for Sammy to never have that bonding he so needed.

Losing her battle with her tears, she switched the light off, and pulled the covers up over herself, her feet cold.

"Why are your feet always so bloody cold in bed?"

"'Cause they know you're gonna warm them up."

If she closed her eyes, she could hear his voice, too clearly, too *exactly*.

She kept her eyes open, waiting for sleep to close them for her – she wasn't going to make the first move, not with all the memories tossing around in her head.

What the hell are you going to do? You can't keep things the way they are. Becca's going to be five too soon, Liam's not far from puberty; blink and you'll miss them growing up.

She turned over to her right. She didn't want them growing up feeling they'd lost something they could never get back.

But they can't get it back.

Unbidden, Jimmy's ridiculous antics around the paddling pool sprang to mind, Becca and Sammy playing, and they hadn't just played – for the first time in a while, they'd played *freely*, as if they hadn't a care in the world. *That's what they need, before they're too old to find it fun and it passes them by.*

The fact that it was Jimmy who had brought all this to the surface – Jimmy who had her stomach fluttering earlier – still left her a little stunned. But Jimmy aside, she wasn't sure she was ready – certainly not ready for love, and then, there was the question of what she could actually give a future lover. Marriage was out of the question; she wasn't sure she could even get divorced, and she was nowhere near wanting that, the mere thought of it bringing a fresh wave of pain to the fore of her chest.

But did it have to be 'love'? She wasn't the sex-only type – there had to be feelings. Was she ready for ... connection?

Maybe. She didn't know. The thought scared the living daylights out of her.

There was one thing she did know, though. And it had never been made clearer than today, surrounded by her family, hearing her kids laugh; finding that attraction to someone else, no matter how tenuous, was even possible...

And right now – lying here in the silence with cold feet...

She didn't want to be alone.

~*~

It was almost six in the morning, and the cancer unit was full. They'd rushed Lauren in half an hour ago, after phoning ahead. She'd woken up coughing, unable to stop, the pain around her chest too much for her to cope with. Because they'd been expecting her, she hadn't had to wait to be seen, which was always a relief after the half-hour drive to get here. That was the sacrifice for having a nice cottage in the countryside.

Lauren was now resting – or trying to. Candy had left Tim with her after she'd requested iced water. Candy was on a hunt for the ice, and the coffee machine would be getting a hello from her, too.

Six months ago, they'd have been scheduling scans for Lauren after a night like that to see if the cancer had progressed any further. Those were no longer needed. It was just a matter of time now, and she tried not to think about it as she made her way down the corridor, already sure she'd struggle to remember her way back, despite the number of times she'd been here. All the corridors looked exactly the same. *Exactly* the same. This place needed some colour. Strange how they never made hospitals bright and cheery when they painted and decorated them – surely it wasn't hard – and Candy was positive it would only be beneficial. Who wanted to look at white walls and fluorescent strip lights for hours on end when they were ill? No one. She'd feel *more* ill at the poor décor.

Lost in her own thoughts, she almost walked right past the ice machine. *Excellent. All I have to do is find the coffee one next.*

She was second in the queue of two, the blonde lady in front of her bending down and peering into the chute the ice came from – was *supposed* to come from.

"Erm ... are you all right? Is it working?"

The blonde started, and half-spun around, still bent at the waist.

"Sorry," Candy apologised. "I thought you knew I was behind you – didn't mean to make you jump." This woman was ... quite beautiful. In a sort of tired and haggard way specific to the cancer ward, whether you were a patient, or a visitor, wretched disease that it was. Candy was sure she must look just as fatigued.

"Hi – that's okay. This machine ... I don't know. I *think* I pressed the right button, but—"

"Is this your cup?"

She nodded, and finally straightened up.

Candy smiled. "This machine's a bit temperamental – I've used it a couple of times before." She placed the woman's cup under the chute, then pushed the two necessary buttons, careful to press the second one with more weight to the left of it, like she'd learned. "It's this button that's the problem."

"You're a star, thanks so much. I wasn't sure who to ask. Everyone who walks past looks in such a rush, I felt stupid asking about such an insignificant thing."

"Not a problem. Here you go." She handed her the filled cup. "Is this your first time here?"

"Second. But my first time using the ice machine."

Candy laughed, then felt herself blush a little because

this woman was looking at her quite intently. She got that quite a lot with her dyed blue, short hair, though. It was looking kind of long and wispy again around the frame of her face, and her almost-black roots were starting to show. It was probably time for a re-style.

Maybe she realised she was staring, because she looked away and cleared her throat. "And this *isn't* your first visit, I take it. Do you have a relative in here, or are you...?" She let that sentence trail off, and Candy suddenly understood the hidden question.

"Oh – no – not me. I'm not a patient. It's my..." She was going to say 'friend'. That's what she always said; how she always referred to Lauren no matter how much she hated to deny their relationship. She had no idea what made her change stance today. Perhaps it was that this woman was a complete stranger – not a friend, or relative, or doctor, or nurse, so it didn't really *matter* what she said. "It's my partner who's the patient – my girlfriend. It's been going on a while now – terminal. They've said she could have up to six more months, but ... I dunno. It's progressing so fast."

She was being stared at again. She found she didn't mind. The stare wasn't anything other than sympathetic. And inquisitive. "I'm so sorry. It's hard, isn't it? I'm usually in the children's ward, but they were full, and my son – Steve – he's fourteen, so ... Well, here we are for the moment, until they have a spare bed."

"I'm sorry about your son."

"Thanks. We're not sure what's wrong though. He had Wilms' Tumour when he was a toddler."

"I don't think I'm familiar with that." Then she wondered if she should be. There was so much information to read just on breast cancer, let alone every other type of cancer.

"It affects the kidneys – more specific to kids. It all cleared up when he was four, though, and didn't come back, and then a few weeks ago, he started getting bruising. Random bruises in random places, and his blood tests showed anomalies, so..." She shrugged. "Here we are."

"Here we are."

She didn't seem old enough to have a fourteen-year-old son. She looked Pippa's age – early thirties. She'd had to have been really young when she conceived.

Candy placed her own cup under the chute and pressed for her ice. "I'm hitting the coffee machine next."

The woman smiled. "I don't blame you. I don't touch the stuff, but Steve's mum is pretty much addicted."

What? Had she heard that right? Candy reached for her filled cup, unsure what to say.

The woman pulled a face. "I just realise how that sounded. Steve's mum is my ex. We raised him together. She gave birth to him, though – did all the hard work," she laughed, this laugh a little nervous. "And I've probably said too much, right? I do this. She used to tell me off – I talk to anyone and everyone, even if they're strangers. Just stop me if I'm going on and on."

"No ... it's refreshing. Most people are just..."

"Kinda repressed?"

"I guess." Candy smiled to put her at ease. "I was going to say pre-occupied. And I think it can be hard to know who to talk to sometimes, especially about illness. It's always so personal how it affects us."

"Right ... and no one wants to be a burden, or for others to think they're complaining."

"I never for one second thought you were complaining, I promise."

They stood there for a second, both smiling at each

other, and then Candy's phone went. She grabbed it out of her small handbag. It was a text from Tim. They wanted to keep Lauren in for the rest of the day, and might let her out tonight depending on how she progressed. She was sure there was more he hadn't put in the text. "That's news about my partner, so I'd better..." She gestured towards the way she'd come.

"Of course. Hopefully, we'll be in the kids' ward soon, but if not, maybe I'll bump into you later."

"Yeah ... good luck with it all."

"You, too. Thanks for the ice."

"No problem." Candy gave a final wave, then turned and headed back the other way, reflecting on how nice it was to just chat, and wondering if the world would be a better place if strangers were more open with each other – perhaps because 'openness' was something Tim had been avoiding of late. She missed it. And she missed chatting; the general 'lightness' to life it brought; connecting with people and places.

When she finally reached Lauren's room, she paused, not entering straight away, but observing through the small, square window in the door. Tim was perched at the edge of her bed, her hand in his, smiling, talking – husband and wife in deep conversation. He had a twinkle to his eye she hadn't seen in a while.

Her joy at seeing him so happy was quickly doused by a sense of abandonment. It almost seemed wrong to go into the room, as if she'd be interrupting something meaningful and private. And perhaps she would be.

For the first time she could ever remember in their relationship, she felt like the third wheel. She felt 'less' than they were.

Because you are. They've been together for ten years.

You've only been with them for five.

Suddenly lost, she backed away from the door, unsure what to do, or where to go. She desperately wanted to be there for Lauren, but she was tired of being pushed to the periphery, and tired of feeling rejected by it; tired of not being able to talk about it because she had no right to – because her own sadness was insignificant compared to Lauren's inevitable future.

It was the ice in her hand that brought her out of her uncertainty. She stared at the cup.

Lauren needs ice.

Pushing all else to one side, she pressed down the door handle, and walked in.

X
The Secret

Can you meet me at the cove down the bottom of Long Lane instead of at the shop? Need to hit the waves & quieter there for talks.

That was the message Pippa had received at 11 a.m. after dropping Sammy and Becca off at her parents', and before dropping Liam off at his friend's house. It wasn't a problem – Liam's friend, Gavin, was only a five-minute drive from Long Lane – but the word 'need' caught her attention: *need* to hit the waves. Jamie always used to say the same kind of thing, as if his life depended on surfing or something, and it almost always meant he was bothered about something he needed to work off.

For the thousandth time, she told herself she should call the lunch off and forget about whatever Jimmy hadn't told her. It wasn't her business to know, and it was obviously hard for him to revisit.

For the thousandth time, her childish inner-voice protested at being the only one left out of this monumental part of his life for the past thirteen or so years.

She looked at her watch, already having parked the car as far down Long Lane as she could before the lane got too narrow, and it was Jimmy's car she'd parked behind. She'd have to walk the rest of the way to the cove – about a fifteen-minute stretch – but she was half an hour early as it was, having not wanted to hang around her parents', twiddling her thumbs and trying not to look like she was the least bit nervous about this meeting. Her mum saw right through her anyway, and she wasn't comfortable with that fact.

She got out of the car and wrapped her cardigan tight around her. The cove was a windy one, which is why it was popular with surfers, but Jimmy was right – it was quieter. Because it was a bit of a wind trap, regular bathers didn't come down here.

She took one of Becca's hair ties off her wrist – pretty much a permanent adornment – and put her own hair up in a ponytail to keep it from whipping around her face. She was glad she'd brought her cardy, but her white sundress had probably been a bad idea, and nothing said so louder than the little bits of stone and grit peppering the backs of her legs. *Why didn't you wear jeans like you do all the time?*

She knew the answer, and it was stupid: she'd quite liked being complimented on her clothes the past few days – it had been a while since she'd received any. And it had been a while since she'd met up with anyone for a lunch date.

Not a date.

Fifteen minutes saw her at the point where the path, which had already given way to a grassy knoll, became an opening between trees and a hedge, from where she could see the beach. And Jimmy.

That was *definitely* him on the surfboard, and 'quieter' was an understatement – *no one* else was here. He still wore a wetsuit despite the growing heat of the morning.

Glancing at her watch again, she noted they still had nearly quarter of an hour before midday. Unsure if being early was a good idea, she stood where she was, leant against the tree, and watched. She didn't think she'd seen him surf since they were teens. He was a *hell* of a lot better at it now. She couldn't remember for sure, but Jamie may have said something about him entering contests at one stage.

It looked like he'd just paddled out and was waiting for the right wave. If she remembered rightly, this beach was notorious for having a good break out by the rocks that jutted just before the coast went inwards again.

She followed her line of sight to those rocks, and frowned at the silhouettes of kids hanging around the top of them, clearly waiting to jump off. Yes, she *had* heard of that rock. She'd forgotten it was also famed amongst danger-fuelled teens.

Then, Jimmy stood.

Her eyes came back 'round to him, and her heart went up to her throat, because standing became something close to flying in the blink of an eye. He was *speeding* along the ocean. This wasn't a leisurely ride – this was every bit like the extreme sport it could be with the waves being as high as they were today. This was like The Cribbar in Newquay – well, nearly. That was a monster Jamie had always wanted to conquer, but his path had led him to Australia instead.

Maybe Jimmy had managed it, though.

He was *just* in front of the swell, racing nature. The wave caught up and curled around him.

Pippa gripped the tree to keep herself steady. She'd been no good with 'potential danger' ever since David's accident, which was a bloody shame, because she'd discovered that danger could be found anywhere if you were predisposed to seeing it. She tried to tame her anxiety, especially around her kids – she couldn't wrap them in cotton wool – and she was reasoned enough to know that 'potential' didn't mean 'actual'. However, her pulse raced right alongside Jimmy, keeping up pace. He was practically riding the wave *in* its crest now, but it was catching up.

He suddenly steered the board left, it literally raced through the air, and for a moment, she thought it was going to flip, but he landed just fine, directing it towards the shore, riding all the way in.

She let out the breath she'd been holding, her lungs hurting a little. *Jesus.* She wanted to go back to 'carefree'. Pointless worries stopped you living, and she'd had too many of those recently – understandably, but still too many.

Pippa drew herself back from view, and fell against the tree, needing to feel a bit more composed before walking down there.

After counting to thirty, she turned back on a final exhale. And froze.

He'd already brought his board up onto the shore. His head was thrown back as he guzzled water from a bottle, his rucksack by his feet, his wetsuit hanging loose around his bathing trunks. There was no denying the eye candy here. All six foot of it.

Shit.

She needed to get a grip, and not on this fucking tree trunk she couldn't seem to let go of.

And she tried to – she really bloody did, and might just have succeeded had he not peeled himself out of that wetsuit the minute he put the bottle down.

There was a stirring in her belly at the sight of him, but she'd have to have been inhuman not to react to … *every single goddamned muscle under the sun – my god!*

So what? It's just a man in Speedos.

She gave her voice of reason points for trying, but no it bloody wasn't – men didn't *look* like this in Speedos. This is what years and years of daily surfing had shaped him into and she suddenly wished she hadn't given up the sport when she was sixteen, 'cause *her* physique was ... not that.

Okay. It's fine. Wait for him to get changed, then go out there. This isn't a big deal.

And it wasn't. It was *not* a big deal.

Until the Speedos came off, too.

Jimmy was now hunching over his mobile phone, dressed in a T-shirt over shorts, not that it made a blind bit of difference to Pippa, because every bare millimetre of him was now etched into her brain. And her brain seemed to be informing every last millimetre of *her* of the visual she'd just been treated to.

She had stood there, unable to move, like an idiot, while he'd towelled himself dry, flicked sand off himself, then put dry clothes on, until there'd no longer been any doubt she was the peeping Tom in this scenario; the illicit voyeur.

Bad, Pippa. So bad.

Not that her body seemed to think so – it was so turned on, it hurt. It had responded as any full-blooded woman would – with unadulterated desire.

Emma popped to mind.

Jealousy surged, so much stronger than before, but this time, the surge carried a frightening whisper, with an even more frightening message: *he's mine – not yours. Mine.*

Hands clammy, she gripped her bag tighter over her shoulder, its handle taking the place of the tree trunk. *But I'm not ready ... I'm not ready...*

And David was never out of her thoughts – how was that fair on anyone? Tears threatened, arrested only by the shrill ring of her phone. A couple of birds took flight. She jumped a little, mostly still dazed over all her feelings ... and the sight of nudity perfected.

Jimmy had his phone to his ear, his rucksack slung over his shoulder as he looked around for something.

Your phone, Pippa...

He finally zeroed in on the opening to the little copse, exactly where she stood.

Because he's phoning YOU, you numpty.

"Shit," she said out loud, finally coming to her senses and scrambling into her bag, her cover blown.

How blown?

Good god, no *way* could she let him know she'd been standing there for fifteen fucking minutes while he'd surfed, and then *watched* him get changed. "Shit, shit, shit... *Hello?*" she answered.

"Are you right *there?*"

Congratulations on answering your phone to speak to someone standing less than fifty metres away. "I ... I ... I just got here."

Lame.

There was a silence at the other end, followed by a small chuckle, as he narrowed his eyes, trying to spot her through the trees. "Are you ... planning on coming out, or shall I throw you your lunch?"

She rolled her eyes, caught herself – went bright red, she was sure, because for her life, *all* she could see was him naked – and then she carefully emerged from the little wood, doing her best to avoid the loose-hanging hawthorn branches from pricking her bare legs.

Phones still to their ears, they stared at each other across the stretch of beach, then Jimmy hung up.

She followed suit, not knowing what she could say that would sound like she *hadn't* been spying on him for quarter of an hour, so she said nothing.

He headed towards her, and she forced her legs to move, so she could meet him half way.

She'd been quite sheltered from the wind amongst the trees. It grabbed at her almost ferociously as she walked forward, and she ducked her head against it, wishing she hadn't left her shades in the car.

The wind only stopped when Jimmy reached her, acting as a windbreak by standing to her left. He slung his arm around her shoulders, pressing her to him as he shielded her, and she couldn't protest (wasn't sure she wanted to) because she was still trying to catch her breath from the wind's sharp pull. "Come on – there's a spot near that cluster of rocks." He pointed towards the top of the beach. "It's protected from the wind – cool box is already there."

He'd made lunch, then. She hadn't really known what to expect when he'd changed plans.

She nodded, and they made their way over. He left his surfboard where it was in the middle of the empty beach.

"Is it usually this quiet here?" she asked, her hair whipping into her mouth as she spoke.

"There's a big competition up in Newquay today – it's usually a bit more bustling than this. I've bumped into three whole other people at a time before."

She laughed.

A fleece picnic blanket lay in the middle of the nest the rocks made, held down by stones and the cool box.

Pippa smoothed the loose strands of her hair back from her face, finally able to see without tearing, and speak without grimacing. "You made lunch?"

"I did."

She sat herself down. He did the same. The beauty in the wildness of this beach could now be seen – now that she wasn't physically caught up in it. The waves looked deceptive from this angle, not the rushing, mini-tempest Jimmy had ridden earlier. The sand was a dark golden colour, and the small cliffs surrounding the bay finished off the scene in a way only nature could. No painting had ever captured it so perfectly for her.

"Beautiful, isn't it?" he said, opening the cool box.

"It is. I really missed being so near the sea when I went to uni."

"Don't think I could ever be anywhere else."

She glanced at him as he momentarily struggled with the lid of the box falling forward. "Did you work it off?"

He looked back, puzzled. "Pardon?"

"Whatever issue you needed to surf away."

He paused. "Did I tell you that?"

"No. I guessed."

"Good guess. Here." He tossed her a filled baguette wrapped in cling film. "Ultimately, no. The issue's still there, but I feel better about dealing with it."

She unwrapped her lunch, and studied it. "Coronation chicken?"

"Is it still your favourite?"

"You know that?"

"I guessed. I remember it was the only thing you ever ate whenever you came anywhere with us."

"Good guess."

There was a yell, and a cheer from a short distance away. Pippa turned her attention to the kids on the rocks on the next beach along – small silhouettes against the sun. A splash carried on the wind from the sea below, mostly hidden from her view, told her one of them had jumped. She let out an angry breath. "That's so dangerous. I can't believe no one's stopping them."

Jimmy shrugged. "It's been happening for years and years. They know to go there when the tide's in – makes it a little less perilous. There's a sign up with a warning, and an instruction not to climb or jump. There's even a railing – they just climb over it. Kids will be kids."

"Has anyone ever hurt themselves?"

"Yeah, a handful of injuries a year that probably weren't as painful as the verbal tirade from their parents once they found out. And maybe a death every thirty years or so."

She stared at him, shocked, having to swallow her mouthful before speaking. "Deaths?" Jesus, she didn't remember hearing about that. "There have been *deaths?*"

"Not for a while. Last one was back in the mid-90s I think; I remember telling Jamie about it. I've overheard a few of the kids I teach talking about it – it's become something of an urban legend: Mike McKinney, a fifteen-year-old boy with asthma who misjudged how cold the water could be. He had an attack as soon as he jumped in. Mike's ghost waits under the waves to pull you under if you don't make it out of the water quick enough, and if you're *really* unlucky, you hear him rasping for breath over your shoulder just before he does."

"Jesus Christ."

"Ironically – maybe poetically – it seems to have made jumpers a bit more cautious. No one wants to injure themselves in case the ghost gets them. Caution's never a bad thing. Mike did some good with his death."

"Poor Mike."

"No one came back here for a while after he died. That's when the railing got put in, and the lifeguards tightened things up by patrolling the cliff, but it's not really their area to cover. It became the usual teen jump spot again after a couple of years."

Another cheer, and another silhouette leapt into the sea.

"God..." she uttered, going back to her baguette. She couldn't watch. Maybe it was the school teacher in her, but it felt so wrong to not go over there and put an end to it. Jimmy was right though, they'd just go back the next day, and the next. It was impossible to police, and danger acted like a magnet to those who felt immortal. All teenagers felt immortal. In some ways she envied it. She wished she still did.

This nest of rocks was a sun trap, and with the wind unable to billow about so much in their corner, she was beginning to feel hot. She eased herself out of her cardigan.

A can of fizzy orange was thrust her way, bringing her back to her lunch and why they were here in the first place. "Listen," she began, as she took the can. "I've been thinking about this lunch and whatever it was that—"

"I want to tell you, Pip."

She furrowed her eyebrows in scrutiny, and also because he'd read her like a book. "You do? Are you sure?"

"I do. And no, I'm not sure, because what happened was shitty and embarrassing and I don't like to think about it, let alone talk about it... But you should know. I think maybe the only reason you don't is because I was so angry and upset at the time, that when I asked Jamie not to tell you, he agreed. Didn't even protest."

"You asked him not to tell me? Why?"

He looked at her, intently. "You know why."

She looked away; down at her baguette. The fact he used to crush on her, though never explicitly stated, was no secret.

"It mattered what you thought of me."

"So, why tell me now?"

He smiled, wryly, as he chewed his own sandwich. "Because I'm not seventeen anymore, and because different things matter now. And maybe ... it matters more that you know, despite what you end up thinking of me."

She wasn't sure what to make of that. The implications of that last statement were both clear, yet unclear – the 'maybe' held a thousand questions. She wasn't certain if he was still attracted to her. They'd gone their separate ways and hadn't spoken too much over the past twelve or so years. But he wasn't acting like he *wasn't* attracted to her. And she couldn't exactly deny her perplexing attraction to him after her little act of voyeurism just twenty minutes ago.

He was about to let her in on something; make himself vulnerable to her. In the hopes of ... something in return?

Because the mere possibility of a 'return' exists, and he knows it. He knows it because you've cared enough to push for this talk.

She had the choice to get up and leave. End the lunch, thank him for meeting up, but state she didn't need to know and walk away. She took another bite of her baguette instead, her heart thudding a little too loudly. This wasn't just him telling her something important – this was her *letting* him.

"You know," he stared out towards the horizon across the ocean, "I feel like anything's possible when I look out at the sea. It goes all around the world, and we can, too. Everything's limitless; goals are possible to reach. I feel it when I surf, too. I didn't get that a lot growing up in my family – everyone put everyone down all the time, and whenever anyone was close to breaking out of that crap, the nail would go right back in the coffin. My sisters, my brothers, my parents ... if you actually showed you could make something of yourself, they didn't want you to, 'cause it made them feel shit they didn't have that for themselves. Better to keep you down in the shit with them, than let you escape."

"It was two sisters and two brothers, right?"

"Yep. I was the fifth – the baby – last one born. By that time, my dad was pretty accustomed to drowning himself in drink every night rather than do something about the fact we faced bankruptcy every day."

"Did drinking make him violent? Did he hit you? Is that what happened?"

Jimmy shook his head. "No. He never laid a finger on me – not once. Not even when he should have." He looked down at the mouthful of sandwich he had left.

She took a sip from her can, and waited.

"My mum was the violent one."

"Oh. I'm sorry."

He shrugged. "Dad got the brunt of it. Sometimes my older brother. I don't really hold my siblings in that high a regard, but they did protect me when I was little – made sure I was out of her way every month when it got bad."

"Every month?"

"PMT."

"Wow."

"Yeah – that was the cause. She'd get into these hormonal rages and not be able to control them."

"Didn't she take medication for it?"

"Sometimes. They helped a little when she bothered to take them – she didn't always bother. I kinda think maybe she liked the power her anger gave her. She saw my dad as financially useless – he was, to be honest – and then she emasculated him in every other way. I always felt it was her way of punishing him for not being more – not providing a better life. He didn't really try, though. Or maybe he did, but her beating him down drove it all out of him. He ended up getting fined and threatened with jail for committing fraud. It was my brother who ended up in jail, though. Embezzlement. He did it to help Dad out; ease the pressure. It's not an excuse, but it's as if once that path is paved for you – by your parents; by how society sees you and treats you – it's really hard to get off."

"But you did?" She didn't really mean that to come out as a question; didn't mean to question his morals, but ... god, he was right – it *did* matter. It mattered that she knew. If walking into anything with Jimmy was even a consideration, there was no way she could do it if he was in any way involved with all of that.

"I did. I barely talk to my family anymore. I'm not in debt, I have my own business..."

Was she imagining the hesitancy in his voice?

"That night when I ended up at your house, sleeping in your room..." He took a sip from his can, shoulders tight; held himself as stiff as his surfboard. He let out a breath before carrying on. "I was seventeen. I came home after a night out with friends – we were celebrating the end of our exams at the beach. Jamie was away, or I'd have probably done something else with him. He was really my only friend – everyone else was just part of a crowd I didn't really like hanging out with, but being out beat being at home. Anyway..." He flicked the rim of his can with his fingernails. Did that for a good ten seconds before carrying on. "When I came in that night, my mum was in one of her moods. Dad had stormed out – they'd just had a huge bust-up, but not about money this time. About sex."

"About sex?"

He glanced at her, warily, and there was a lot of pain

there behind the blue of his eyes. "Or the lack of it. She went into this huge tirade about how it was all my fault they hadn't had sex in years, why I was the reason Dad was out every night and slept around, how I was an accident – was never supposed to be born – and then..."

"And then?" Instinctively, she placed a hand on his thigh in comfort, only hesitating after she'd done it, but he put his own hand on top of hers before she could move it.

"No, it's fine."

It wasn't fine, 'cause he was fidgeting where he sat, clearly not comfortable in his skin, and not wanting to re-live the memory. Why the hell had she pushed this?

But they'd gone too far now. She needed to know, and it seemed he needed to tell her.

She stroked his leg with her thumb in reassurance that ended up feeling ... like it was something more. "What happened next?"

He gripped her hand, suddenly becoming still, and then laced his fingers through hers.

She didn't stop him, her mother's words coming back to her: *don't make this hard for him to talk about.*

Jimmy didn't look at her, but out to sea. "What happened next was, she came onto me."

Jesus Christ! "She did *what*?" But she'd heard him per-fectly well. Anger rose sharp at the thought.

"It was just like one of her rages – like she was in some kind of blind fury – but she was letting it out a different way. She wasn't even cautious; didn't even test the waters. Just threw herself on me, tried to kiss me, and her hands were...

"I wasn't wearing much, you know – I'd just come back from a beach party. I was in shorts and a vest. I pushed her away, but she kept lunging at me, said I *owed* her, and I didn't know what to do. There was no one else in the house and I didn't want to hurt her. I was disgusted and scared, and it all went through the roof when she grabbed me between my legs." His words came out fast now. "That's when I pushed her hard. She fell. I felt like shit for doing that, but she was up again – like I didn't even break her stride – and she took the kitchen knife from the counter, and I fucking froze. I didn't know what she was going to do."

Pippa's hand hurt. She couldn't tell who was gripping who harder.

"She hit me. That was the first time she ever had – I was all grown up with no one to protect me this time. She punched me hard across the face. It's a fucking weird feeling when the person who brought you into the world hits you – everything as you know it sort of ends in that moment. I landed on the ground, unprepared, then she was on top of me, and the next thing I saw was the knife aiming straight for my dick. She was screaming something like, 'if you won't give it to me, you won't give it to anyone'.

"I turned right at the last minute – couldn't slide away 'cause she had my legs pinned and ... I dunno if rage gave her some kind of inhuman strength, or if I was still frozen, but turning's all I could do."

Pippa studied his face. Red patches rested high up on his cheekbones, making his eyes look hot. From the memory, the anger, or from holding back tears? She wasn't sure.

He pulled his hand from her grasp, lifted the hem of his shirt up and pulled the waistband of his shorts down over his left hip.

She looked down.

There it was – a huge, ugly, star-shaped scar, marking

the area above his hip-bone. She hadn't noticed it earlier from the distance she was at.

"The blade hit bone. I was damned lucky it hit nothing else. I wasn't thinking anymore. I remember yelling out in agony, and then I think I might have even hit *her* – I think she was on her back on the floor when I ran out the kitchen door, the knife still stuck in my side. I pulled it out; it only crossed my mind afterwards that maybe I shouldn't have done that. I had no idea where I was going, I just knew I needed to get the fuck away. I got on my bike – clambered on it half way down the driveway, and cycled..." A dry laugh escaped him. "Can't believe I stayed on my bike now that I think about it."

Her hand moved from his thigh. She grazed the scar with her fingers, and just like that, just with one simple action, the line was crossed.

His breath hitched when she touched it.

She glanced up at him, to find him staring back, intently, many questions in his eyes. This was his secret; the most private part of himself exposed. She was consciously stepping in.

"I ended up at your house. It's the only safe place I knew. It was 11 p.m. and I was banging on the door, trying not to bawl my eyes out. I *did* bawl my eyes out the minute your mum answered the door, 'though it was the blood covering my lower half she was shocked at. I must have been a sight."

"She was a nurse. She'd have seen it all."

He placed his hand over hers once more, pressing her palm into his hip, right over the scar – an act of trust.

She felt overwhelmed, and strangely calm. Calmer than she had for a while. Perhaps because his story was so turbulent.

"She saved my life that night, Pip, in more ways than

one. She wanted to call an ambulance, but I was near hysterical – said she couldn't; begged her not to. The police would've gotten involved, and if they'd put my mum in jail, my nan would've ended up in a home, and my dad would've stolen her money."

"Bloody hell."

"My nan had been diagnosed with MS three years beforehand. She'd been living on her own, my granddad having died, so Mum and Dad moved her in with us. I didn't mind 'cause I *love* my nan. She's one of my favourite people in the whole world – always there for me no matter what, no matter what I did, or what was done to me. I can't figure out how my mum's related to her, but there you go.

"After she moved in with us, Dad sold her house, and she didn't see a penny of it. That wasn't enough for them, though. My dad and Rob – that's my oldest brother – they'd been talking about trying to convince social services my nan wasn't mentally capable of looking after herself or her finances. They wanted in on her will; they wanted right of attorney. My nan *was* mentally capable – nothing wrong with her mind at all; not back then. My mum had put her foot down about it over and over again – maybe it was the one good thing she ever did. I think she assumed *she* was getting all of Nan's money after she died, and didn't want my dad touching it given how quickly he'd spent the money from the sale of her house. I didn't know how far Dad and Rob would've taken it, but I can't say I was ever happy at the thought of them alone in the house with my nan. 'Accidents' occur far too easily."

"You really think they'd have *done* that?"

"Bunked her off? Don't know, but I never put it past them. Money's a temptation that makes them weak; makes them do crazy things. I told your mum all this. Garbled it out. Didn't even know if I was making sense, but she listened anyway. She's good at listening. And whether she understood or not, she made the decision to stitch me up there and then, at home."

"She didn't call an ambulance?" She had trouble picturing it. Her mum was, for the most part, a quiet and mild person, and she'd always done things by the book. At least, as far as she knew. Obviously, she didn't know it all.

"No, she didn't. She took my blood pressure, my temperature, dosed me up on vitamin pills, did the whole shebang, gave me painkillers – she had the heavy-duty stuff stored as shots."

"For my great-granddad, if I remember rightly. She was looking after him at his home, and making daily trips – he needed morphine at the time."

"Lucky for me. Morphine's fucking bliss. She cleaned me with alcohol, and sewed me up herself. Don't know if she broke some code of ethics or whatever by doing all that – probably; I never asked her – but that's what she did. And she had your dad's support in the end, too. He wasn't keen. I'm guessing her job would be on the line if anyone found out. She told him she wasn't budging. I'll never forget it. I'll never forget what she did. Your mum is ... I don't know anyone stronger. Except maybe you." He stared at her again.

She couldn't hide her blush, but her own vulnerability sort of seemed irrelevant after everything he'd just told her.

"She stitched me up in your bed. That's where she put me 'cause it was the only spare bed, and because the sheets were already clean. I was in there for the best part of a week, until I could walk around sure the stitches weren't going to come apart. In that time, I heard your mum went over to my house and 'had a word' with my mum."

"Had a word?"

He smiled. "She didn't elaborate. But when I finally returned home, my mum was in tears, grovelling for forgiveness, quite literally going out of her way to give me anything I wanted. She never touched me again – not even for a hug. I'm under the impression your mum put the fear of god in her."

"I'm stunned. With it all. And I can't picture Mum being so assertive. She's so—"

"Quiet?"

She laughed. "I guess so."

"Don't be fooled. You get your strength from somewhere."

"I'm not str—"

"Don't."

"What?"

"Don't do that – don't put yourself down. I've seen you, Pippa. I've seen the hell you've been through the past year, and no one less could have dealt with it. You *are* strong. You're strong every single day, and those three kids of yours – they know it. They do. They feel it. And when they're all grown up, they'll remember it and cherish it. You're their rock."

Taken aback, she found herself blinking back tears. "I'm not a rock," she whispered. "Every day I feel like I'm breaking."

"And every day, you don't."

A tear slipped, stupid thing. Jimmy wiped away the track it made with his thumb, his other hand still firmly on top of hers, resting on his hip.

Her anger rose again for what his mother did to him; for what his family were like. "It's not your fault – you know that, don't you? What your mum did, and how you had to fight her off – none of that was your fault."

"I know," he said, softly. "I do. But there's still some demon that likes to sound off in my head sometimes; to make me feel guilty, and tell me it is."

David's mangled car invaded her vision; their last kiss as she'd practically pushed him out the door to his meeting. "Yeah ... I know."

"I've tried to let it go, and I *have* let a lot of it go, but sometimes..." Regret, tinged with anger, was audible in his tone. "Sometimes, I wonder if that was the exact moment I started shooting blanks. Her aim with that knife... I felt so cold. Just thinking about it now, I feel like I'm shrivelling up down there; like some part of me's still in shock – still stuck there." He laughed. "Not sure how scientific that is, but that's how I feel at times."

"*I'm* still in shock." And it shocked her a little to say it out loud. She'd only really ever talked about David's accident with her counsellor, but those sessions had ended months ago. "Like I sprinted into a glass wall I didn't see, and it knocked me to the floor, and I still haven't got my balance back. I'm standing, but disorientated – might fall over any moment."

He looked at her, listening, but no more words came out of her, her throat closing up around them before they formed. She really was shit at talking about it.

His hand was still on her cheek. She only just realised it, and before she could think about it, she leant her face into it, taking comfort from his touch.

His eyes heated with something much more dangerous than lingering anger at his past.

Her breath quickened.

"Pippa." He'd whispered her name, and somehow made it sound like the single most important word in the universe.

She closed her eyes, afraid to meet his gaze; just wanting to ... *feel.*

His thumb brushed across her lip. "Pippa ... what are we doing here?"

She didn't have an answer: sharing something, reliving something, trying to let something go ... starting something that would end nowhere, 'cause she had nothing she could give him.

She shook her head, but he cupped her face tighter, arresting her movements, thumb still pressing her bottom lip, and it felt too good – too *important* – to turn away from. It had been so very cold the past eight months; winter had stayed with her – with that part of her still stuck. Jimmy was warm. He was the sun and the surf; carried it with him everywhere he went. God help her, she darted her tongue out and flicked it over his thumb, his salty taste intoxicating her senses as needed heat stirred, melting ice.

He made a low sound that might have been words, then gently pushed his thumb between her lips.

She opened and let him in, circling his digit, sucking it into the centre of her mouth.

"Fuck..." His voice was hoarse in a way she'd never heard before; in a way that sparked every cell in her body awake. *Traitor* ... whispered the demon in her head.

"Pip ... please look at me."

She did. Forced her eyes open, half-dreading what she'd feel at the sight of him.

God... He looked ... *like something you need.*

The blue of his irises were as dark as she'd ever seen them. "I'm still crazy about you, Pippa – that's never changed. But you've never once in the past given me the slightest indication you might be interested in me, so I have no idea what you want. I don't want to take you anywhere you don't want to go, 'cause it's a place I won't wanna come back from. Do you understand?" He was completely sincere.

Jesus, *what* was she doing? She pulled away, and drew back her hand from where he'd plastered it on his hip. She pulled his palm from her face.

He looked both confused and disappointed – it echoed her own feelings, but she just couldn't *give*. "I'm sorry. I ... I like you. I do. And I'm attracted to you. But I'm married, and ... I'm always going to *be* married." Reality sank in with her words, spoken aloud for the first time. There couldn't be divorce papers, because David couldn't sign anything, so it didn't matter. Yes, she still loved her husband, and exactly three days ago, she'd begun to explore the future (or perhaps very present) possibility of being in love with *more* than one man, or at the very least, in love with one, and attracted to another. Because she wasn't even thirty-three, and if she had a long life ahead of her, five-plus decades was far too long a time to be alone. But it didn't *matter*. Two years, ten years, fifty years – this was it. She'd still be married, unable to promise that same commitment to anyone else.

She dropped his hand, but it came right back up, encircling her arm, Jimmy's voice as steady as his grip. "I know exactly what I'm walking into here. I'd never take your marriage from you, and I don't need to exchange rings to know you're in my heart."

That threw her. She hadn't expected that answer from him. "But ... I can't give you all of me."

"And I can't give you all of me – I can't give you children." It was clear how much that cut him.

She decided not to mention she hadn't exactly been planning on having more after Becca. "I can't believe you've thought so far ahead – that we're having this conversation."

"This is the only conversation of this sort I'd have with

you, Pip. I've liked you since we were *kids*. Do you think that in the past twenty-odd years, I've never once thought about a future with you? I have. Other girls, other women, they've come and gone, and none of them have held a candle to you."

"So ... what are you saying?"

He let her arm go; leaned back a little, but didn't look away from her. "I'm saying, whatever you have to give, it's enough. I don't need promises of marriage, or forever, although you can bet your last penny I'll be aiming for forever – I don't see anything less with you. All I need, is for you to *want* to try. With me."

She felt dizzy. Her mouth was dry. In the past three days, Jimmy had gone from 'little brother's slightly annoying best friend' to 'hot guy who wants forever with her'. What happened? Had a cyclone lifted her life and dropped it in Kansas? Maybe she *had* fallen ill, and this was some kind of mirage. Maybe he'd cast a spell on her, because the thought of giving it a 'try' with Jimmy was pretty much the only thing on her mind right now. But ... the kids. What if it hurt them?

Fine. Choose fifty years alone, then, Pip.

Shit. "I don't know what I want."

He leaned forward again. His hand went on *her* thigh this time, the way hers had been on his, and his touch wasn't just warm, it was fire personified. "Do you want *me*?"

She stared at him, wide-eyed, wondering if she looked like the frightened rabbit she felt.

His eyes suddenly gleamed, taking on a mischievous glint. "Did you like what you saw earlier from the safety of the woods?"

Whaaaaat? Fire personified her fucking face. *Crap!* She shut her eyes against her embarrassment. Jimmy let out a chuckle, and anger chased humiliation. She opened her eyes in frustration. "You should have told me you knew I was there."

"Bollocks. You should have stepped out of your hiding place and staked your claim."

His desire-fuelled words woke her earlier possessiveness, just as unexpected now as it had been then. How the blazing *hell* did he know?

She was suddenly against him, with no time to fully manifest her annoyance. He'd pulled her right in to him, practically *on*to him, and any air left in her lungs gushed out at the feel of him. The feel of him was everything it promised to be: hard, hot, and *hers.*

If she wanted it.

He trapped her there, his hands on the small of her back, holding her firmly on his lap. All that fire went south, and she clenched her thighs in response, only succeeding in trapping his thigh between hers, and *that* felt *too* good. A small, strangled moan escaped her.

Great – you can't speak, but you can moan.

Mortified at her lack of control, she let her earlier temper rise a little – her only defence.

He recognised it in her face; saw right through her – something he seemed to be bloody good at. "Shush. Don't you dare. Don't avoid the question."

"Jimmy," she growled, thoroughly pissed off. She pushed against his chest to no avail, though she couldn't say she was really trying, because his skin under her hands set her alight in ways she'd forgotten. Better not to touch him at all.

Haha – yeah, right. Bit late, love. You gave his thumb a blowjob.

She felt his palm travel from the small of her back, up her spine, finally touching her skin at the base of her neck.

He cradled her there, then pulled her further in to him. It felt divine. And hazardous. She could feel his nipples through the front of her dress, which meant he, without a doubt, could feel hers.

"Pippa..." He all but groaned her name into her ear, his stubbled cheek against hers.

Don't ask me again. She couldn't answer his questions.

You can't avoid them forever.

"Did you like what you saw?"

Everything fell silent for a moment, the rush of her blood in her ears the only thing she could hear.

He kneaded the back of her neck with his fingers; eight months of grief-laden tension seemed to melt. Another tear slipped onto his shoulder. She nodded against his cheek. It was the only way she could answer. To hear herself say it ... she couldn't quite face her betrayal to her husband so directly. Not yet.

Her nod was enough. She felt his lips brush her temple, then he kissed her there.

She sighed, half-resigned, half-exhausted. Fighting was so *hard.*

Guilt dominated her being; battled with desire. She wrestled with both, too aware a faint ray of hope had awakened. A future might actually exist – a potentially happy one, where she wasn't sad, or alone.

"Do you *want* me?" he asked.

She nodded again.

His breath shuddered against her hair – it felt like an exhalation of relief. "That's a good place to start."

"Start," she repeated, automatically, dazed over his every touch.

A gust of wind found its way over the nest of rocks and sprayed grains of sand over their forgotten lunch; over them. She felt nothing but Jimmy's next kiss on her neck, more determined than the last, and the scorching lave of his tongue as he tasted her.

She moaned louder than before.

His hand left the back of her neck, and both found their way under her dress to her backside, pulling her further in.

All hesitation gone, she followed where he led and gasped when his cock, fully hard behind his shorts, replaced his thigh between her legs.

The noise he made at the contact sent her stomach into a flurry; a rush of warmth into her underwear. His hands were over her dress again, massaging her hips, and sides, feeling her out; his lips did the same to every inch of her neck.

Reality must have pierced his bubble for a second, for he slowed down and looked up at her through misty eyes... "Is this all right?" he croaked out.

She only saw him through half-closed lids, not wanting to come back. Her bubble could stay for a while longer. "Yes. God, yes." She had no problem speaking this time. A lover's touch was something she'd taken for granted; missed greatly.

She found his warm hand on her ribcage, just under her left breast. She took it; moved it up and placed it directly on her breast.

"Jesus," he uttered. His cock stirred against her crotch.

She groaned with want; was *alight* with want.

He enveloped her breast; squeezed it; rubbed it.

"Please," she encouraged.

"You're so fucking beautiful." He pulled the strap of her dress down, slowly, right along with the strap of her bra until her breast was bared, and she didn't really hear what he said next – her blood was rushing in her ears again, the sound only getting louder when his wet lips found her nipple.

"*Ooooh.*"

His teeth grazed it.

She was gone. *So* gone.

Another yell from the teens by the rocks was the only thread keeping her from fully falling. She doubted they'd be able to see her and Jimmy from this angle. Nevertheless, the thread offered enough of an anchor to have her glance up towards them, just to make sure.

The blood rushing in her ears turned into a faint ringing, like a telephone handset, or a car alarm, or any alarm ... getting louder...

She blinked, trying to figure out what was wrong. It wasn't Jimmy on her breast – hell no – that felt unbelievably right. So right, she wondered if she might actually orgasm. *Keep grinding yourself against him, and you won't have to wonder for long.*

She blinked again.

When it hit her, it was like finding out about the accident all over again. The entire world crumbled; washed over her like iced water as it fell, leaving her cold as death.

Jimmy froze, sensing her change. "Pip?"

She scrambled to her feet, pulling her dress back up, her eyes glued to the silhouette on the rocks – the one a head shorter than everyone else. "That's Liam," she breathed out, her voice barely sounding.

"What?" He followed her gaze, blinking his own way back to the wretched world.

"The shorter one."

"Are you sure?"

Then, another short one stood beside him. "And that's Gavin, his friend. I dropped Liam off at his house this morning, not far from here."

"Pippa—"

"That's *him*. I know it, I know my own son." And she did – his shape, his gait, the way his hair haloed his head – every single thing about him screamed Liam. *What the hell?* He wasn't a teenager, he was fucking *ten*. What was he *doing* there?

She couldn't move; couldn't tear her eyes away from her son, three hundred metres away – too far away.

She got her answer as he stepped towards the edge of the cliff. "No..."

Everything happened at once.

Jimmy leapt to his feet and raced for his board.

"NO!" But she could stop it no more than she could stop that dreaded phone call.

To a round of cheers and applause, Liam jumped.

XI
Jump

"Liam."

A raging stomp from upstairs told her Sammy had just about had enough of his homework. She looked skywards in exasperation, but couldn't blame him. Her and Jamie had never gotten homework at the age of six – the education system had taken a rather rigid turn the past decade. They seemed to expect little Einsteins from the moment they could talk nowadays. "Liam!"

Her eldest appeared from around the corner, seemingly unperturbed by the almost constant chaos that was his brother. *Why did Sammy have to go and inherit my genes? Good job Liam had inherited David's calm collectedness, and Becca reminded her of Jamie more and more each day – joyful, with a maturity beyond her years that nothing seemed to ruffle.* You're damn lucky only one of them has your temperament.

"Sweetie, I need you to lay the table, and get the drinks." She hated asking him to do that – he'd only just turned ten. With all the homework they had to do, she figured she would wait 'til they were a bit older before starting the household chores, and usually David was back in time to help her sort out the little details while she got dinner ready and on the table.

Liam took it in his stride the way he always did, and, as

usual, offered his reply with as few syllables as possible. "Cool," he shrugged.

How he and Sammy were so different was beyond her.

"I'd better go sort Sammy out," she mumbled, with a reminder to herself that she needed to put the tray of oven chips down first. A full-blown Sammy-tantrum wasn't too far away. "Where's Becca?"

"Watching TV," said Liam as he walked towards the sideboard to get the plates.

Damn that box. It was turned on far too often in this house. Entirely her fault – she'd been too lenient, and too dependent on the daily respite it offered her on collecting all three of her kids and trying to manage the home routine after her own gruelling day at work. She made a mental note to speak to David about TV on-and-off times.

The phone rang.

Bloody great. *But maybe it was David explaining why he was running late. She looked back at the kitchen, all its counters cluttered. She could put the chips back in the oven...*

"I get it! I get it! I get it!" Becca came sprinting down the hallway from the living room. "I get it! I get!"

"Becca – give the phone straight to Mummy, okay?" Last time she'd answered it, Pippa hadn't even known, and the little chatterbox had ended up speaking to a market researcher for half a bloody hour. God knows what information she'd given them.

Chips, chips, where do I put the fucking chips? They'd burn if she put them back in the oven and the seasoning needed to go on them now.

"MUMMY!"

"Becca," she admonished, "there's no need to scream, I'm right here – what is it?"

"It's a policeman on the phone."

"What?"

Right – the chips were coming with her. Honest to god, the police had phoned two months ago because the neighbours had put in a complaint about Sammy shouting and kicking the walls. If this call was because the neighbours had a bee in their bonnet about Sammy and his current thumping, they had too much time on their hands. He hadn't even let rip yet tonight.

"It's snowing!" squealed Becca, gleefully, pointing to the little of it that could be seen out the panes of the storm porch.

"It is?" Please, lord, let it be a light fall with all the schools still open tomorrow.

Becca dropped the handset on the hallway table and ran to the glass panelling by the front door to gawp at the snow. She attached herself to the pane like glue.

Pippa picked up the receiver, resigning herself to the fact the chips would probably be ruined. Throw cheese and ketchup on. They'll eat anything with cheese and ketchup on. "Hello?"

"Mrs Fellows?" came the deep voice from the other end. Oddly, it sent a chill up her spine.

"Yes, is this about my son? I'm sorry if the neighbours complained again, but look, he's only six, and going through a tantrum phase. He's finding his homework a bit frustrating – I was just about to go help him, but I don't want to burn the dinner, so if it's the neighbours who called you—"

"Um, no, it's not about your son." There was a pause, and another shiver snaked up her spine. "It's about your husband."

The next pause was laden with gravity. "My husband?" A cold knot formed in her gut.

"David Fellows is your husband?"

She had to force herself to reply, that cold knot taking up all her focus. "Yes."

"Mum?"

She turned to find Liam behind her, his eyes questioning, clearly picking up on the topic of the phone call. She shook her head. Everything slowed down, and she must have been shaking, because the chips on the tray were trembling. The baking tray made a 'clang' as its metal cooled and buckled.

"Mummy!" Becca's oblivious exclamation came from very far away – every sound had become muffled, as if the world had draped a thick blanket over her. "The snow's falling faster!"

"Mrs Fellows? Can you hear me?"

"Um ... sorry ... yes, I'm here – I can hear you."

"I'm afraid there's been an accident."

"Pippa."

It was snowing now, right? 'Cause she was really fucking cold.

"Pippa!"

She shook.

No – she was being shaken.

"Hey..." Jimmy's voice softened with forced serenity. She assumed he was purposely hiding the panic in it. "Pip, he's fine."

She shook her head. He couldn't possibly know that.

"He *is*. I hear no screaming, no one shouting for help, I also hear no silence – just the usual chatter from that rock. Listen."

He was right. *Her* hearing had changed – her senses,

every last inch of her sent into overdrive – but now that she *made* herself listen to what he was pointing out – their high-pitched voices, faint on the wind – there was no discernible sound of panic from anyone else. The logic calmed her a fraction. "Okay," she managed to breathe out, reason flooding back, along with some relief.

"I'm gonna go out there on the board – I'll be there in under ten minutes, I'll make sure he's okay, and I'll wait for you."

"On the board?"

"Done it before – not a problem."

"The rocks."

"I can navigate them, I know exactly where they are. Tide's in anyway. You gonna be all right driving?"

Driving. *Shit.* She had to *drive* to reach Liam, and it was going to take her fifteen fucking minutes to get the car in the first place. Anger simmered, slowly replacing her terror. She nodded.

After she knew he was all right, she was going to ground that boy 'til kingdom come.

"Good. I'll see you there."

She was suddenly engulfed in the heat of his body as he brought her right in to him and landed a kiss on her forehead. She was pretty sure he would have done it anyway, even if they'd not shared a moment earlier, but in that second, the gesture wasn't just reassurance – it was a pillar she took strength from. There'd been no pillar when she'd received that phone call; no one to meet her at the hospital when she'd walked through the sliding, glass doors.

She wasn't doing this alone. "I'll see you there," she whispered back, not really meaning to whisper, but barely able to speak, her throat was so tight.

His warmth was suddenly gone. She followed his movements as he ran back to where they'd been sitting and grabbed her bag and cardigan. She felt more than a little useless – her car keys were in that bag. Her head was all over the place. *Time to act like a fucking grown-up, Pip.*

She took them from Jimmy, then he actually spun her around so she faced the little copse she'd come out of. She felt another swift kiss on the back of her head, then he gave her a gentle push in that direction. "Go."

Perhaps it was daft, but she needed the instruction – it gave her focus.

She walked towards the path that had led her to the beach, worry for her son, coupled with frustrated anger towards him, fuelling every step. Before too long, she was running.

~*~

There was only one time he could think of when he'd seen Pippa upset beyond reason. She'd been sixteen and drunk at the time, and she probably didn't know that he knew about it given she kept calling him Jamie the entire time he'd held her hair back for her while she'd puked into the toilet. And she'd *kept* calling him Jamie while he'd held her as she'd cried over her idiot-boyfriend who she'd discovered making out with another girl *while* he'd bragged to said girl about the bet he had going with his mates to see if he could pop Pippa's cherry. The girl had apparently been in on it. Nice fucking couple.

He hadn't popped anything of Pippa's. He had, however, received a black eye the very next day, not that Pippa, or anyone, knew how it had gotten there. The one advantage of being the fourteen-year-old, ginger-haired dweeb was that the sixteen-year-old class prince would never in a hundred years admit he'd been knocked down by said dweeb. And it had been the one time the 'bad' reputation of his family and older brothers had been to his benefit. It turned out people could actually be slightly afraid of him.

This went far beyond Pippa being upset. 'Upset' didn't cover the palpable fear radiating from her. It was more than disconcerting, and it gave him a small glimpse into what it must have been like for her that night she'd found out about her husband. Half his panic was for her, not Liam. No way in hell did he want her to go through all that again.

She visibly calmed in his arms as he kissed her forehead, much to his relief. He needed her able to drive and, more selfishly, he needed not to worry about her while he made his way to Liam. The waves were much less ferocious now, the wind having died down, but it was still a bit of a pig to navigate his board to the next cove. He'd have to take the rip out, then pull himself around and make sure he kept away from the rocks, and he'd be doing it all without the protection of his wetsuit, but it was the quickest way to Liam. He wasn't about to tell Pip any of that.

Handing her her cardigan and bag, he gently turned her around, hoping to draw her focus to where she needed to go and what she needed to do. "Go," he said gently, with a not-quite-as-gentle push, after dropping another kiss on her head for reassurance.

She did – striding off in that Pippa-on-business way, and when he was sure she wasn't going to look back, he grabbed his board from where he'd dropped it, and headed out to sea.

Eight and a half minutes, according to his watch. That wasn't bad going all things considered.

Jimmy scoured the beach by the rocks for Liam, spotting him straight away with a small crowd gathered around him. He was sitting up, which was a damn good sign. From this distance, he couldn't see anything immediately wrong with him.

Relieved, he dragged his board up the shore and peeled his soaking T-shirt off, laying it out on the board. He didn't want to feel the chill of the water. The sun's heat was getting blistering now it was just gone 1 p.m. and the sooner he got warm and dry the better.

He was finally noticed by one of the kids. All heads turned to him one by one. He was pretty sure he could see a couple of 'we're in deep shit' looks.

Too bloody right.

They knew who he was, and they knew he knew their parents. He counted three he gave surfing lessons too. He allowed one of his more thunderous looks to shine through as he stared at them.

They suitably winced and looked away.

Liam looked pale. And he was wet and shivering, and sitting in the goddamned shade. Other than that, he seemed okay, but until he got a chance to properly examine him, he couldn't be sure.

Never mind that they were kids – he didn't mince his words. "What the fuck d'you think you're doing?"

Heads went down, and Liam and his friend – clearly the youngest two in the group – looked alarmed at his tone and language. His friend was bone dry.

"He *wanted* to jump," said Bobby – one of the boys he taught – with a couple of others sounding off in agreement.

"He's *ten.*"

They shut up.

"You telling me you'd be okay with your little brothers

and sisters jumping off this thing?" He gestured at the large, jutting rock behind them. "Are you telling me you'd lead them up by the hand and give them a bloody good push to boot?"

They all looked down again. "No, sir," someone mumbled.

He went straight for the fear-of-god approach, and pointed directly at Liam, feeling only slightly guilty 'cause he wasn't sure who was to blame here, or why he'd gone and done the crazy jump. But he needed all the others to know they'd made a bad decision letting him, and he also needed answers from them right now. "Your mother is going out of her mind, because she just saw you jump from the next beach over."

That did it. Liam's eyes filled, even though he was still shivering, his friend went white as a sheet beside him, and there was an intake of breath from some of the other kids, too.

Aaah – he'd forgotten they'd all know who Pippa was; that they'd have heard about what she and Liam had been through, which made this whole thing even more unacceptable.

He still felt that twinge of guilt though, and pushed it to one side. He was completely unfamiliar with the whole parenting thing, and that was sort of the problem here: this was *Pippa's* kid. The need to both protect and soothe him was there, whether he'd asked for it or not. It was slightly uncomfortable, not least because it was met with an unexpected and sudden wash of sadness over the children he could never have.

Putting his own issues away, he strode towards Liam.

Everyone else moved to one side, and made a path for him. As he walked by, he heard a quiet, "Sorry, Jimmy," from the only girl in the group, and one he also tutored.

For the moment, he ignored her, and knelt down in front of Liam, sat there on the rock in nothing but his trunks. "Are you all right? Are you hurt?"

He shook his head, eyes still watery, although the tears remained unshed.

"What's this?" He gestured to a few cuts on his legs, only one of them seeping a bit of blood. He guessed he'd scraped them on the sea bed, or perhaps even on a couple of the rocks. Fucking hell.

"They're just scratches," he said defensively, although his voice was shaking – whether from fear or because of his shivering he wasn't sure. "They don't hurt."

"Somebody get me a towel."

One of the kids scampered off to do just that, returning in a nano-second, and Jimmy silently cursed that none of them had thought to wrap him up to ease the shivering, then place him in the sunshine for a few minutes. They should all bloody know better.

He threw the towel around the boy, and wrapped it tight. "Hold this," he said, giving him the ends. It might not be enough, given the amount of time he'd been exposed to the cold, but he was clearly with it, and mentally alert, which could only be good. "Didn't you go in and test the water's temperature first before jumping? Get your body used to it and what to expect?"

He shook his head, and a tear finally fell, his lips tightening, as he tried to hold it together.

Yeah ... that kinda got you in the gut, that look.

Jimmy stared at Liam for a beat, and he stared back, clearly worried about what he was going to do.

Pip would be here in five minutes or so. Liam didn't need shame added to his mistake. Jimmy turned to the other young kid – Liam's friend whose name he'd forgotten. "He staying at your house?"

The kid nodded, looking almost as upset as Liam.

"Right – you sit over there up the beach where I can see you while I talk to Liam, and gather your things – anything you both brought with you. The rest of you: show's over. Get out of here."

No one protested. The boy who'd given Liam his towel looked at it as if he wanted it back; one look from Jimmy and he decided not to say whatever he was going to say.

They scarpered fairly quick, and Jimmy waited 'til they were out of sight, not wanting to baby Liam in front of them. He then knelt back down. "You need to be warmer, okay?"

He nodded, still crying quietly.

"Come here." He held his arms out.

Liam shuffled forward as best he could while shaking and cocooned in the towel, and Jimmy pulled him in the rest of the way, hauling him into his arms and lifting him as he stood. He walked them both out into the sun.

Shit, that was better. He'd been getting cold himself in the rock's shadow.

He rubbed Liam's back through the towel, wanting to get his blood flowing, and scanned the beach. Liam's friend, who had followed his instructions, was sitting further up the beach. He'd whipped out something that looked like an iPad from his rucksack, and seemed immersed in that. No sign of Pippa yet. He was pretty confident now that Liam was going to be fine – just needed warming up – but he didn't think Pippa would do well seeing him shivering like this. It always looked far worse than it was.

All at once, he stopped, sensing a change in the boy – a different kind of tremble. Then sobbing. The racking, snotty kind.

His friend looked up from his iPad, uncertain, then went back to it.

After a moment of awkwardness, Jimmy started rubbing his back again. The sobbing became greater. But Liam's head sank onto his shoulder – he wasn't pulling away. Instead, he kinda nestled himself in there, seeking out comfort. He could feel his tears fall down his back.

A heaviness ached his heart; surrounded them despite the sun they were bathed in. This release wasn't just about regrets over jumping off that rock; this was something much deeper.

He pulled him up a little from slipping down; found a better position, and held him closer, only resisting the urge to drop a kiss of comfort on his head 'cause he didn't know him that well. "You're fine, kid. You're gonna be fine."

Jimmy felt him nod against his neck.

He sighed. Sod the shoulds and shouldn'ts. He dropped that kiss anyway, then went back to rubbing his back 'til the sobs started to quieten down.

Still no Pip.

She'd better be bloody okay, and not have wrapped her car around a lamp post or worse.

Liam was now quiet.

His shivering had stopped. There was just the rise and fall of his chest.

"You wanna tell me why you did it?"

Silence.

"Waves could have bashed you against those rocks, you know that? Or even taken you out to sea – the wind was up; ocean's rough today. I'm guessing you know all this, though, 'cause I know you're not dumb. So, why d'you do it?"

Not a word.

And his arm was starting to go numb, but never mind. He carried on pacing around with the boy, and scanned the area again for Pippa.

"I wanted to see what it's like," came the whisper, which he wasn't sure he'd have heard if Liam's mouth hadn't been right by his ear.

"See what it's like to do the jump?"

After a pause, "To not be able to stop it."

Jimmy looked at the rock, trying to see the jump from Liam's eyes, the water coming at him fast, the uncertainty of the outcome, the rising fear he—

"The way Dad couldn't stop it."

He almost hadn't heard that at all, it was even less than a whisper. His heart broke for the kid. *What a fucking mess.*

"You know he'd have stopped it if he could have, right? And he probably tried. In fact, I know he tried, 'cause he wasn't the kind of person who wouldn't try. He's still trying now – trying to learn how to live his life again, and 'cause it's probably one of the hardest things in the world to do, that kinda makes him a hero."

He felt another nod against his neck.

"But your dad didn't put himself in front of that truck on purpose. He wouldn't want you jumping off that rock, Liam – not the way you did today."

One more hint of a nod. "I'm sorry."

Liam's weight tested the strength of his arms. The emotional weight surrounding them, though, seemed to have lifted a little. The sun made the ocean glitter, and they both stayed as they were, not saying anything else, Liam all but draped over him, unmoving, to the point where he wondered if he'd fallen asleep.

Liam's friend was still on his iPad.

Finally, Pippa came walking towards them from the top

of the beach. She stopped in her tracks when she saw them, then resumed her steps, stopping to say something to the boy while he hurried to pack his things away.

Liam didn't stir.

"Jimmy?" she said on approach, her voice tight – fearing the worst, he suspected, because that's what she'd been dealing with the past year.

"He's fine, he's fine."

"Is he..."

"Sleeping, I think." He kept his voice low so as not to wake him.

She walked around him to look at her son. When she reappeared in front of him, her face showed both relief and ... something he couldn't place. "He hasn't slept like that on someone since he was ... I don't know, maybe five or six."

"He's exhausted – body took a battering with the cold of the water. He's nicely warmed up now, but he was shivering when I got to him. No injuries from the jump. A couple of scratches on his legs, which you might want to put some antiseptic on, but the sea salt would have washed them pretty well. He's fine. Tough kid."

Pippa sighed, and blinked back tears.

He wished he had four arms.

"What the hell was he *doing*?"

What could he say? "Talk to him, Pip. He didn't tell me much, but I think he's going through stuff, and trying to figure things out."

"Stuff?"

"About David."

She looked distraught all the sudden, and he almost wished he'd said nothing.

"Just talk to him."

"You think I don't?"

"Hey, that's not what I said."

"I've *tried*, but ever since it happened, he's just gotten quieter and quieter, and every time I bring up the accident, he goes mute. He won't tell me anything, and then he goes and does *this?* What was he trying to do? Kill himself?"

"What? No. Shit." He inched towards her, wanting to hug her, but unable to with Liam in his arms. "I don't think it's anything like that. He's just trying to understand what happened and why."

"So am I!"

"Sshhh."

She sucked in a breath, and bit her lip.

"Look – I know you've got to discipline him over this, and you should, but don't go in all guns blazing. You should have seen his face when I told him you saw him jump. It was like despair, and not because he got caught. He was really sorry, Pippa. I don't think he's going to do it again."

And there was that look on her face once more – the one he couldn't figure out. She stared at him, almost as if he was speaking a foreign language.

"Why are you looking at me like that?"

She blinked, coming back from wherever she was, but her answer never came, because Liam lifted his head, eyes half closed. "Mum?"

Thank fuck – his arms were about to fall off.

Liam turned and reached for her, and she took him from Jimmy's arms with a grunt.

Liam wrapped himself around her neck in a tight hug. "I'm really, really sorry, Mum."

Jimmy met her eyes before she looked away. "We'll talk about it after I've dropped Gavin home."

Gavin! That was it!

"Okay," came his meek reply. He knew there was no way

out of it.

With arms now free, Jimmy took a step towards her.

She took a step back.

His heart took a dive. That was it now, was it? Her defences were up, and while it was understandable given the circumstances, he was bummed he'd have to break them down all over again.

She must have read his thoughts on his expression. She put Liam down. "I can't carry you, Liam, sorry – you're way too heavy."

The boy rubbed his eyes, still coming around.

"Can you walk okay?"

"Uh-huh," he nodded.

"Go help Gavin with your things. My car's in the car park. You can both wait for me at the top of the beach in front of it, where I can see you."

"'Kay, Mum."

He waddled off, and she turned back around to Jimmy, straightening her back and crossing her arms. "Thank you for what you did. For swimming out and getting Liam."

"There was no way I wouldn't." He reached out for her, but she moved away.

"Jimmy ... the kids."

He attempted a smile, though he felt shitty inside. "It wasn't going to be more than a hug."

"Not in front of Liam."

Hell... He crossed his own arms. That kinda hurt.

Her look softened. "I need some time. I'm sorry." She lowered her voice, looking back to check where Liam was. "What happened earlier – between us... It's not just about you and me."

"You think I don't know that?" he said. "It's about your whole family – you're a package deal, I get that. I don't *mind* that."

"Well, they might."

Breathing was getting hard; his chest was starting to hurt. *This is why – remember now? This is why you never, ever, ever, tried to start anything with Pippa, EVER. Because you knew it would hurt when she turned you down.*

"And you know, it's not like everything's perfect at your end."

"What?"

"Emma."

"Emma? I told you, we're not even—"

"I can't do the carefree, open relationship thing, okay? I'm the jealous type – I freely admit it – I can't be with someone who's with someone else."

"Jesus, Pippa, I *know* that. I don't want that with you – I want the real thing."

"Well, Emma can't be a part of that."

"You think I'd want that?"

"I don't know what you want." She looked in Liam's direction again, and he was starting to feel pissed off about that. Yes, the situation was sensitive, but he wasn't a fucking leper. "Beyond a teenage crush, I don't know what you feel for me."

Oh, he could tell her. He could lay it all out, right now, except he bloody well knew she wouldn't listen. She'd run the other damn way, and then he'd *never* get her back.

Ha! Listen to yourself – you haven't even got her in the first place!

He sighed, suddenly feeling tired himself. Too tired. "Look. I'm going to head back."

She looked surprised, as if she'd expected him to argue it out. "Erm ... okay. I can give you a lift back to—"

"I'm not leaving my board here. I'll just paddle back, and

grab the food and my car from the other beach."

He wasn't imagining it – she *did* look disappointed.
Damn this woman.

He turned his back to her so he could gather himself,
because for the life of him, he didn't want to walk away. He
wanted to get in that car with her and make sure both her
and Liam were all right.

But she wasn't ready, no matter how much she might
want to be.

Shit, she had a whole fucking world to let go of. She was
so far from ready he'd be waiting for her 'til the four horse-
men rode in, and now he'd had a taste of her, suffering any
more years of her looking the other way was something he
didn't think he could do again.

And then, there's the world you *have to let go of.*

His thoughts darkened. Yeah ... there was that. She was
right to an extent – not everything was perfect at his end.
He really needed to sort the Cait thing out.

Earlier, when he thought they might be starting something – *really* starting something – he'd even decided he'd
tell Pippa about it; after all, laying all that crap out about
his mum was dehumanising – the thing with Cait didn't
quite reach that low.

Now, he was glad he hadn't. He *did* remember her jealous streak. If she was like this over Emma, she was going to
go ape-shit over Cait.

She'll find you disgusting.

Yep, she probably would. And that was something he
didn't have the strength for.

He turned back around to say goodbye, and almost
didn't.

She looked forlorn, and more fragile than he'd ever seen
her, until she realised he'd turned back and pulled herself

together. "Thanks for lunch," she said with a smile.

He couldn't find it in himself to smile back. "It was nice to share it. Hope Liam sorts stuff out. I'll catch you around."

He walked off, feeling like a bit of a jerk for doing so, but not willing to play the doormat to Pippa's yo-yoing emotions – not right now, anyway. He really was tired from the sudden panic and the swim out to get to Liam. And he had shit of his own to deal with.

He leant down and picked up his T-shirt from his board.

Shit he was going to deal with tonight.

XII
Sorry Doesn't Cut It

Tim yawned as Candy shut the front door behind them.

After a flash of hope back at the hospital, riding on the promise of Lauren's release, it was finally dashed when the doctor decided the concluding test results of her antibodies and electrolytes and lord knew what else, weren't stable enough for her discharge. They wanted to keep her in for a full twenty-four hours, which meant she wouldn't be released until tomorrow morning at the earliest, providing any further tests came back okay.

"Thank god it's Sunday." Tim dropped his wallet on the kitchen counter, and flicked on the switch to the kettle.

"I know. Half of me wants to sink into bed and stay there for the rest of the year."

"You can if you want."

"For the rest of the year?"

"For the rest of the day, perhaps."

"You gonna join me?"

He yawned again, but shook his head. "Not sure I can sleep."

We don't have to sleep. But Candy kept her mouth shut despite the prominence of that thought. She wondered if she should bring up the porn thing, but reminded herself she'd promised to give him time to mention it. It had only happened last night. "I doubt I can sleep either. My mind just keeps turning. Lauren despises the hospital, and I hate leaving her there."

"Me, too." He brought down two mugs from the cupboard. "Did you want a drink?"

"What are you having?"

"Coffee."

"Another one?"

He snorted. "That stuff you get from those dispensing machines at the hospital is *not* coffee."

She suddenly thought of that woman by the ice machine. "I think I'll pass on the drink – I'm more hungry than thirsty."

"Shit. I think the fridge is just about bare."

Candy groaned. "We should've gone to the supermarket before coming home."

Lauren was the one who usually organised the food, needless to say, the fridge had had a habit of going bare for quite a few months now.

Tim sighed as he stirred sugar into his caffeine hit. "I'll do the food shop in a couple of hours."

"No – I'll go." He was exhausted. He didn't look like he could lift a bagel right now, let alone bags of shopping. "I feel restless anyway. I might as well go do something useful."

"What about your sleep?"

"Sleep? What's that?"

Tim grunted.

She looked towards the bedroom. Truth was, she didn't want to sleep alone knowing Tim was in the other room, when he could be between the sheets with her. After walking in on him yesterday, that would make her feel shitty, *especially* considering what he might be watching while *she* was in bed. She wanted him to share himself with her, not with the TV. And she wanted to share herself with him –

her fears, and her doubts, and her grief. And her love. "You know," she started, already scolding herself for pushing him, but her thoughts had now surfaced and brought a good amount of insecurity with them. She needed ... *something* from him. "We could *both* go to bed." She threw a smile in for good measure. "It's been ages since we shared a bed – I mean, *just* you and I."

He stared at her strangely, then frowned, not seeming too happy. "While Lauren's in hospital?"

Her heart fell, right along with her smile, mortified he'd read her that way. "That's not what I meant. How could you... Not *because* she's in hospital – Jesus. I just thought..."

He looked down from her to add the milk, his face stony.

"I thought it would be nice to ... be together." *And held, and comforted.*

Right, maybe if she were a porn star; some detached and distant figure on the screen – no commitment, no effort, no responsibility.

"And Lauren wouldn't mind, Tim – you know she wouldn't. Of *course* she wouldn't." If anything, Lauren had been pushing for them to talk and spend more time together recently – never something they'd had problems with in the past – and getting less and less subtle about it as she became more ill. Tim had ignored every hint, and Candy's armour was wearing thin. Whereas at the beginning of Tim's emotional withdrawal, she'd practised patience and prudence, his rejection of her – no matter if it came from a place of self-preservation – just plain hurt now.

"It doesn't feel right."

Yes – it hurt. "Why?"

"Just..." He put the teaspoon down a little harder than was necessary, his annoyance at the subject – and perhaps being made to talk about it – very clear. "It doesn't feel right to be *loving* you while she's dying."

Her shocked silence followed.

Hell, she was wrong – it didn't hurt, it *skewered*. Tears surfaced fast, but at last, so did her anger – every bit of it she'd been swallowing back for the past few weeks –   finally too exhausted to carry on the act. "But getting your rocks off to some nameless, faceless, boob-injected porn actress – *that's* okay?"

He froze, and then looked at her, realisation setting in, guilt colouring his features as it did.

She hugged her arms to her chest, ignoring the tickle of her tears on her chin, and ignoring her own guilt for erupting, knowing Lauren would be devastated at their arguing. "Making love to me disgusts you so much you can't get it up, but watching two women you don't even know, copulating, has you coming faster than the tax man on payday? Did that feel *right*?"

To his credit, he looked as upset as she was. "You saw me yesterday."

"Yes, I saw you. Looking not very impotent at all."

"God, I ... it wasn't what you think."

"It doesn't *matter* what I think! You've just said what *you* think." Shaking, she made herself move, and grabbed her bag from the seat she'd put it on when entering the kitchen. "It doesn't feel right to love me."

"No," he shook his head. "That's not what I meant. Candace, please ... I'm so sorry."

"I'm going out."

"Where?"

"I don't know." She turned away from him towards the door. She felt like she was suffocating; like she'd just lost everything.

"Wait—"

"No." She spun back around. "I've *been* waiting. For days and weeks and months. I've been waiting for *something* to hold onto from you."

"You have it."

"I have *nothing.* I have your guilt, and your grief, and now your revulsion."

"Candy, I didn't *mean* it the way it came out."

"You know, no matter how hard I'm racking my brain, I can't think of another way to interpret 'it doesn't feel right to love you while she's dying'. Seems pretty straightforward to me." She strode away.

He reached for her.

"*Don't,*" she yelled. And perhaps it was because she didn't yell often that he did as she asked. Or perhaps it was because it didn't *feel* right to love her. "Leave me alone," she said, defeated, and didn't look at him again as she left the house – their house.

No. His house. His and Lauren's.

Whatever the three of them had shared, he'd just obliterated it. Had she been living an illusion this entire time? All these years? She'd never felt like the spare wheel in their relationship; she'd never felt like the 'second' of their little pack. She'd always felt they'd worked equally *as* equals – that that was *why* they worked as a polyamorous unit.

The click of the door closing behind her reached her ears.

A sob threatened. He'd shut the door. *He actually went and shut it.*

She got into her car, slammed her own door, switched on the engine, and tried to breathe through her crying.

She had no idea where she was going.

What the fuck happens next?

~*~

Pippa stopped along the kerb of her parents' road, a little further down from the house, not wanting to pull into the drive in case Becca or Sammy spotted them and wanted to come out.

She and Liam hadn't spoken yet, her head was a mess, and she was *steaming*.

Dropping off Gavin and bringing the entire thing up with his mother had been shitty to say the least. Both boys had stood there with their heads down during the conversation, then after Gavin had been sent up to his room, the woman had made clear implication she thought Liam was a bad influence. Liam. *Liam*. Quiet-as-a-mouse Liam who always studied hard, got almost straight As and was a pillar at home was a *bad influence*.

Fuck that!

Except she couldn't say a damn word, because Gavin hadn't been the one to jump off that bloody rock – Liam had. While Pippa was angry at Liam for his antics, the real reason for her steam at this moment was that little disagreement with Gavin's mum, and unfortunately, it was already riding on her agitation from having every single button pressed by Jimmy. The way he'd *held* her son...

She'd screamed inside – completely bloody lost it – first because she thought something horrendous had happened to her boy, and then because she'd found herself wrapped up at the sight of them both – needing it, wanting it, not ready for it...

So she'd done what she always did when her trigger was pressed: her tongue had lashed and she'd cut him. She'd hurt Jimmy with her words – had known it as she'd done it – and she'd ignored the part of her telling her not to. The part that was becoming louder, and more persistent.

Only now did the sadness at her actions override the panic of the afternoon. She'd hurt him, and she wished she could take it back. More than that, when he'd walked off, she'd been thrown – hadn't wanted him to. Had wanted him with her for the rest of the day and *in* her life, the vision of Liam on his shoulder, so right, it caused a new kind of hurt – the kind that needed a conclusion; satiation.

She'd stalled, and then had run the other way. She was falling behind in this race – hadn't trained for it.

The final nail in the coffin, and one that had left her ex-tra jumpy, was that she *thought* she'd seen that blue Ford Focus three cars behind her after she'd driven back from the beach. At first, she'd been too wound up to pay attention, and when the hairs had finally pricked at the back of her neck, she'd looked more closely in her rear-view and side mirrors, but had been unable to make out the driver or the number plate from the angle she was at.

About thirty seconds later, the car had turned right and she hadn't seen it again. She'd spent the next five minutes telling herself she was being daft, and then she'd pulled up outside Gavin's house and *that* had become the centre of her focus.

Right now, Liam needed to be the centre of her focus. He sat, silent, in the seat next to her.

She drummed her fingers on the steering wheel, bringing her mind back to the most present source of her anger. "Liam ... I'm sitting here, trying to figure out what the hell to say, but all I can focus on is *not* blowing my lid. I'm so mad with you, it's unreal."

There was a pause before he spoke, quietly. "I'm sorry, Mum."

"Sometimes 'sorry' doesn't cut it. Do you have any idea what could have happened to you? 'Sorry' wouldn't matter then; 'sorry' would come too late."

"I won't do it again, I promise."

"*Why?*"

His head still hung. He did look genuinely upset, but it did nothing to temper her anger.

"*Why* did you do it?"

This time, all she got was silence.

She huffed out her sigh and hit the wheel in defeat.

Liam winced beside her.

Sod this. She'd been pussy-footing around him ever since the accident, not bringing up the car crash directly because, despite being the eldest, Liam was sensitive. She hadn't wanted to bring him more pain. He was a deep kid who thought about things other kids his age might not give the time of day to. While his friends were trading game cards, he was looking at the constellations and trying to understand the universe. So, she just figured she'd give him time; give him the room to come to her when the time was right, rather than push to get his feelings out of him – that almost never worked anyway. And what did he do? Jump off a fucking cliff!

Might has well have been a cliff, anyway.

The time for subtlety was over. "Jimmy said you were figuring stuff out about Dad." She looked at him pointedly to gauge his reaction.

He fidgeted in his seat. It was better than nothing.

"Did you? Figure stuff out?"

Nothing. Not a fucking word. Just the tops of his ears going a slightly deeper shade of red.

She swore under her breath, running through dialogue in her head – any dialogue that didn't sound desperate, or loaded, or ... god! There must be some magical key to his voice box! And she needed to find it 'cause she'd failed him.

She blinked back tears; stared straight out of the windscreen.

Today, she'd failed him – big time. "Talking isn't easy. I get that. Because I'm sitting here trying to keep my voice from shaking, and my hands hurt from being clenched the past hour, and my heart's pounding so loudly, I wonder if it'll just give up and stop. But doing what you did today ... when I thought for the briefest second I'd lost you ... do you have any idea how—"

"I didn't want to be angry with him anymore."

She turned to see him.

He was huddled in his seat, but he sniffed, and looked up at her, eyes wet, guilt writing over every story on his features.

"With Dad?"

He nodded, and his face crumpled.

"Hey..." She undid her belt, and damn the fucking gear box in the way. She reached for him the best she could.

He took her hand, and sort of hugged it, still crying.

"It's okay to feel that way, even if he's not to blame. He's been taken from you, and feeling angry's natural."

"I was angry at him for being stupid, and clumsy, and not driving differently. 'Cause he let it happen, and maybe he could have changed it, and it would all be different now."

She held his hand as he wept through his words, her policy of never crying in front of her kids, straight out the window. Seeing him hurting like this was too much.

"When I jumped off the rock, I stopped being angry, because ... I got it. I got that Dad couldn't change it. And he couldn't stop it. It happened too fast, and he couldn't stop it."

"You know he would have if he could have."

"That's what Jimmy said."

"He's right."

"It's not fair."

She swallowed back a fresh wave of tears. Oh, how many times she'd screamed the same words in her head. "No – it's not fair."

He let out a few breaths, steadying himself.

She stroked her thumb along the top of his hand in comfort.

"Mum..."

"Yeah?"

His voice was a bit calmer now, the shuddering, less. He stared at her to ask the next question. "Dad's not going to get better, is he?"

Pieces of your heart broke every day when you were a mother. Even now, knowing the answer, which he surely must, there was a flicker of hope in his eyes that she'd say something other than what she was going to say. "No, honey. The doctors have said now that this is as good as he's going to get. They're still trying though – they try every day, because ... well, we don't give up on people, no matter what."

He contemplated her words, and this time, looked away when he said, "Sometimes, I feel like I don't want to see Dad anymore. The way he sits in his wheelchair, and the way he is..."

She squeezed his hand. "That's okay, too. None of this is easy. It's okay."

"Do you think he's sad? Like ... do you think he still re-members everything, and is the same inside his head, only different outside?"

"I've wondered that myself. I don't think so, though. I

think the accident changed the way he is inside, and the way he thinks about things, and what he knows and remembers."

"Do you think he still loves us?"

"Oh, Liam..." Fuck life. Just ... fuck it. "I *do* think he still loves us, and I think a part of him will always love us, but I also think the new part of him since the accident, maybe loves us in a different way to before. That's all. But he's *always* loved us, and that can never be taken away. Ever."

Liam nodded.

Pippa wiped her wet cheeks on her shoulders, not wanting to let go of his hand. "It would have been okay to tell me you've been angry. I've been angry, too."

He looked at her, surprised. "At Dad? You have?"

"A little. And at myself. Wondering what I could have done differently for things to have happened ... differently. And the fact that there was nothing anyone could have done, is sometimes a bitter pill to swallow. We always like to think we can fix things, even impossible things."

They fell silent, digesting her words.

She ignored the way her shoulder was starting to ache from her position. "I was going to take us all to see Dad tomorrow at the care home. You don't have to come if you don't want to. If you'd rather stay here with Gran, that's fine."

He furrowed his brows as he thought. "Becca and Sammy are okay with seeing Dad the way he is. They don't mind."

"I wouldn't exactly say that. Sammy's having nightmares, and Becca ... well, she's young. I think she thinks Dad's going to just learn how to do all the things he used to all over again, and be fine eventually. Even Sammy might be thinking that. You're older than them. Those few years offer you a bit more insight and awareness as to how things are. In some ways, that makes it a little harder for you 'cause you get to meet reality face-to-face."

He chewed on his lip, his tears now dried on his cheeks. "I want to come tomorrow."

"Really? Are you sure?"

He looked at her and blinked, then nodded. "It's all right."

"Okay then. If you change your mind in the morning, just let me know."

"I will."

"Right," she squeezed his hand a final time, "I want Gran to look at your scratches and make sure they're okay."

He grimaced. "That means—"

"Yep. That means you have the honour of telling her what you did."

"Muuuuum." He looked horrified.

"That's in exchange for me only grounding you for a week, and not a month."

"You're still grounding me?"

She smirked, leaned forward and planted a large, loving kiss on his head. "You betcha. You and Gavin left his cul de sac when you were asked not to, sneaked away to that rock, and shaved ten years off my life. A week off yours is nothing."

He pouted, but sighed in acceptance. "Fine."

"Good." She leaned across him and opened the door for him. "You go on into the house. I've got to grab things from the boot."

He picked up the towel by his feet, and his rucksack, then got out of the car.

"Oh, wait..." She suddenly remembered something. "Yesterday at the barbecue when you came out of Gran's room –

were you looking in my bag?"

He tightened his lips, and looked sheepish, but nodded.

"What was that about?"

He went red. "It was nothing."

"Liam." Her tone was a warning. And he knew he was all out of chances after the stunt he'd pulled today.

The colour of beetroot, he shuffled on his feet. "You usually take your wedding ring off when you're in the kitchen."

She was confused. "Yes, I do – always have – to keep it from getting damaged."

"And you put it in your bag if you take it off at Gran's."

Pippa frowned, not understanding. "You were looking for my wedding ring?"

He nodded. "Or Dad's. I thought it might be together with yours."

She was more than surprised. The doctors had taken David's ring off at the hospital after the accident because his hand had been half-crushed. It was lucky they hadn't had to cut it off. Naturally, she'd been handed his possessions to manage. Weeks wrapped in plaster and bandages, and the ring had never gone back on – in the end, because he wouldn't have known what it was, what it symbolised, or why she was putting it on his finger. "Er ... I keep Dad's ring at home. He's got this small memory box he keeps – used to keep – by his bedside table."

"Oh."

"Why the ring, Liam?"

He prodded his toe into the pavement, then sighed. "It was supposed to be a secret, but I guess it doesn't matter now. Dad said he was going to give you a surprise Christmas present – one of his secret ones he never says anything about until you find it."

What the... Her heart pounded so hard it hurt. That had been one of David's things. He occasionally liked to plant 'surprises', and it could be months, even *years* later until you discovered it, and he'd smile like a school boy when you did, at the look on your face. How the hell he didn't break and blurt out the surprise, she'd never fathomed. No way could she keep anything secret that long, but he did, and he had, and it had been one of the things she'd loved most about him. "Something he told you about?" Fuck, her throat felt too dry. She needed a drink. The conversation suddenly felt too real; too hazardous. Ironic really, considering she'd finally prised everything out of Liam. Half of her didn't want to talk at all right now – didn't want to know the secret. Wanted to crawl under her duvet and stay there forever.

"Yeah. But I never knew if he got it done, 'cause of the accident."

"And it's to do with my ring?" she whispered, failing to speak normally.

"And his. He said he'd been meaning to do it after Becca was born, but it never happened."

For fuck's sake, just tell me! "Do what?"

He stopped abusing the pavement, and stared at her, nervously, and a little sadly. "He said he was going get Sammy's, Becca's and my birthdays engraved in the rings – his ring and yours – but he wanted it to be a surprise for you, but he needed to swipe your ring when you weren't looking, so he told me about it in case I could do it."

She was gripping the steering wheel harder than ever, and glad she was, because it was the only thing keeping her from collapsing. "Did you?" She forced her mind to go back to before last Christmas – before the accident. Was there a time she'd been without her ring for—

Shit – yes! Yes, there was! It had been around Becca's

fourth birthday – she couldn't find her ring for two days, and had been scared she'd lost it baking the cake, although she'd sworn she'd taken it off for baking... She'd looked all around the kitchen sink, down the sides of the dishes, then had searched every room. She'd found it in the fruit bowl two days later, and hadn't a clue how it had gotten there. She'd put it straight on. Hadn't looked *in* it at all.

"Yes." His gaze dropped to her wedding band.

So did hers.

Hell, she couldn't look inside it now – she just couldn't. This was the kind of stuff you needed armour for. Or vodka. She cleared her throat. "I'll check Dad's ring when we get home."

He looked disappointed, and she felt bad, but she *couldn't* look now with him there – with anyone there.

"I'll let you know when I do, okay?" And she couldn't hide the tremble in her tone.

Liam seemed to read it right. "Okay. I'll go see Gran."

She nodded, and attempted a small smile. "Thanks, honey."

He went to shut the passenger door, then stopped. "Mum, I almost forgot to say ... there was a guy earlier who stopped to talk to me and Gavin when we left his house."

What? Her warning bell went off. "What guy?"

"I don't know. He said he knew you. Said he'd heard about the accident and asked if I was okay. I thought it was weird."

Oh, hell... "It is weird. What did he look like?"

He shrugged. "Kinda tall and thin, with blond hair. I felt safe being with Gavin, but I didn't stop to chat or anything 'cause ... well, you know."

"You did the right thing walking on. I can't think of who he'd be. Listen, if you see him again, get me, or Gran, or anyone straight away, okay?"

He nodded, gave her a reassuring smile, then shut the passenger door, and she didn't move a muscle until he'd made his way five doors down, and had disappeared from view walking up the driveway.

What the bloody hell is going on? She mentally went through the list of people she could immediately think of, trying to figure out if she knew anyone of that description who her son didn't know. There were so many parents that saw her and recognised her, but she never caught onto who they were straight away. It was probably just that, but it still left her feeling unsettled. That, however, could also be put down to everything that had happened today, and the bombshell Liam had just dropped.

Her eyes went straight back to her ring. *Like you're not going to look right now.*

"God damn it." Pulling her shaking hands from the wheel, she leaned back into her chair, and slid the band off her finger.

She closed her eyes, took a deep breath, turned it in her hands a couple of times, then finally looked at its inside rim as she held it against the light.

The air rushed out of her.

There it was – three sets of finely etched dates, taking up half the band: *29/01/06 05/04/09 20/11/11*

And on their tail, two more words: *Our family.*

She waited for the tears; waited for herself to fall apart.

It didn't happen.

She stroked a finger across the engraving. What a beautiful gift. 'Family' had always been a big desire for them both – had cemented their relationship in those early stages – all three of their children, loved and wanted before they'd even been born. It was a big thing for her now, too – family.

She looked at the dates again. She still had her family. It was the 'our' that was missing – at least, to an extent. And pretending, or wishing things were as they'd always been was serving no one. Today's events had waved that in her face with shocking clarity.

"Thank you, David," she said quietly. "It's a beautiful present. I love you."

And she did – as much as ever. But for the first time, there was a change; some intangible shift she wouldn't have predicted could take place while she continued to carry that love, but it had.

Love itself was a restless mistress, needing as much nourishment as it gave.

Pippa still gave, but she was malnourished. Her love for David remained, despite his inability to reciprocate, but the storm of their passionate sea was fading, the tide ebbing; the turbulence of lovers finally easing into the trusted safety of past friendship; of history.

Her phone sounded its text tone, making her jump in her seat.

Curling the ring into her palm, she reached into her bag to pull her mobile out: *Jimmy.*

> **Hi. Wanted to make sure you got home safely after everything. Thanks again for the chat earlier. J x**

She stared at the message, reading the words as carefully as she'd read the engraving in her ring.

He'd worded it with thought, not giving much away – not wanting to sound pushy, but wanting to know she was all right.

Theirs was no longer a 'safe' friendship; no longer history.

Tides turned.

XIII
Restless

A steaming shower back at the shop had done nothing to lift his mood. Tonight's pending visit to Cait's – one he wasn't going to confirm with her because he didn't want to give her time to prepare – hung over his head like an axe waiting to drop, and the unusually quiet Sunday in the shop was the bitter icing on the cake. He needed a fucking wage – where the fuck was everyone?

He side-eyed his part-timer, just to make himself feel better.

She was completely oblivious to his current state, which wasn't a bad thing since none of it was her fault. Luckily, she was used to him and took everything he said and did with a pinch of salt. Amanda was the daughter of an acquaintance of a friend – he'd been teaching her to surf for about two years now, before he'd even started his lessons officially. He'd given her a job here last year to help her out with cash, and hadn't regretted it. She was a hard worker with an almost inappropriate sense of humour, which suited him just fine. Humour made everyone easier to work with, especially when he was being a crabby bastard, like now.

Throw into the mix the fact he could still remember the feel of Pippa under his hands, and the taste of her on his tongue, and he was as good as a loaded pistol.

Good analogy there, Jimmy.

He grunted under his breath. Maybe he should have had a cold shower instead.

He couldn't shift the wound her dismissal of him had caused, although he tried to let it go. Her son mattered most at that moment – that was completely understandable.

It's her you need to let go of. Go back to the 'just friends' thing – forget the idea of a relationship with her. If you do that now, you might still be able to salvage the friendship.

Except thinking about letting her go made him angrier. And restless.

It was too late, he knew that – knew it as soon as she'd walked out of that little copse and onto the beach. Something had shifted. He'd moved forward in the past couple of months; changed – ending things with Cait was a big part of that, but he'd be lying if he denied that the more recent possibility of starting something with Pip hadn't lit his fuel.

"Oh, Jimmy, I forgot to say when you walked in – your accountant called."

His side-eye became a full-blown stare.

The eighteen-year-old raised her eyebrows at him.

"Sorry," he mumbled. *Accountant. That's just wonderful.* His accountant was nice – she was – friendly, numerically accommodating (god knew, he needed her to be) and a whiz with the books, but accountants phoning you was never a good thing, no matter how nice they were. "Did she say what she wanted?"

"Something about a discrepancy; she asked you to phone her back. Here." Amanda, held a piece of paper out for him to take. *THAT* piece of paper.

He scowled, and snatched it from her. "What's this?"

Those eyebrows went up higher. "I wrote down her number for you."

"On this? Why on this?"

She looked at him like he was insane, then down at the burnt piece of paper in his hand. "It's a scrap piece of paper, right? It was on the side of the till, and it looks ready for the bin."

There it was, scrawled on the back of the poem he'd found in the alleyway:

Rachel Collins
accountant
07957 234890

He knew he was being completely unreasonable, but that irritated the fuck out of him and no mistake. *Why* in god's name, out of all the bloody notepads in the shop, did she have to write on *this?*

He said nothing because he didn't trust himself to say anything that didn't sound odd.

The silence was just as odd, though.

"So..." Amanda wrinkled her nose, "it's not scrap paper, is it?"

He sighed, unable to explain himself. He just *liked* the poem, that was all. And he hadn't solved its puzzle yet.

"So, what is it? Like, Shakespeare or something?"

"I don't know. It's just ... it's personal."

"Oh," she grimaced. "Sorry."

He placed the paper, poem side up, on the counter. "Don't worry about it, it's no biggy."

"Really?" she asked incredulously.

"Just don't touch it again, okay?"

"Not a problem. Don't ever want to."

The restlessness he felt suddenly shot sky-high. He needed to *do* something. After this afternoon with Pip, he couldn't go back to some stalemate – that had been his whole life: he had a stalemate with money, he'd had a stalemate with his education, he had a stalemate with his nan, with his family – fuck – every relationship he'd ever had had been a stalemate; some means to an end that obliterated his goals.

He was done with it. Whatever it might mean – even if he lost everything he had – he was done with being stuck. "Listen, I'm sorry to run on you, but it's so quiet here and with two hours until closing, I think you can handle it – can I leave you to cash up?"

"Er ... I've only done it twice before, but I guess."

"You'll be fine. Instructions are in the blue folder if you need reminding, but just do your best, and you'll be fine. You remember the alarm code?"

"Yeah."

"Cool. Use the spare keys to lock up, then chuck them back through the letterbox."

"Okay, no worries."

"Thanks, Amanda."

"Hope you sort it out."

"Sort what out?"

She stared at him, bemused. "Whatever it is stressing you out."

"Right ... sorry."

"It's cool. Next week I have my period, so I'll get my turn then."

"Nice." But he grinned. Her candidness was welcomed, and lifted him a little out of his funk.

Forget this evening – he was going to go end things with Cait *now*. Then maybe he'd spend the evening with his nan and give her carer a break – no doubt she'd appreciate going home early on a Sunday.

He wandered back into his bedroom to grab his jacket, wallet and phone. He wondered if he should take anything else.

A chastity belt.

He let out a dry laugh. Nope – not going to happen, not this time.

He looked at his watch. Cait had said her husband's flight was today. If he took the usual flight he did on Sundays, he could catch Cait on her way home from dropping her husband off at the airport, even if it meant he had to wait in the car for a while. Without a doubt, she'd be hugely pissed off he'd sprung himself on her, allowing her no time to prepare herself the way she did for all her 'visitors', but for the first time in twelve years, that wasn't the reason he was going there.

Visitors. Another laugh. He wasn't even sure there was a name for what he was to her. 'Toy boy' didn't really fulfil the position.

A small wave of sadness caught him unawares. Twelve years with her hadn't meant nothing; it hadn't been purely functional. But it *had* been mutually beneficial, and it no longer was. He liked her; she'd helped him – had given him what he'd needed in more ways than one, and he'd reciprocated with time, youth and vigour. She'd helped him feel secure, he'd helped her feel young – both had gained some independence from that.

At one time, their symbiotic relationship had served his emotions; closed wounds without really trying. And the money, as well as being the reason for their agreement, had been a bonus. A really big, fucking wonderful bonus he'd been more than grateful for. Now, all there was was the money.

And his fears surrounding it. Inherited fears he needed to put to rest.

"Amanda," he called out from the hallway as he pulled up his jacket's zipper.

"Yeah?"

She was tidying up one of the clothes racks when he walked back onto the shop floor. "If Rachel calls again, tell her I'll phone her back tomorrow, and tell her to find something better to do on a Sunday."

"I'm not telling her that!"

"You disappoint me," he teased.

"It's not like *I'm* doing anything better on a Sunday."

"Touché. Guess you won't be wanting that double-time, then?"

"Hey ... I deserve double pay. I've been giving you free wit."

He laughed. "If I could swap places with you right now, I would."

"Your pending mission is that bad, huh?"

"It's been a long time coming – gotta be done."

"Oooo, those are the worst missions – the ones you put off until forever. Good luck, Captain."

He returned the light-hearted salute she gave him, then sent her a silent apology as he walked out of the shop, because after this meeting with Cait, he wasn't sure he'd be able to afford to keep her on.

~*~

"My goodness, Pippa..." Her mother's gently scolding voice brought her out of her thoughts, although she hadn't a clue what she'd been thinking, the rhythmic pounding of the steak sending her into some kind of trance.

She looked down at the cuts of sirloin in front of her.

Her mum took the steak hammer from her. "I asked you to tenderise the meat, not kill the cow all over again."

"It's *extra* tender," she replied, defensively. Bugger. It looked kinda wrecked.

"What on earth's the matter?"

"Sorry. Nothing. I just feel ... restless." And her wedding ring was burning a hole in her pocket.

She hadn't put it back on because it suddenly felt ... not quite right to wear it – after all, David hadn't worn his for eight months. But her finger felt strange, not yet used to its new freedom.

"Anything I can help you with?"

She could see Sammy and Becca in the garden, heads locked together in some secret project they'd taken to.

Liam was sitting in the living room with her dad, having had his scratches looked over by her mum. It was as if a burden had lifted off him a little, and despite his being grounded and having to explain what he did, he was in good spirits.

She was glad – very glad – but she wished she was in the same place. "No."

Her mum placed the steak in the dish to soak in the sauce for an hour before cooking it. "Well, if you think of anythi—"

"Why did you do it?" she asked, all the sudden, not really knowing she was going to.

Her mum, unsurprisingly, looked at her with confusion.

"Jimmy told me what happened that night. You could have gotten into so much trouble. Why did you treat him here, and not take him to the hospital? If anything had gone wrong, or he'd become infected after a stab wound like that

... you could have lost your job."

"I would have taken him in at any sign of infection. It's true, I'd have had some explaining to do, but I wouldn't necessarily have lost my job."

"But you *could* have."

She closed the cupboard door having put a couple of sauce jars away, then looked at Pippa, and smiled – a sort of sad, understanding smile. "He would have lost more."

Pippa turned back to what she was doing – cleaning the kitchen top of bits of steak juice. She hadn't expected that answer, although she wasn't sure why. She had never known her mum to be so bold. But perhaps what irked her most, was that she'd never known Jimmy had been so *influential* in their lives; so dear to them. Clearly, he had. Where the hell had she been hiding all those years? She'd never known she was so oblivious.

"I wanted to be a nurse so I could *help* people. Sometimes help isn't black and white – you know that, Pip. Jimmy was almost like a second son – he was here all the time, Jamie adored him, he adored you..." Her mum laughed. "I'm assuming he told you about his mother, and what his dad was trying to do with his nan." She shook her head in disgust at the memory. "My decision might have led, not just him, but his family down a road they wouldn't come back from unscathed. I had to do what I could, and it wasn't a decision I made lightly."

"You knew Jimmy had a thing for me?"

"Everyone knew Jimmy had a thing for you." She glanced at Pippa sideways, curiosity in her eyes. "Does he still have a thing for you?"

She blatantly ignored her mother's question, not wanting to go there right now. She hadn't responded to Jimmy's text yet, which was a bit cruel of her because he obviously wanted to know if she was safe, but she was teetering on the point of no return where Jimmy was concerned. She liked him a hell of a lot more than she ever knew, and she had yet to decide what to do about that. "How did you know? Back then, I mean."

Her mum laughed again, louder this time. "Are you kidding? It was clear from every look and every action."

Pippa rolled her eyes.

"He hung on every word you said, remembered it all, too. I recall when you were all quite young – you must have been around fourteen; he and Jamie were twelve – you mentioned in passing once you preferred fudge to chocolate, and after that day he *always* brought back fudge from the candy store every Saturday, and left it in the cupboard next to Jamie's chocolate so you'd have some."

She stared at her mum, speechless. "What?"

"Oh, yes, that's why you always found fudge in the cupboard."

"I thought *you* bought it when you went into town with Dad for the weekly shop."

"Nope."

She had no idea what to say. She went over to the sink instead to rinse out the sponge in her hand.

"Poor boy," her mum laughed, with a sigh. "You never noticed."

"I..." She had no defence. She *hadn't* noticed him for the most part because... "He was just Jamie's annoying friend."

"Oh, I'm not blaming you, darling, you were teenagers. Siblings and their friends – yes, I remember how irritating it can all be. Irritating or not, he cared for you a great deal."

"It was just a crush."

"It was more than that. Goodness, there was that time you were blind drunk – *you* of all people – up in the bathroom."

She'd only been drunk enough to puke once, so she remembered that night. Ugh – that had been over Danny Foreman. *Jerk.* "What about it?"

"You don't remember?"

"I remember it was a horrible night," she scowled.

"Hmmm. Well, Dad and I went out to the cinema leaving Jamie and Jimmy home alone – it was only for two hours and they were fourteen, so old enough. Little did we know that on our return, the one causing havoc wouldn't be either of them, but you."

"I had good reason."

"We came back to find Jamie out on the front door steps trying to fix a paving slab you loosened as you'd stumbled in, and Jimmy upstairs holding your hair and rubbing your back while you threw up into the toilet."

"Nope. No." She squeezed the sponge dry, then chucked it on the side of the sink. "Jamie was holding my hair back."

"No, Pippa, Jamie was fixing the porch, and looking ever so guilty about it in a bid to defend you so you wouldn't get into trouble."

"No ... Jamie was in the bathroom with me." Although she suddenly wasn't so certain.

Her mum looked at her, then blinked. "Then who was downstairs fixing the porch?"

She was stumped. Again. "Jimmy was ... helping me puke?" It's not as if she remembered in *detail* what had happened after downing shot after shot of Jack Daniels, with full encouragement from her then best friend after they'd caught Danny admitting to *another* girl he was snogging, that he only went out with Pippa to 'break' her virginity.

Git.

She'd never been able to drink Jack Daniels again. "But ... I told him all about..." She stopped short of mentioning Danny, not sure if her mum even knew about all that. Bloody hell, she'd bawled her eyes out to who she thought was Jamie, she remembered that much. "And then, he ... didn't he—"

"He carried you to bed – as good as, since you could barely walk. He took off your shoes, and made sure you were tucked in, then came downstairs and assured me you were fine so I wouldn't be worried. 'She'll need some water or milk first thing when she wakes up so she's not dehydrated,' that's what he said." She snickered. "As if I wasn't a nurse. Sweet child."

And on the Tuesday morning, Danny had come to school with a black eye.

"Fuck me!" *Jimmy* had done that?

"Pippa." Her mother frowned at her swearing.

"Sorry."

"Well," she brought the jug of Pimms and Lemonade out of the fridge, "I'm glad he finally told you about what happened between he and his mum – gosh, that night was horrific. And I'm glad Liam's safe. To think neither of you might have been there. Thank goodness Jimmy was."

"Oh, Mum, Liam said some guy stopped him in the street this morning to talk about David's car crash?"

"Really? That's a bit strange."

"It is. It was probably a parent of one of the kids I teach, or something. Everyone sort of knows everything that happens around here – at least they *think* they do, like Chinese whispers. The boys are fine, and they walked on, and whoever this guy was didn't press or anything, but I thought I'd let you know to keep an eye out."

"Of course."

All at once, she felt faint, her chest tight. Breathing became hard. She raised her hand to her head to ease the sudden sense of overwhelm. There was a gentle snag against her wrist, then a clatter on the floor.

Her bracelet had fallen off again. *Never did get it fixed.*

"Darling..." Her mum was standing there holding the bracelet out for her to take. "Are you all right?"

She took the piece of jewellery, but couldn't stop her hand from shaking. "It's just been a long day."

"Certainly an adventure. Perhaps after dinner you could—"

"Do you mind if I go out?" She felt awful asking. As if they didn't look after her kids enough. But the restlessness she'd felt earlier had grown tenfold, and she didn't think she could sit through dinner without ... *doing* something. She wasn't sure what needed doing, though.

"Um, of course not. Where to?"

"I ... er..." One of the bracelet's tree charms dug into her palm. "I think I might go see David."

"Are you not seeing him tomorrow?"

"It might be good to see him on my own, just to..." *To what? Say hello? Say goodbye?*

Her mum squeezed her arm. "Of course it's fine – you know you don't have to worry about a thing at this end."

"Thank you. I'll head off in ten minutes; I'll just make sure the kids are okay first."

"Right you are. Will you grab dinner out?"

Oh – dinner. She hadn't even considered that. "Yeah, I'll just grab a sandwich from the supermarket."

Her mum didn't look best pleased about that. "That's hardly dinner."

"I'll be fine. I'm not too hungry anyway." She pocketed her bracelet next to the ring, gave her hands a quick dry with the tea towel, and made towards the kitchen door.

"Pip..."

"Yeah?"

She turned around when her mum didn't reply to find her staring at her with love. And an element of concern. *About my lack of dinner?*

"I don't know if I've ever properly told you how proud I am of you."

Oh... She didn't know what to say. She clenched her hands together, slightly embarrassed. "Erm..."

"When you were kids, Jamie was the one who got all the praise with his good grades and academic achievements – they're things that are easy to see. But *you* inspired him, did you know that? He was a little different to his friends – far too sensible, emotionally intelligent – and he was comfortable being that way, because *you've* always paved your own way. He grew into the confident man he became because his big sister was confident in herself."

Okay ... cue the waterworks. "You trying to make me cry?" she teased, light-heartedly.

Her mum smiled and approached her with arms out for a hug.

She hugged her back.

"You're not lost, Pippa," she said quietly against her ear.

Fuck – yeah – waterworks. She tried to blink them away.

"You never have been. You always knew what you wanted. You fought to marry at twenty-one because you *knew* it was right for you, no matter that you'd only just finished your degree. You knew exactly what you wanted, and you still do. You're not lost."

"Mum..." She pulled back, wiping her eyes with her hands.

"I know you're going to figure things out – that's what you do. And *everything's* going to get better."

She wiped them again, and sniffed. "Thanks."

Her mum reached for the tissue box on the counter behind her. "Here."

She took the tissue she was offered.

"I'm going to grab George to get the potatoes ready – he's so much better at them than me. Don't you worry about anything here. I'll see you when you get back."

She was choked – couldn't say anything else, but silently thanked anyone listening that she had the best parents in the world. And the best brother. And the best kids.

Her heart hurt.

Things *could* be so much worse, and she hadn't figured everything out yet, but her mum was right – she would. Right now, she just needed to see David.

She smoothed her hand over her pocket; over the bracelet and ring.

There had been this growing sense the past few days that she'd forgotten something, or missed something. Something important. An urgent pressing on the corner of her mind she couldn't decipher. And David had always been the one she'd gone to with problems, so despite all the complications of his situation, that's where she'd go.

XIV
Broken Spells

Candy stood outside The Boat Shop feeling about as miserable as you can get, not really sure what she was doing here, but here was better than home right now, and she didn't want to be too far away in case Lauren needed her.

Tim had texted her about a dozen times, and she had yet to return any of the messages – hadn't even read them all – which she did feel a little bad about, but she was also mad. Really fucking mad at his aloofness and distance. Oh, yes – and the lying.

She caught her reflection in the glass of the shop window.

Subconsciously, she ran her fingers through the short curl of her blue hair at the back. She'd thought of growing it long again – waist length and naturally dark like it used to be. It didn't look too bad like this, though, and she *liked* the blue. The ends were a mystical, lighter shade of indigo.

But she suddenly felt stupid. *You're almost thirty. Who dyes their hair blue at thirty? Act your age.*

Something her mother would say, no doubt – she'd said the same about polyamory – and she really didn't want to sound like her mother.

Hands in the pockets of her khaki shorts, she walked into the shop, kind of wanting to see Jimmy even though she didn't really know him at all. He seemed to be fun and jovial, and she could really do with the pick-me-up.

He didn't appear to be on the shop floor. A girl, about eighteen or so, stood behind the counter on the phone, looking somewhat fed up with the phone call she was taking. "Yes, I know we're *called* The Boat Shop, but we only *hire* boats, we don't sell them." She raised an eyebrow. "Hello?" She shook her head as she put the phone down, mumbling to herself. "Goodbye to you, too. Every. Bloody. Week."

She finally looked up at Candy and smiled, closing the blue folder on the counter in front of her. "Hi."

"Hi." Candy hoped she didn't look as miserable as she felt. "Annoying customer?"

"Annoying question. I get it at least once a month. 'Do you sell boats?' I tell them no, and I'm met with some stuffy reply about how we should because we're called The Boat *Shop* – not The Boat *Hire*. I mean, I kind of understand – *why* this place is called The Boat Shop, I have no idea – but I'd never be so rude as to tell a company to change their name. Anyway ... what can I do for you? Please don't say you want to buy a boat."

She laughed. "No. I was wondering if Jimmy was in?"

"Ah. Nope, you've just missed him."

"Oh." Her face fell. She felt it fall.

The girl looked at her, unsure.

It was all a little awkward.

"Erm ... you're not Rachel, are you?"

"Rachel? No."

"Oh, good," she said, sounding relieved. "Jimmy's out for the rest of the day. Is it something I can help you with instead?"

"Got a cure for a shit boyfriend?"

"Ugh. No, we're all out of Frog-to-Prince potions. We've

had a new batch of shark teeth come in though."

"For real?"

The girl grinned. "Yep." She pointed at the far corner. It was full of friendship bracelets, shell and surf jewellery, and a display shelf filled with tumblestones and fossils.

Ah – maybe she'd have a look.

"Tough day, then?"

"Tough year."

She wrinkled her nose. "You're not the only one. Jimmy was stomping around earlier with a face-on, too."

"Maybe it's something in the wind."

"Right."

"I'll have a look at the stones and stuff. Maybe I can make my own Frog-to-Prince potion."

She laughed. "You might be joking, but there's a woman that comes in here at least once a week, all dressed in black. Witchy type – wears a pentagram around her neck. She buys a handful of the fossils and a couple of stones at a time. I'm *dying* to ask her what she does with them. She's kind of creepy though, and I don't think she's much of a talker."

"Hmmm – your job sounds more exciting than mine. I just have crabby business men and women as clients."

She smiled again. "Jimmy's cool to work for. Just let me know if you need any help. I don't know any spells though, so, no-can-do in that department."

Candy threw her a thanks, and wandered over to the knick-knacks. She knew a spell or two thanks to Merri's mum, but she couldn't say, hand on heart, that anything had ever 'happened' when she'd performed them. Merri, how-ever...

"Oooh – hey!" The shop assistant's sharp whisper had her turning around. "Speak of the devil. That's the woman I was talking about." She nodded at a figure standing just outside the shop, and, sure enough, dressed in velvet blacks and purples.

She found it quite admirable. Cutting her hair short and dyeing it blue was as brave as she got, and the occasional stare was something she'd had to get used to at first, because people did that – judged you on a fraction of a thing that made you who you were. It had given her a thicker skin, and she hadn't regretted the experience or the lesson – she often felt she was too sensitive. *This* woman though... Candy would never have the guts to go full goth like her. She looked like she'd stepped straight out of an Anne Rice novel.

The woman walked into the shop, and Candy turned back to the gemstones and fossils, not wanting to get caught staring like all those judgy people she found so challenging.

Odd though, how the hairs on the back of her neck and arms rose. The woman had a presence about her and no mistake.

Too late, she realised what the shop assistant had said: *she buys a handful of the fossils and a couple of stones at a time.* And Candy was standing right in her way.

She froze to the spot like an idiot. If she moved now, would it look like she'd moved *because* of her?

You are *moving because of her.*

But why? She was just a customer.

Nevertheless, her heart thudded, and she still had goose-bumps. Surely this wasn't shyness, although she *was* a naturally shy person – she dealt with strangers every day at work.

"Excuse me."

Shit. "Oh. Sorry." Candy stepped to her right, and the woman stepped *into* her space – totally into it. Or maybe it was her magnetism that took up the whole area.

She set to work, feeling out the fossils with her fingertips, occasionally picking one or two up and rubbing them between forefinger and thumb, putting them down again, moving onto the next... Whenever she settled on one, she transferred it to her left hand. It was quite riveting to watch – she was so focused. Not *completely* focused, though. "Wow – you're really sad."

It took a second before Candy realised she was referring to her. She looked up, shocked, to find the woman staring back. Her eyes were very blue – a similar blue to her own – and she also had black hair and pale skin. In fact, if this was some weird alternate universe, she might just be some evil version of herself.

Really? You're non-judgemental? Did you just call her evil?

Hell, she hadn't meant to, but the thought had come from somewhere, and the shop assistant was right – she *was* kind of creepy, and it wasn't because of the clothes. It was in her demeanour. Candy knew many witches and Wiccans and pagans who weren't creepy. Merri's mum had been one of them. "I ... am?"

She smiled. Or was it a smirk? "You know you are. I just can't tell if it's because of a him or a her, but it's definitely a lover. This kind of sadness is *always* because of a lover."

She had no idea what to say; felt stunned at her bluntness.

The woman bored her stare into her, then the stare travelled down her from head to foot, and bloody hell – Candy felt naked. It was like some weird energetic violation. She visibly shivered and wished she hadn't.

Rooted to the spot, she dumbly watched as the woman turned back to the merchandise and picked up a ribbed Ammonite. She pressed the pad of her thumb into the dip at the centre of its spiral, the action strangely erotic.

Candy's stomach dipped the way it sometimes did when she was aroused, except she *wasn't* aroused ... was she? *What the hell is going on?*

The woman put the Ammonite in one of the organza pouches meant for the tumblestones. She smiled at Candy, then picked up a rose quartz tumblestone and a snowflake obsidian, then literally *threw* them both on the floor, hard.

Candy jumped out of her skin.

"Hey!" shouted the shop assistant, her hands up in the air, in a what-the-fuck gesture. "You can't do that!"

She ignored the girl who looked as stumped as Candy was, picked up the broken pieces of tumblestone off the floor, and added them to the pouch. "What's your name?"

Don't say your name.

"Candace."

What... She shook her head. She swore she hadn't meant to speak.

"Carry it with you until the problem's gone." She handed Candy the pouch, and because she'd become a robot or something, she took it.

She stared at Candy again, in that intrusive way, then smiled, her perfectly applied, dark red lipstick on full, se-ductive lips.

It disturbed her that she noticed that.

The woman took a step towards her, cocked her head, gaze still boring into hers, then said, "See you soon, Can-dace."

She didn't reply.

She strode towards the shop assistant, who still stood there, agape. "I'll pay for those," she pointed to the pouch in Candy's hand.

Candy literally just stood there, clutching the pouch, as money was exchanged, feeling all kinds of wrong. *Wrong,*

wrong, wrong. And now it was worse, because money had changed hands. That was like sealing the deal, or something, although Candy didn't really understand what the deal was. But she was now indebted to this woman, even though she hadn't asked to be. "Wait," she croaked out. Too late, because she'd already strode out.

The shop assistant hurried up to her, looking as spooked as she felt. "Are you all right?" she asked, disbelief in her tone.

"I don't know."

"Jesus, that woman... I *told* you she was creepy."

"Yeah."

"'Though I've never seen her do *anything* like that before. What are you gonna do with that?"

Candy looked at the pouch she was pointing at, then suddenly thrust it towards her. "Put it in the bin." She felt nauseous.

The girl jumped backwards away from it, clearly not wanting to touch it. "Bin's right there." She now pointed behind the till. "Feel free."

Candy walked towards it, every step she took making her feel like she was going to throw up. She felt dizzy; strange.

And just a little turned on, and *that* freaked her the fuck out.

"I'm going to go get the dustpan and brush to sweep up the bits of tumblestone she left on the floor."

The girl disappeared out the back as Candy walked around the till. She suddenly stopped, something catching her eye. She didn't get what it was at first, but when she finally did, unexpected relief flooded her; relief which outweighed her confusion. *That's Merri's spell! 'Once times thrice...'*

But it couldn't be – what on earth was it doing *here*? Last time she'd seen it had been just before Pippa had sneakily taken it from her dining table. And there it was, upright on the counter this side of the till. It was *definitely* the spell – she'd know Merri's handwriting anywhere – but it did look different. The paper was burnt for one thing, and it looked as if someone else had written the final word of it: Start.

Re-written it more like. That hadn't been Merri's word.

She couldn't say exactly why she did what she did next. Perhaps it was because it belonged to Merri and she was feeling possessive for her friend; perhaps it was because it reminded her of Merri's mother, or perhaps it was because the immense sense of relief she felt at looking upon those words made Merri's spell a bright, shining beacon that cancelled out the disturbing events of the last ten minutes.

She opened her bag, made sure the shop assistant was still gone, then took the piece of paper and tucked it away into one of the inside pockets.

I'm not stealing it – I'm just taking it back.

Footsteps sounded.

Fuck.

Her guilt rose, and she sped away from the counter, sticking the pouch in her bag, too, because she'd blown her chance to chuck it. She'd throw it away at home.

"You know," started the girl as she appeared around the corner, dustpan and brush in hand, "the more I think about it, the more I think it's just for show. I mean," she waved the brush around before getting on her knees by the tumble-stones, "why do all that? And the outfit, and everything... Seriously – it was creepy, yeah, but I don't think you should lose sleep over it. Just forget about it. Not giving people like that the time of day is what annoys them the most."

"I hear you." Although doubt still remained. Perhaps she was right, but Candy couldn't shake the disconcerting sense of personal infringement at what she'd done. Maybe it would all seem less of a big deal by tomorrow. "Hey, listen, I'm going to head off."

"I don't blame you."

Candy laughed. "No, really, I've got a million things to do."

"Okay, well, it was nice to meet you, even if under bizarre circumstances."

"Never a dull moment. Just like I said – your job's way more interesting than mine."

She stood with the pan, and smiled. "Do you want me to let Jimmy know you stopped by?"

Candy shook her head. "Nah, it's cool. I'll catch him another time."

"All right. Hope the rest of your day is ... normal."

She grinned. "Yours, too."

They waved their goodbyes, and as soon as she was out the store, Candy took in the biggest gulp of air.

The sun shone; the breeze seemed to make everything a little better, although she did note the dark clouds a few miles to the south. *Looks like there might be a storm tonight.*

Automatically, she scanned the area, looking for the creepy woman, and couldn't find her. *Thank goodness.*

She took her phone out of her bag and noticed another two text messages from Tim.

She sighed. She'd put the phone on silent after his first three, needing time to think.

Please, please let me explain. Candy, I love you, you know that, and I'm a first class

> idiot. Are you still coming with me to the
> hospital later? Please talk to me. I've been a
> shit. I'm ready to talk now. Love you. xx

Oh, he's *ready to talk now. Good for him – it only took* months *and getting caught out.*

But she hit reply and began typing. Lauren shouldn't suffer because of them.

> I'll meet you at the hospital at 7pm. We'll talk
> after that.

She left her phone on silent, then put it back in her bag. She had three hours to kill.

She was going to go back home – *her* home. She hadn't returned to her house since Merri had gone back to London, and she had yet to find someone who wanted to rent it after the last guy. She was currently two months short on the income it brought.

She made her way to her car, feeling sombre. The way things were going with Tim, she might not have to find anyone after all.

XV
Moments In Time

The best time to come to the care home was before or after meal times, and Sunday was no different. After an overdue and embarrassing talk (more like a telling off) from the nurse about how she'd run out of there last time after David had lashed out, she now felt calmer and as prepared for such a thing as she could be, should it happen again. She was assured it had been a rare occurrence and would likely remain so.

He'd been very calm today, apparently, and in good spirits.

She felt stupid for not being able to tell. *How did they know?* 'Happy' on David, kind of looked the same as any other emotion nowadays.

Nevertheless, she'd been sitting on the armchair next to his wheelchair, with her shoes kicked off and her legs tucked under herself, fiddling with the tree bracelet she'd put back on her wrist, as she told him all about the past few days – the barbecue, and Liam's little near-suicidal adventure.

He made noises a couple of times, but whether they were in response to what she was saying she didn't know. She'd left Jimmy completely out of the conversation, partly owing to guilt, and partly because that just wouldn't be fair on David. In this version, she'd been at the beach with

Jamie, and he'd been the one to surf out to get Liam.

"There's a noticeable change in him now. Since we got him home, he's been happier, and ... he's really loosened up; relaxed a bit. It's nice to see. He really misses you. We all do. And Becca's chewing at the bit to see you tomorrow." She studied his expression, hoping to become suddenly psychic, or something, so she could decipher his thoughts – if there were any. "The nurses said you've had a good day today – that you've been in good spirits."

Another noise – a grunting sound she was starting to become familiar with, but found untranslatable.

With a small grunt of her own, she unfurled herself from the chair and stood to stretch her legs. It still hurt, even now, to be sitting here speaking with him so familially, and yet have no recognition from him, or so little it was barely there. God, she missed him. But she didn't want to carry the hurt anymore – didn't want to hold onto it *because* she missed him, *because* she loved him. That wasn't love. Love was acceptance, wasn't it? She could still love him, and be free of the hurt, couldn't she?

A clatter on the floor had her looking down. The damn bracelet had fallen as she'd stood. "It keeps doing this. I've been meaning to get it fixed."

The wheelchair creaked. David moved on it, or tried, and for a second she held her breath, thinking it was going to be something similar to last time. But he didn't lash out. Instead, his grunts became more pronounced, and this time, she did get the sense he was trying to say something.

She looked down at the bracelet she'd just picked up, then back at him.

Yep – that's what he was looking at, and it was one of those unusual moments where he was actually focused on something. "This?" she asked, holding it out towards him, flat in her palm so he could see it. "I still wear it. Don't worry, I'll find a way to get it fixed."

He spent another few seconds *really* trying to get some point across she couldn't fathom, and then sat back in his chair, the more usual blank look, glazing his features once more.

Half of her was disappointed. Half of her was relieved. She should probably let the nurses know, though – stay in their good books after the mad dash to escape she'd made the last time.

"David, everything's okay. Listen, I'm going to go and speak to the nurses quickly, and then I'll be back, all right?"

It was strange how she still expected him to nod, or something, after all this time.

She slipped her canvas deck shoes back onto her feet, and left his room. She scanned the hallway for a member of staff, but found it pretty empty. *They must be sorting out everything for dinner.*

Opening her bag, she pulled out her phone, feeling the inexplicable urge to call Jimmy, just to have someone tell her everything was all right. And he would, wouldn't he? He had earlier with Liam.

"Pippa." Nurse Kelter sang her name in greeting from two doors down the corridor.

Pippa smiled, and put her phone away. "Hi."

"How are you, my darling? I wasn't expecting you until tomorrow morning with your horde."

She laughed. She'd always liked Nurse Kelter – matronly and kind. "I just thought I'd swing by and get some one-to-one time in."

"Too right."

"He ... erm ... seemed to recognise something a minute ago, although I can't be sure." She showed her the bracelet in her hand. "This. He gave it to me years ago."

"Oh, I see. Does it mean something special?"

"Sort of, yes. It's, um, a bit of a silly story. After we bought our first house, we used to have this favourite tree in a little patch of woodland nearby. We were so young," she laughed. "It had a hollow trunk, and we kept a large jam jar in it, sealed with all these bits of paper where we wrote our hopes and dreams and stuff."

"Oh, goodness. Mrs Fellows, that's a beautiful memory to have."

And for a flash of a second, it wasn't a memory, but a dream. A dream she couldn't quite remember.

"Is the tree still there?"

She shook her head, trying to come back down to earth so she could answer the nurse's question. "You know, I'm not sure. We stopped going there after a year or so because the whole wood got cornered off while they built a new housing development next to it. That's when he bought me the bracelet – to remember it by because we no longer had access. I heard they built into half the wood, but I'm not sure which half. It *might* still be there."

"That's a story for the grand-kids, surely. It's like a fairy tale – what a lovely thing to be able to tell."

"It is."

"And maybe David *does* remember it, or parts of it. Even if he doesn't remember in detail, perhaps he still re-cognised the bracelet has significance."

"It seemed so."

"That's encouraging. Are you staying a bit longer?"

"Half an hour or so."

"Good, I'll try to catch you before you leave. I have to hurry on to my shift now."

"Of course. Is the visitor's bathroom okay to use today?"

"Yes, yes, yes – no problem. You know where it is."

"Thank you."

"See you later."

She waved her goodbye, then walked towards the washroom, needing to collect herself after that trip down memory lane. She walked past the reception area, and smiled at a more surly looking woman manning the desk, who didn't smile back, but seemed a bit put out by the phone call she was taking. She let out a soft curse when she accidentally knocked a pile of papers off the desk.

Pippa hurried over to pick the pile up, and ended up staring at it instead, or more specifically, at the red envelope that had fallen out of it.

"You didn't want me to write it, but I had to."

"What are you talking about?"

"The tree."

"You went back to the tree?"

"Oh, my god."

"Excuse me?"

"Huh?"

"Miss?"

Pippa looked up from the pile she was holding.

"Can I have my paperwork?"

Oh. She handed it to her. "Yes – I'm so sorry, I got distracted."

The receptionist put the pile back on the desk.

Pippa noted the fact she hadn't even received a 'thank you' – not that that was why she'd helped. But that was far less important than the red envelope, and the playback of the dream it had triggered. It was the dream from a few nights ago, wasn't it?

Bloody hell ... was that all of it, or was there more? She couldn't remember. But she *did* now remember the red envelope. And David mentioning the tree – the one she'd been talking about *just now*.

Coincidence?

Maybe, but it didn't matter, because all at once, she had to know – *had* to know if that tree was still there. Despite the bracelet being a reminder of those times, she wore it so often, she hadn't really thought about that tree for so long.

Freaked out, yet buzzed with a sense of excitement, she entered the washroom and dipped her hands straight under a cold running tap to cool herself down.

"I felt it was important. They were things I wanted to say. I want you to open the envelope..."

She splashed some water on her face, her heart going at the rate of knots.

No – she wasn't expecting to find a red envelope in that jar, but it now seemed that *all* she could think about was that tree – their old, favourite spot.

Half an hour with David, then she was heading straight there.

-*-

Only when he walked through his front door, and threw the keys into the pot on the little rattan box that sat in the corner of the entrance hall, did he realise he was shaking.

He'd held it all in; he'd held it all together. He'd ended twelve years, and he hadn't caved in.

Almost two hours of waiting for Cait to come home had shot his nerves; he'd almost left – turned his car right around and driven home. It was the ultimate sense of failure he knew he'd have to live with that had stopped him from doing so. That, and the fact he couldn't continue on like this.

"Mr Darling?" His nan's carer, Claire, popped her head around the frame of the living room door. She was the only one who ever called him 'Mr Darling', because she was the only one that ever made it sound right. On anyone else's tongue, the surname always sounded like a joke or jibe, or at the very least uncomfortable. Perhaps it was her soft-spoken nature, or perhaps it was because she looked after one of the most important women in the world to him, but she managed to make the name sound like it fit him. Maybe here, it did. This was more his nan's home than his, only because he'd made it that way so she'd feel safe and would never want for anything. He'd taken to 'living' at The Boat Shop more and more so that his nan could have her independence and space, not that those things were on her priority list nowadays. But he loved it here *because* it felt like her home. It reminded him of his childhood visiting her – one of the only times he ever felt safe. The least he could do was reciprocate.

"Yes, Claire, just me. How has today been?" Jimmy kicked his shoes off and shed his jacket, trying to keep from showing he was shaking. There'd been so much tension today, from meeting Pippa, to the scare with Liam, to his ending things – finally – with Cait... He could do with hitting the sack and not waking up for a week.

"Mmmmm," she shrugged her shoulders, "a little hard. She's been more aware than usual that she keeps forgetting things, and there have been some frustrating moments. All in all, though, you know I love her."

"You and me both." He looked at Claire and smiled.

God, he felt shit, because he might have to let her go now he'd severed all ties with Cait. She'd be the *last* thing he lost though, he'd see to that for his nan's sake. "Thank you for today, I really appreciate it. Feel free to go whenever you like."

"An unexpected early night," she smiled.

"I know, I'm so generous making you work nine hours on Sunday, rather than the usual twelve."

She laughed, and it was a pleasant sound in the silence of the house. He wondered what it would be like to hear Pip laugh like that in some place they could call home.

He quickly pulled himself out of *that* ruinous thought. She hadn't returned his text – it left him feeling heavy – and he'd had quite enough upheavals for one day without adding to the mix some vision of a rose-tinted future that was never going to happen.

"I love my job, Mr Darling. There are hard parts, but I also get to pop my feet up and put on the TV, make myself cups of tea, and bake, and sit in the garden. There's lots to be grateful for."

Claire was one of those people you never, ever noticed. Her husband was the same. Pretty, in a nondescript way, she was quiet, never troublesome, seemingly happy most of the time, and never minded her lack of recognition for anything. It had always been quite beautiful to spend any amount of time with her, because she was one hundred percent ego-free. Bloody refreshing in this day and age. His nan had been the same. He hoped the future brought Claire someone able to look after her if she ever needed it, in the same way she looked after all her patients. That was the only problem with people like Claire and his nan – no, the problem wasn't with them, it was with the world: if they got trodden on, they never said a bloody word, sometimes even accepting responsibility for it. People like his father and brother took advantage of people like that.

"Well, thank you again. Now, go and spend the rest of your evening with your husband."

"Yes, sir. I plan to."

"Good."

"Oh, Mr Darling, the MS has been a little better today. It's the dementia that's caused her most frustration. She's been hobbling about without too much bother. All the medication's been given except the bedtime one."

"Okay, that's good – thanks. I'll go see her now."

"I'll let myself out. Goodnight."

"Goodnight."

He left her to gather her things and made his way to the living room where he knew his grandmother would be. She'd been diagnosed with dementia a year ago now, brought on by the Multiple Sclerosis. Rare, they'd said – so rare, it hadn't even been diagnosed as dementia when symptoms had first occurred five years ago, but cognitive 'difficulties' brought on by the MS. Symptoms had been mild, and easy to bear – mood swings, moments of displacement, she'd forget things ... but hell, so did he. She'd taken a turn for the worse twelve months ago, and it hadn't happened slowly. She'd forget things for longer and longer stretches – whole parts of her life, whole years, and then, one day, she'd forgotten who her grandson was. Not only that, but she'd filled in the blanks with delusions she believed to be completely real. It had been a downhill slide that had had doctors unable to give him any information on *why* this was happening. It's 'rare' with the MS, they kept saying, and that was it. This was all research to them.

The only good symptom, if one could call it that, was that when her dementia was bad, her MS seemed to be bearable to the point where she was able to move around in her zimmer frame.

His sense, having lived with her for twelve years, and having seen her mental decline over the last twelve months, was that she didn't have long left of this world.

He missed her.

He missed the chats they'd had, and the stories she'd tell him. She still told him stories, although he could never be sure they were factually correct nowadays. And sometimes he was pretty sure they were, because she wasn't talking to *him*, but to her husband who had died almost fifteen years ago.

It had broken his heart at first. Now, he just took joy in the memories *she* found joyful, even if she didn't realise they were memories. Even if they turned out not to have ever happened.

He found her sitting on her chair, frowning in concentration at whatever was being said on the radio. Or maybe she was frowning at something else – he wasn't sure. "Hi, Nan."

She looked up, surprised, and completely ignored his greeting. Or hadn't heard it. "Andrew, they're talking about Syria." She gestured to the radio. "I don't quite understand what Syria has to do with Vietnam. I know they all say Britain aren't on the ground, but we know from your friend, Thomas, that they are. I don't understand why Harold Wilson isn't addressing people. There's this Cameron person talking about Syria, but no mention of Harold or Vietnam."

Aah. It was going to be one of *those* evenings. "Nan," he walked over to the sound box, "why don't we turn off the radio for a bit. It feels like I haven't spoken to you in weeks."

She gave him a rather reprimanding look. "We spoke this morning, Andrew, and you know I like keeping up to date with current affairs."

"I could tell you about my day at work instead."

"At the factory?"

He sighed under his breath. "Yes, at the factory."

She lit up a little, because she liked it when her husband discussed his work with her – as if she was being let in on a part of his life she was usually not privy to. "Yes, all right, that would be lovely. Shall I get us a cup of tea?" Sometimes, she also forgot it pained her to walk.

"Is that a cup of tea you've already got there?" He pointed to her china cup, and the brew in it that Claire had undoubtedly made.

She furrowed her brow. "I don't remember making that at all," she muttered. "Perhaps it was Barbara."

"You saw Barbara today?" Barbara, he had learned, had been her best friend from the 60s – she'd lost touch with her in the 70s. She often thought Claire was Barbara.

"Oh, yes. She came to visit. She brought biscuits, but we ate them all." She looked up at him apologetically, and somewhat sheepishly. He almost laughed, and silently thanked Claire for feeding his nan's sweet tooth – little things that made the days passable. She'd always loved her biscuits and cakes.

"I can't see anything wrong with that."

"It's because of the rations, you see. I was only eight at the time of the war, but I remember it well – the hunger. I was *always* hungry once the rations began, and when they ended ... goodness, I remember my first taste of bacon after that. And butter. Then, in my teens and twenties, everything was so different, and we had so much. Life bloomed. That's why I like the biscuits – it reminds me of the good times after."

"I'll tell you what. I'll go make us fresh, hot cups of tea, then we can talk."

"Thank you, my love."

Leaving the radio on, he went into the kitchen, and pulled two teabags out of the container. As the kettle boiled, he slipped his phone out from his back pocket.

Nothing from Pippa – not a peep.

He felt a sudden tendril of fear. What if something *had* happened to her? She'd been stricken watching Liam jump like that, and she hadn't exactly been with it straight after when she'd left for her car.

His more logical and, sadly, realistic self cut right in without pause. *You'd have heard about it if something had happened. Her mum knew she'd seen you today; she would have phoned you.*

Yes, Helen would have. He had no doubt about that at all.

Which means she doesn't want to talk to you. It's over. Your only saving grace is that it never really began.

He spent the next three minutes forcing his mind to go blank as he stared at the teabags floating on the water.

When he walked back into the living room, he stopped dead in his tracks with a cup in each hand. His grandmother was crying, dabbing at her tears with her handkerchief. She looked up on hearing him enter.

"Nan?" He walked quickly, trying not to spill hot tea.

"Jimmy..."

Fuck. He knelt on the floor where his nan was seated, and placed the cups on the carpet, far enough away so he wouldn't kick them over. He took her hand.

"Jimmy, I keep ... I keep forgetting."

"It's all right. Everything's fine." The last time she'd called him by his name had been almost a week ago now, and the periods in between were becoming longer.

"No, no, no. I think he's alive, and then it's as if ... I wake up, and I have no idea where I am, and then I remember he's gone."

"But *I'm* here. It's all right."

She shook her head. "I'm scared."

"We're looking after you – me and Claire – you don't have to be scared, I promise."

She took a shuddering breath in, then started to sob into her handkerchief.

"Nan..." He rose on his knees and pulled her into his arms, trying to soothe her. He wasn't sure he was succeeding, until the crying eased, and she pulled back from his chest. "I'm so glad you're not out there," she croaked, her voice tight from her emotional release.

"Out where?"

She looked at him. "In Vietnam, of course. I remember my mother, alone, as my dad fought for our country. I love our country, but I love you more, Andrew, I don't know how I'd bear your absence if you had decided to stay in the army."

So ... he *had* succeeded. In a way. He never knew which was worse – her remembering, or forgetting. But her distress, at least, had faded.

"Come now... I have your tea." He put her cup in her usual spot, on the side table by her chair.

"Thank you so much, darling."

"We were going to talk about my day at the factory."

"We were?"

"We were."

"Oh," she smiled a small smile, "how was it?"

He stared at the clock on the wall, and weaved a tale in his head, for the millionth time wondering if the lie was worth her happiness and peace of mind, and for the millionth time deciding that it was. "We had our yearly health and safety inspection today," he began, not knowing where it would end.

XVI
The Tree

*A*re you expecting this to end well?

Pippa looked up at the sky having felt a huge drop of rain on her shoulder. Great. She hadn't noticed the blackest of black clouds creep in, and she'd left her cardigan in the car. All she had on was the same short, white dress she'd worn earlier when meeting Jimmy for lunch. Where had her head been?

With the tree.

Which is exactly where she was standing now – thirty metres away from it, anyway. It *was* still standing. And if she didn't want to be driving home in what looked like was going to be a torrential downpour, she had to hurry.

An angry, and far too near, clap of thunder filled the sky.

You're crazy, Pippa. Why exactly are you here? What are you expecting to find?

She didn't know the answers, but now that she remembered the dream in more detail, she couldn't get it out of her mind. Half of her couldn't believe the tree was still here – although she'd had to walk through an unfamiliar housing estate to get to the small bit of woodland that remained.

She looked at her watch: 20:32. She'd gotten here a bit later than intended, but the evening traffic hadn't been great. And her mum was right – a sandwich hadn't been enough for dinner, but she was too nervous to be bothered about her slight hunger.

She had about an hour of sunlight left, but the rain was imminent, and those clouds had darkened the sky anyway – the sun might as well have already set.

It took such a ridiculous effort to move forward now she was here, staring at that tree without David by her side. This must be the first time she'd ever been here without David.

Another fat drop of rain forced her forward, her canvas shoes already feeling a little damp from the moisture in the air.

In some ways, the wooded area looked much the same, if a little neater and better looked after now.

Someone must have found the jar – there's no way it's still there.

The tree, she could see, still had the hole in its trunk. The hole was head height, and only now did she remember David had always been the one to reach inside it, being taller than her. *Damn.* She'd never been able to reach the jar without his help.

Now standing right in front of it, she looked around its base for some kind of foot hole that she could use to lever herself up. There wasn't one, but she did spy a small log a few feet away.

Another roll of thunder had her ducking as she ran for the log, it was that loud.

The log itself was small enough for her to pick up, albeit with a small huff. She carried it back over to the tree and dropped it in front of the trunk. Rain now fell persistently – just a drizzle right now, but she knew the worst was coming.

Taking care not to slip, she climbed onto the log and peered into the hole. It was far too dark to see all the way down, but if she remembered right, the jar – if it was there – sat about a foot further down.

Refusing to think about all the creepy crawlies that might nest in that hole, she grimaced, squeezed her eyes shut, and put her arm in, feeling for the glass container she wasn't even sure was there.

She almost screamed when something brushed across her wrist, but her nails hit what felt like the top of a steel lid. *That's it!*

Her eyes flew open and her hand flew out, clasping the large jam jar, and promptly dropping it when she saw about six *things* on it with far too many legs. And one on her fore-arm. With a squeal, she smacked it off herself, then rolled the jar around with her foot until the others came off. "Yuck."

She shivered. But it was partly from the cold now. A flash of lightning speared the black sky. The rain came down heavier – far too heavy for the trees to give her adequate cover. She was getting very wet.

But the jar called to her. The jar and...

She caught her breath.

The red envelope in it.

She couldn't believe what she was seeing. *How is it even possible?*

She hadn't put that in there, which meant David had, and he'd done it on his own. Their usual game had been to write their thoughts on slips of paper cut thin and long. Not envelopes.

A rain drop dripped into her eye and she blinked it out.

"What did you write?"

"You didn't want me to write it, but I had to."

No... He didn't.

He must have.

"Damn it, David." Their one rule with this game had been to write only positive things down – a 'happy' jar if you will – lots of good hopes and wishes for the future.

When she'd become pregnant with Liam, he'd come to her one day and suggested they write their 'final' hopes and wishes – what they'd like the other to read after their death.

She'd point-blank refused, finding it macabre – and why spoil the happy jar?

His reasoning had been the life growing inside her – their first true commitment to the world at large. He'd said the baby had made him feel unexpectedly mortal. *'None of us are around forever, and we can still write positive things. Wouldn't it be nice to have a 'final note' from one to the other? It would be like closure.'*

Nice...?

She stared at the red envelope through the glass of the jar, and had no idea whether she wanted to rip the damn thing open, or rip it apart. "But you're not dead. You're not dead."

She was still half thinking this was all a dream, and she was going to wake up any second now.

The next crack of thunder and lightning both played out at exactly the same time, but it was the lightning's deadly bolt hitting another tree a few metres to her left that had her leaping out of her skin and for the jar, before sprinting towards the exit of the woods. It led her back onto the housing estate she'd had to weave her way through.

At least she was away from the trees. *Silly girl, Pippa – that wasn't safe at all.* She should have known better, but finding the jar had evidently knocked all sense out of her.

A movement higher up to her left had her looking that way. Someone seemed to be staring at her from their window. The curtain twitched closed.

Bloody fantastic. She must look a mess; she was definitely waterlogged. She was also the only insane person wandering around in a thunderstorm.

And wearing a white dress.

Alarmed, she looked down to find *everything* showing through it, her white bra under the dress not quite enough to keep her modesty.

She cursed, and crossed her arms over her chest as best as the jar would allow, walking faster, head down, and wishing the jar wasn't quite so big and bulky. *It's fine – just get to your car.*

Her head was *so* far down, she didn't see the Ford Focus straight away, parked right behind her own car.

She froze, staring at it, less than a hundred yards away, then turned and ran into a gap between two houses, the first sense of terror over that car taking root. This was no longer coincidence – no way.

She hadn't seen the owner of the car, just the car, and she hoped to god wherever he was, he hadn't seen her just now. *Maybe he lives around here.*

She recalled the twitching curtain. That didn't make her feel better.

Shaking, she pressed herself against the wall of the house that stood between herself and the car, until she was sure she'd gained the least possible chance of being spotted, then reached into her small handbag – too stupidly small to fit a jam jar in – and clumsily pulled out her phone. She almost cried when she saw the one pip of the battery left. Not a chance her phone would survive a call to emergency services with the questions they asked, and she wouldn't be able to stay on the line. Texting would take too long. She had one chance to get this right.

After another quick scan of the area, she hung her hair over the phone in an attempt to shield it from the relentless rain. She went straight for her text messages and called the first name she saw, not because it was the first, but because she knew he'd be there in a heartbeat if she asked; because she was taking a chance he had an answering machine; because she knew he'd pull out all the stops to find her if it sounded like she was in trouble.

Jimmy .... please, please pick up.

~*~

His nan slept like the dead. That, at least, was a blessing, despite the fact it was most probably down to the MS drugs and sleeping pills.

He'd been told that most people with dementia or Alzheimer's found sleep was often interrupted; elderly people needed less sleep anyway. Not his nan – even before she'd fallen ill. She'd always been a very active person, and a very heavy sleeper. He'd always seen it as her necessary 'recharge' from everything she'd managed to fit into a day, and although she was no longer physically active in the same way, her mind certainly was.

The drugs might very well sedate her, but as long as she got the rest she needed – and the peace (especially the peace) – Jimmy wasn't too fussed on the reason. Tonight, he felt thankful for it as the thunder violently cracked outside and the rained poured down so heavily, he could barely make out anything from his window. He'd helped his nan with her night time wash routine, and had gotten her into bed not ten minutes ago. He hoped she was asleep already, 'cause he'd find it hard drifting off to that noise outside.

His mobile rang from downstairs.

"Fuck." He put the folded towel he was holding into the wardrobe and came out of his own bedroom, having just put the dried laundry away. Despite the phone being all the way downstairs, and the rain beating on the roof and windows, its ring sounded far too shrill.

And he suspected it was Cait. He had *no* intention of speaking to her – they'd finally reached a semblance of closure earlier and he wanted that to settle.

He poked his head as quietly as possible into his nan's room. She hadn't stirred at all – seemed out of it. *Good. Stay out of it until the morning.* She usually slept at least ten hours.

He looked at his watch. Nearly 9 p.m. *Definitely Cait. Or Emma.* Although Emma he hadn't heard from since she'd hung up on him a couple of days ago, other than a quick text to say she was back at home and looking for a job while she waited for her university degree. Traditionally, he only ever caught up with her during the school holidays. Now she was working, he suspected their non-relationship would sort of just fizzle out, and he had no problem with that – they'd always known that would be the case, and it felt something of a relief after the crazy day it had been.

Which means it's Cait. No one else ever phoned him at this time on a Sunday, damn it. When was she going to understand the meaning of 'it's over'?

Jimmy let the voicemail get it, and finally let out a breath when it stopped ringing, still staring at his nan to make sure she wasn't disturbed by the sound of it, or the cacophony of the small apocalypse happening outside. When he was happy she was out for the count, he shut her bedroom door.

Did he want to hear Cait's message now?

You don't want to leave it until tomorrow – start tomorrow on a clean slate. Get it over and done with now.

He felt sullen as he walked down the stairs towards his phone. At least he'd bought himself some time to think about how to respond to whatever he was going to hear.

How very wrong he was.

Pippa's number glared at him under the 'Missed Call' instruction above it. *Shit. Should have fucking answered it!* He phoned her right back, not even bothering to listen to the message, but her phone went straight to her answering machine.

Biting back another curse, he hung up, then phoned his voicemail box. *'You have one new message. Press 1 to hear the message, press 2 to change your answer-phone greeting, press 3 to—'*

He growled impatiently as he hit number 1.

Impatience quickly turned to a sense of absolute dread on hearing Pippa's rushed, breathy, panicked voice. "Jimmy, it's Pippa. I need you to come get me. I'm parked at the end of the road of that new housing estate – The Brambles. The road leads into the small wood. Someone's been following me in a blue Ford Focus. He's parked behind my car, and I'm really scared. I think he's been following me for a few days. I'm on my own. I don't kn—"

He stared at his phone, the silence more deafening than any other sound. Her line had gone dead, and his heart was about to do the fucking same.

He looked up towards his nan's bedroom, then out at the monstrous weather. *She's out in that. Alone. Or ... not alone.*

Her words finally sank in. His fear for her lit a spark of anger. *Some guy's* following *her?*

With a silent apology to his nan, and a prayer she wouldn't wake up, he pocketed his phone into the back seat of his jeans, grabbed his boots from under the coat rack, ramming his feet into them; didn't bother with a coat because he didn't want the weight of waterlogged clothing to worry about, and snatched his keys from the top of the rattan box.

As a last thought, he also grabbed his wallet from the jacket he'd worn earlier. He had no idea what he'd find – he might need quick cash.

'I think he's been following me for a few days.'

Anger overtook his earlier fear as he replayed her message in his mind. Why the fuck hadn't she *said* anything about being followed?

'I'm on my own.'

She wasn't on her own – all she had to do was wait ten minutes. *You're not on your own, Pip.* He locked the front door behind him, and raced to his car under the downpour.

You're not on your own.

XVII
The Car

Pippa tried not to read anything into the way her phone had died. *It's not ominous, it doesn't mean anything. All it means is that you were an airhead who forgot to charge it earlier.* And she'd blown it.

Maybe.

She'd barely been able to hear herself over the sound of the rain on the cement, and she had no idea whether Jimmy would understand her message. She didn't even know *when* he'd get it. Tonight? Tomorrow?

She couldn't wait any longer. She was soaked through and she'd catch her death if she stayed out in the rain.

Fuck. She really wished she'd phrased her thoughts differently.

Slipping the phone back in her bag, she looked for a weapon. There were only her car keys, her phone and her wallet – that's all she had. *The* one *day I decide not to carry the big, heavy handbag... Jam jar it is, then.* She clutched the container tighter, the glass slippery under the rainwater, and pulled her bag back over her shoulder.

Cautiously, she peeked around the wall of the house towards her car. The Ford was still there behind it, but she couldn't tell whether anyone was at the wheel for the force of the rain. Damn it, she could barely see a few feet ahead.

Maybe you're blowing this all out of proportion.

In her mind's eye, she envisioned the man she'd seen at the petrol station – the car's owner, she assumed. Tall, thin, blond. *Just* as Liam had described the man who'd stopped to talk to him.

"Oh, no..." Why hadn't she put two and two together before?

Knock on a door. Tell them your car broke down and you have to call recovery, then wait for them to turn up so you don't have to go to your car alone.

And then what? Her phone was dead, and the number for breakdown recovery was on her phone. *All* her numbers were on her phone.

So call 999. Call the police.

Maybe she should, and had her entire dress not gone translucent, she probably would have, but she really didn't fancy showing her assets off to complete strangers. Not when her car was right there and she could just get in it, and drive home.

She wished she hadn't left her cardigan in the car.

She wished she'd worn *anything* else today.

Fuck it, Pippa, just get to your car.

Bettering her grip on the jam jar, and crossing her arms tightly over her chest, she stepped away from the house she was leaning against, half of her still thinking herself ridiculous for the way she was acting about this entire thing. The likelihood of that car owner being some kind of murderer, or rapist was very small.

But she couldn't think of a single damn reason why anyone would be following her around, much less speaking to her son. *That* made her angry. Angry enough to walk up to her car, because a part of her needed to keep him the hell away from Liam. *What if he's actually after Liam and not you?*

That thought left her cold. If that were the case, she *definitely* wanted to keep him here, and not anywhere near Liam, or any of her kids.

She scolded herself for her wild imagination, her car just fifteen feet away now, and no sign of the tall guy anywhere, although she still couldn't see that clearly through his windshield. It was also dark now, as well as raining. She could make out the number plate, though. It ended EKN.

Shit, shit, shit...

Nevertheless, with him nowhere in sight, her confidence grew, and she quickened her step, wanting to be within the safety of her locked four doors with wheels beneath her.

With her breath held, she looked over through his windshield once more when she was right in front of his car, ready to sprint if she saw him there.

No one.

Breath gushing out of her in relief, she sprinted anyway to the driver's side of her car, unzipping her bag and reaching in for the key, trying not to drop the glass jar as she did so.

"Mrs Fellows?"

She froze, her heart in her throat. His voice didn't come from his car to her left, but from her right. Was he standing in the rain?

She finally looked up to find him emerging from the hedge by the side of the road, a little further up from where she'd parked her car, the hood of his jacket over his head, but definitely the same man from the petrol station.

"Stay there!" she shouted over the rain.

He stopped, but he was still far too close for her liking.

She brought her arms back across her body, aware she might as well be naked.

He brought his hands out of his pockets and held them

up slightly. In a gesture to show her he had no weapons? That he meant her no harm? "I just want to talk. We can talk in your car if you'd like." He took another step forward.

"I said *stay* there."

He stopped again.

"Did you approach my son this morning?"

He didn't give any indication he was surprised that she knew that. "I did."

"Why?"

"I wanted to know how he was."

"I don't *know* you. My family is none of your business."

"Can we please speak in the car?"

"No."

"It would be easier out of the rain." And there he was fucking walking towards her again.

"I said, *no.*" She held the jar in front of her, her dress be damned. She was ready to swing the thing at his head if he got any closer.

He stopped walking again, and let out a sigh of frustration. Up close, she could see he looked worn and gaunt in his face, dark circles under his eyes. "I'm not going to hurt you. That's not why—"

"I know you've been following me. I've seen you, so you'll have to excuse me if I don't believe a word you say."

He studied her silently. "It's true."

"I've called the police," she bluffed. "Before I came back to my car. Do you think I'd have just walked out here without some kind of plan? They'll be here any minute."

"I don't want to be your enemy."

"Well my *friends* call me on the phone when they want to meet up with me, they don't follow me in their car and accost my son."

"I didn't accost him." He stepped forward.

She stepped back. "You so much as lay one finger on me, and you'll live to regret it."

"That's not..." He sighed again and dropped his head, shaking it, then looked up at her, the rain cascading between them both, his expression unreadable. "I'm the truck driver. I'm Paul Matheson. I'm the one who hit your husband that night."

She'd been prepared for anything. She hadn't been prepared for that.

This, she had no defence for. Everything in her seized; her world fell away as his words sank in. Not just his words, but that night itself – the one that liked to replay in her mind over and over again in never-ending torture, even though she hadn't been there.

But he had. *He'd* been there. She remembered his name – in police reports – but she'd never seen his face; had never met him because there'd been no court case, and no reason to. "No."

"I just want to talk."

"No." She shook her head. She was going to throw up. God, she was going to throw up. She doubled over, retched, bringing nothing up but a past she couldn't change.

"It's all right." He reached for her and this time, she screamed.

He jumped back. "Please, I just—"

"Why? *Why?*"

"Why talk?"

"Why any of it? Why?"

"It was an accident."

"Why are you here?" Damn it, her voice broke, and she couldn't stop it, tears of anger joining the rain already marking her face. "What do you want from me?"

"I—"

"You destroyed my family," she bit out, her anger finally finding a home; a target. "Do you have any idea what I've been through, what David's been through, what we've *all* been through the past eight months? And you're here, *following* me ... do you think that's okay?"

He shoulders hunched in defeat. "I'm sorry. I wanted to say I'm sorry. I destroyed my family too. My wife left me with our daughter two months after it happened."

"Why are you *telling* me this?"

"I haven't slept since that night – not properly. I just..."

She shook her head in disbelief. "You ... what? You want to put me through it all again? What do you *want* from me? Forgiveness?"

He looked at her, haunted, and his own voice broke. "All I can see is his face when I lie down at night. All I can see is his face before I hit him. And I'm sorry."

Jesus.

"I do." He wiped at his face – rain or tears, she couldn't tell. "I do want your forgiveness. Please forgive me."

Jesus. Christ.

Everything spun. She barely registered the sound of another car pulling up, its door opening... "Pippa!"

Jimmy.

Relief flooded her, but she couldn't move, even though she wanted to. Wanted to run as far as possible.

She was spun around, until the face she was looking at wasn't her husband's crippler's, but Jimmy's, his gaze both panicked and furious as it searched hers out, simultaneously glancing up in warning at the man now behind her.

She placed her hands on his chest, partly to keep him from lunging at him, but mostly just to feel him – solid. "Jimmy," she said, not able to speak any louder. "Get me out of here." The thunder sounded in the distance, faint now, but the rain still fell hard and fast.

"Mrs Fellows..." The driver's voice held a plea.

She couldn't. Couldn't look at him. Couldn't give him what he wanted.

She felt Jimmy tense under her palms, ready to attack. She shook her head and buried it in his chest. "He's the one who hit David in the car. Please just get me out of here."

She felt his shock at her words, then, after a pause, Jimmy's arm came up around her and he cradled her in to him as he turned and hurried them towards his car. "We'll come back for your car tomorrow," he said.

She nodded.

Jimmy opened the passenger door and she got in, robotically.

The driver – Paul – didn't call out. Didn't say anything else. Neither had he moved. She could see him in the side mirror. He stood there in the rain, watching her.

She was shaking. All over. Or was she shivering? She wasn't sure. She was freezing. At least she thought she was – it was hard to tell through the numbness.

The driver's door slammed shut after Jimmy got in, he started the engine, and they were off, the truck driver's reflection in the side mirror growing smaller and smaller, and so did everything else.

Sound faded into silence – a deafening void of nothing; then, slowly seeped in again – an echo through a tunnel.

"Pippa... Can you hear me?"

The jam jar rolled across the footwell with the car's movements, occasionally knocking into her left foot.

"Pippa."

She turned to look at Jimmy. He looked like he was waiting for her to do something.

When she didn't, he mumbled something, looking worried as hell, then turned left into a lane, and pulled to a stop. "I asked you to put your belt on."

She knew this lane. They were in the middle of the countryside between the housing estate she was at and the main town. They must have been driving for five minutes already. She'd zoned out.

Jimmy killed the engine, undid his own belt, then reached over and took her hands, rubbing them in his. "You're bloody freezing. Pippa, I need you to respond. Talk to me. I have no idea what happened there. I have no idea where to take you – the police station? The hospital?"

Why would he take her to the hospital? She hated hospitals.

She looked back out the window. It seemed like she was seeing everything through a TV screen.

"Damn it." He got out of the car, she heard the boot lid release, then slam shut, and he was back in the car with her, throwing a fleece blanket over her shoulders. It smelled of the beach. She stared at it. It was the same one he'd used earlier today for the picnic. Had that been just today?

"I can barely see the fucking road in this rain and in the dark, and I don't know if it's flooded up ahead – it was getting that way coming down to get you. The best thing to do would be to stay parked here 'til it eases, but I don't know if you're okay."

Am I okay?

"Pippa." Her head was turned, Jimmy's hand cupping her face. She found herself looking straight into his eyes, nothing but concern in them as he looked her up and down, his voice taking on a gruff note. "Did he hurt you?"

She'd been hurting for months.

"Fuck it, Pippa," his thumb traced her cheekbone, "did he *hurt* you?" He looked down her again, then back up at her eyes.

She remembered the state of her dress. Oh – *that* kind of hurt. She shook her head. "No," she whispered, her voice as diminished as she felt.

He let out a sigh and dropped his head in relief. When he lifted it back up he seemed a fraction calmer. "How do I make this better? How do I fix this?"

He'd come. She'd phoned, and he'd come.

It was a simple realisation, but one that eradicated the TV screen she'd been looking through, and brought the world back, full force. And Jimmy was in it.

"I don't know what you need, Pip. Tell me what to do."

She twisted herself around, rose onto her seat, left leg stretched out until she straddled Jimmy's lap, facing him, his look now one of surprise...

"Don't give me time to think." She crushed her lips to his.

~*~

It turned out that when you took a good dose of panic, a fair amount of anger and pending exhaustion, and mixed it with a kiss you've waited two decades for, from the only wo-man you've ever secretly (or not-so-secretly) loved, some kind of cataclysmic surge took place inside you.

Her tongue brushed across his lips.

Shocked, he automatically parted them.

Everything soft, yet firm delved inside – she tasted di-vine – and he was ruined. Ruined for all other women for all of eternity because this was *exactly* how he'd dreamed she'd feel. Twenty-plus years hadn't made a liar out of his subconscious, or wild imaginings.

Cataclysmic was correct. He was no longer the same,

undone in the space of two seconds.

And cataclysms brought destruction. He could handle his – he'd done it before. He couldn't handle hers. "Pippa…" He wasn't even sure he'd spoken aloud.

Her mouth was on his cheek, his ear, his neck, her hands everywhere her mouth was not.

"Pi—"

She swallowed her name from his lips with another kiss, just as fervoured, almost desperate.

He groaned. Too good. *Too good.* And also not really how he'd envisioned this finally happening in the moments he'd dared to. "Pippa, you're hurting."

"Make it stop."

"I—" Nope, that sentence also got devoured by her mouth, his groan this time much louder as she reached beneath her and cupped his erection through his jeans. God, he ached; everything also pinched a little because of his damp denim and underpants. The rain smacked the car's roof.

"You always make it stop."

He did?

Another protest lay on the tip of his tongue, and went no further, because she pulled herself back and looked him directly in the eye, this time with focus. She was one hundred percent there, and looked like a goddess in the dim light.

Not dim enough. Despite his doubting anyone would be able to spot them through the rain, he reached up and switched off the car's inside light, plunging them both into the murky shadows of almost-black.

She cast the fleece blanket aside, and her white dress seemed to beam in the darkness, and then she was pulling it down off her shoulders, not dropping her gaze from his at all.

She looked almost ghostly with her dark hair framing her beautiful face, far paler than usual. It piqued his worry for her. "Pip—"

"You asked me how to make it better." She reached behind her, undid her bra and pulled it off. "This is how."

He'd seen her half-topless earlier, but now she was fully displayed, and proudly so, dark nipples on ivory, and every word failed him. She was stunning.

She pressed herself in to him, kissed him again, then rose, her left breast brushing past his chin. "Jimmy, please."

It was her stark plea, clearly a plea, but spoken so surely, that lost him the fight. He couldn't deny her; had never denied her, but she'd never asked him for much before.

His hand found her breast, and she moaned as his thumb pressed her nipple, part of him still in a state of bewilderment... He darted out his tongue and flicked her nub, tasting her desire in the air, wondering how that desire would taste between her legs.

She gasped.

That did it. Her sweet noise coupled with that last thought set him alight, and he drew her breast into his mouth as he drew the rest of her onto his lap.

She didn't follow his lead, remaining on her knees, and he was suddenly scared he'd read her wrong until she grabbed his hand and pulled it down to where his mind had already ventured; guided him straight to her core, flattening his palm against the carnal heat behind the cotton of her underwear.

The cool, clammy wet of rain became the slick, warm wet of want.

The sound that left her lips at his touch was pure, feminine desire.

Arousal surged through him in a wave of raw hunger. Still teasing her breast, he drove his fingers past the seam of her knickers and found her soft centre, already opening for him as he eased his way inside.

Jesus...

She clutched his hair and keened, head thrown back, then rode on the reprieve he offered, no vulnerableness in her open need. Up, down, she turned him inside out with every movement, slight or bold.

Hands grasped at his belt and tugged ... released. "Jimmy..." His name, a hoarse demand that scratched the humid air.

His left hand joined hers, unbuttoning his jeans and struggling with the rain-sodden material; too heavy, too tight...

He removed his other hand from its perfect place.

She moaned in protest, then held her breath, and bit her lip in the most luscious way when he brought his fingers to his mouth and tasted her.

Mother of god! He almost came right then.

Everything became frenzied.

All hands tugged at his jeans and pants, determined and desperate. He lifted his backside off the seat and they were hauled down, inch by inch.

"Hurry... Jimmy... God..." Urgency dripped off every syllable she sounded, and then he was finally freed.

She half-moaned, half-whimpered, half clambered up his body to get into position, her lust alone about to set him off.

He threaded his fingers through her hair, brought her lips down to his where he locked her into the kiss he should have given her two minutes ago; the kiss he'd *always* wanted to give her – had given her many times in the realms of his fantasies.

She moaned when his tongue swept across hers; moaned louder when he pulled her forward, arm tight around her waist, 'til she was flush against his chest.

He gripped the base of his cock, holding it steady as she aligned herself above him. Its crown swept across her entrance, and he let out a sigh at how phenomenal that felt; at how she was so wonderfully wet, he went and slipped in half an inch without even meaning to. He took in a sharp breath.

They both ceased all movement, and stared. At each other. At the re-writing of their friendship in this crucial, present moment.

She slid down amid both their groans; a tear slipped through her lashes.

He wondered if he should wipe it, but she got to his first, running her thumb across his cheek to catch the bead he hadn't known he'd shed.

This was it.

By god, this was it.

The plea was on the tip of his tongue... *Don't leave me broken; don't let this be the one and only time...*

His whispered words said something else. "I'm here. Take what you need, baby."

Another tear, a small smile, an almost-sob, and she *moved* right along with the earth (or perhaps it was the car), driving herself down, down, up and down again, one hand gripping his neck, the other on the ceiling to keep her head from getting bashed, her momentum building fast.

He met her thrust for thrust, furious and fast, nipping at her breasts to distract himself from coming far too soon. But the taste of her, the scent of her – an exotic, sweet honey – he was lost in her drug; hadn't prepared for this;

hadn't readied himself for this. She was wild, and he was deep. *Fuck*, was he deep in her.

Close. *Too close.*

She was closer.

Her near-savage cry of release claimed their surroundings a second before his own.

He pressed her down against wave after wave, and held her as she rocked, every grunt of his muffled by the curve of her neck as his climax chased hers.

Just as frenzy had held them captive, slowness now seeped into every swell and sway.

A lighter rain fell.

Hands in hair and short of breath, they moved into stillness, and neither let the other go.

XVIII
Not Alone

Visiting hours were over, but Candy and Tim had hung around for as long as possible, dragging out the minutes, because two hours wasn't enough time to spend with anyone if you weren't sure you'd ever see them again.

Lauren scoffed at their fuss as she always did. "I'm fine. You know they'll send me home tomorrow – got to cut costs; save the beds for those who count."

"You count," bit out Candy, a little more irate than she wanted to feel, but she and Tim had not had the chance for that talk yet, and she didn't know where to start. She caught him glancing at her every now and then, but Lauren was the priority right now.

All opportunities to avoid the situation had pretty much run out, though. The nurse came into the ward. "Time's up, now. Let Lauren rest."

Lauren made some kind of disgruntled noise. "The amount I rest you'd think I was already in my grave."

The nurse ignored her, obviously quite used to Lauren's sharp tongue.

Candy smiled despite herself. "Okay, hun – we'll see you tomorrow. Tim's just outside on the phone. I'll get him to pop in and say goodbye." She leaned in and gave her a kiss.

"Candy, wait." Lauren lowered her voice. "What's going on with you and Tim?"

"What do you mean?" She looked over at the nurse, not sure if she wanted to discuss any of it in front of her.

"Don't play me for a fool – you know exactly what I mean."

She sighed. Fine. "Nothing's wrong, Lauren, it's just a bumpy patch."

Lauren took her arm and dragged her nearer so she could lower her voice. "Candy, listen. Tim's skill at avoidance is second-to-none, and what he needs is your directness which he won't be able to wriggle his way out of. He's always been that way, right from when we first met – he's a bury-your-head-in-the-sand type, and too often he realises he should have dealt with things earlier. His parents always argued, and he was an only child. I'm pretty sure that's where it comes from. He shut it all out because he could; because he had no siblings to look after, or to look after him, so shutting it out wasn't a problem. It's his learned coping mechanism, not suitable for every situation." She held her hand. "What I'm saying is, don't give up on him. And don't be afraid to push him, Candy. He needs it. Maybe one day, he won't, but right now, he does."

The nurse practically barged into them. "All right then, visiting hours are over," she said with finality. "We'll see you tomorrow, Candy."

Tim walked into the ward, and made his way over.

"You're being kicked out," Lauren told him.

He looked suddenly unsure, flitting his gaze from Lauren, to Candy, then back again.

Lauren looked bemused. "You're being kicked out by the nurse."

"Oh." His relief was evident.

Candy's anger towards him faded a little. Lauren was right, and she didn't *want* her and Tim to be this way. She took his hand, and squeezed it in a truce. He looked so grateful she almost teared up. "I'll leave you to say goodbye, and wait for you at the entrance downstairs." She needed fresh air.

"Thank you," he replied, the two words holding a world of meaning.

She left them to it, and walked out of the ward. She decided to take the stairs rather than the elevator, not wanting to stand still because the movement helped to keep the mostly horrible, hurtful day she'd had at bay. She still felt kind of shaky about the incident at The Boat Shop. She hadn't said a word to Lauren about it, or Tim, and now, looking back, it all seemed so bizarre she was starting to wonder whether she'd blown the whole thing out of proportion. The shop assistant was probably right – the woman was just unhinged and needed to make a show of things for attention, or some other obscure reason. You got strange people in every town and village, even sleepy ones like hers.

She reached the bottom of the stairwell, and took the double doors that led to the front of the hospital.

"Hello?"

Stopping in her tracks at the voice that called out – to her? – she turned to see the 'ice machine' woman from this morning. "Oh, hi. How are you doing?"

"Holding up – still here, although we're getting kicked out now."

"Same. You've been here all day?"

"Yep. Brought my work with me though, to keep me busy."

"Ouch. On a Sunday?"

"Better than waiting and twiddling my thumbs."

"I suppose it is." She spotted Tim walking through the same double doors she had. *That was quick.* Maybe Lauren hadn't spoken to him so much, then. "I've got to go, my ... friend's here."

She'd almost said boyfriend. She'd caught herself just in time, remembering she'd already mentioned having a girl-friend.

"No problem. It was nice to see you. Have a good night." She offered her a bright smile, and made her way to the ladies' room by the entrance's revolving doors.

She felt a twinge of sadness at not being able to stop and chat.

"Who was that?" Tim asked, seemingly in higher spirits than he had recently been.

"I don't know her name. I met her this morning at the ice machine. Her son's ill. He's only fourteen."

"What a shame. I can't even imagine going through any of this with a child."

They fell into silence, both fidgeting a little on their feet.

She made the first move and took Tim's hand, lacing her fingers through his. "Let's go for a walk outside before we get in our cars."

He smiled at her, apologetically – presumably at what he had yet to say. "Okay."

The woman came out of the toilets just as they stepped into the revolving doors. Candy saw her stare at their inter-locked hands, but she quickly caught herself and threw Candy another friendly smile, accompanied by a wave of goodbye.

Candy smiled back, although her hands were otherwise occupied with holding Tim's and pushing the door.

She had no idea where they were going to walk. It had been raining a downpour while they'd been visiting Lauren, and although it had stopped now, the sun had also just set.

It was dark.

Tim read her mind. "If we go through the car park up that end, there's a small path that leads into town. Probably not much open other than bars, but if you wanted to walk..."

She squeezed his hand, warmed at the thought that they were finally on the same wavelength, even if it was over something so banal as which direction to head in.

"I'm an idiot," he finally said when they were halfway across the car park. "And I really need to explain to you what I meant when I said that awful thing I said."

It doesn't feel right to be loving you while she's dying. Her heart panged at the memory, but she said nothing and let him continue.

He stopped, and pulled her around so she faced him. "It *is* right to love you, and I *do* love you. My more recent behaviour has been appalling, but I hope I've never in the past given you any reason to think I don't love you just as much as Lauren, because I do, and that's ... that's what I've been scared of the last few months. I've ... I don't even know if I'm explaining this right. I've never been in a monogamous relationship before. Never. When Lauren and I started out, we were young – in our first year of uni – and she was already ... well, she was more experienced than me, let's say." He smiled. "You know how she is – fun, outgoing and outspoken – she's always known her own mind and desires. I had always been more reserved, but we had an attraction, and, at the time, she was straight-off-the-bat very clear that she wanted to keep an open relationship with me, and I went along with it. I didn't mind, but I also had nothing to compare it to. I just knew that watching her be a free spirit – watching her love others – was this huge release for me because all I'd really ever known was arguments and disagreements between my own parents.

"In time, we fell in love, and an open relationship became a polyamorous one, our commitment and loyalty to each other being paramount and a priority, and I could honestly say that I'd never been happier. Of course there were difficulties, but it worked. We did meet others, were involved with others, and were happy to be because it taught us new things about ourselves and brought something new into our own relationship each time, but Lauren and I were still ... the 'main' couple, as it were. There was a sense of her and me against the world. Until you came along."

She went to cross her arms, suddenly feeling a little too raw, but he didn't let her hand go, and tugged her a little more towards him.

"Candy, you changed everything. Lauren loved you, and I loved you, and when I fell for you, it was quick – hook, line and sinker. Lauren teased me about it – said she'd never seen me react like that with anyone before, and she was right, I hadn't. And now, I'm terrified. And I realise that's no excuse for what I said to you earlier, or the way I've been with you, but I'm *terrified* of going from three to two, and of you being the centre of my world. Because you will be – because I love you. We've already ended up arguing."

"Because you pushed me away."

"I know. I see that now. I saw it then, but I refused to pay attention. I'm scared of being monogamous with you, because that *is* what we'll be."

"We will?" Her head was sort of spinning. Sure, she'd thought about this to an extent, but it seemed that Tim had been thinking about it *far* more than she had.

"We will, because..." He hesitated. "Because since the spring, I've been thinking about how it would feel to be in an open relationship with you, the way Lauren and I were at the beginning."

"You have?" Shit. That kinda hurt.

"Yes. I've looked at other women. I've flirted with other women."

"Oh, my god." She stepped back.

"Wait. I need to be honest, please. I don't want to push you away anymore."

She stopped, but she was holding back tears, her arms going right across her chest like she'd tried to do earlier. *To stop your heart from falling out.*

"I haven't been with anyone else, I swear – there's only you and Lauren. I thought about it, I did. But I didn't do it. I couldn't; more importantly, I didn't *want* to. And I should have told you. I should have told you what was going through my mind and what I was feeling. What I was looking for in those thoughts was escapism from the fact that I love you *so much* I'm terrified of what happens if it doesn't work out. I don't know *how* to be in a monogamous relationship, Candy, I've never done it – my parents are my only role model. But I damn well know I don't want an open relationship while with you, and I'm realistic enough to know we're not just going to find the perfect polyamorous arrangement after Lauren. We might *never* find that again."

She stood there, dazed. She and Tim had been thinking the same things all along, only in their own ways, but to have him voice everything out loud ... there was a sense of finality to it all. "Am I ... enough for you?"

He stepped towards her and pulled her right in to his chest.

She didn't resist the embrace.

"When I said that loving you feels wrong while Lauren's dying, what I meant was that loving you *as much* as I love Lauren makes me feel guilty and scared knowing she'll be gone soon. But I'm admitting it. I'm saying it now, and I want to get through this, because I *don't* want to be without you. The question is, whether I'm enough for you. And whether you can forgive me for the way I've been acting."

She held him a bit longer, trying to gather her thoughts, and finally, she pulled back. "I'm scared, too. I've been scared of what we'll be without her, how our dynamic will change as a couple instead of a trio. I'm scared it won't work out and we'll break up, and honestly, the thought of that right now," her voice cracked, "after everything we've been through, and after Lauren's gone … I just can't…"

"Hey." She was back in his arms, now crying into his hug. "I'm not letting you go easily, Candace."

"Good. I don't want you to. You've been so distant, I thought maybe you wouldn't care if I disappeared, too."

"Not care? Jesus, I'd fall apart. Please don't leave me."

"I'm not going to."

"Thank fuck." He held her tight and kissed the top of her head as she tried to sniff her tears away. "Please forgive me."

She nodded. "I do."

He noticeably relaxed against her, although his hug didn't ease. He nudged her head back and kissed her forehead, then her eyes, then her mouth. "Please stay home tonight – don't go back to yours. I need to be with you."

She smiled. "I'd like that." A weight lifted. Even if they didn't, or couldn't make love, just to lie next to him, *with* him … and this very talk they were having… It was her light at the end of the still long tunnel. "I don't want to go back to mine."

He returned her smile, and pressed his forehead to hers, his eyes shining and most likely as red as her own. "Then let's go home."

~*~

Jimmy pulled his car into his drive. Everything was quiet and all the lights that should be off, were. He assumed that meant his nan was still fast asleep in her bed.

He breathed out a sigh of relief, and turned to Pippa in the seat next to him. Her cheeks had a bit more colour to them after their little make-out session earlier – he was still kinda thrown by it – but she was still too pale for his liking. She was soaked through and through, much more than he, and occasionally, he thought he saw her shiver. She'd catch a chill if she hadn't already.

"We're here."

She blinked herself out of wherever she'd disappeared to, then looked at the house, then looked at Jimmy. "You live here?"

"Yes."

"I thought you lived at the shop."

"There's a room at the shop if I ever need or want to stay there, but this is my home."

"Oh. I never knew."

He smiled. "I never said." He switched off the engine. "Let's get you in the shower and all warmed up. I sometimes get stock delivered here – there must be some kind of clothing I can find for you, although it'll probably not be as nice as the last lot." He smiled again, and she almost returned it. It fell short, but she did meet him in the eye. He was somewhat consoled to see no sense of regret there at what had taken place earlier.

"Jimmy, I need to phone my mum. My battery went dead, and she must be worried, and I didn't say goodnight to the kids, and—"

"Pip." He took her hand in his.

She didn't pull away.

"I'll phone her. I'll explain everything. I'm more worried about you right now – I want you warmed up and dry."

He thought she was going to protest, but she squeezed his hand instead, and nodded. "Thank you." He hoped her acquiescence was brought about by her trust of him, and not because she felt too ill to fight him over it.

"Come on," he said, then they both got out of the car, Pippa clutching that jam jar to her and looking ... gorgeous and ruined all at the same time. Sod the shower – he just wanted to get her under his covers and hold her until she was fighting fierce again.

Nope, she needed that shower – mud and grit from the splashing rain and wet ground had stained her legs and dress.

He listened for his nan as he opened the front door, and was greeted with the sweet sound of silence. "Okay, bathroom's down here, first door on the left. I'm going to get us some clean towels and phone your mum." He noticed her staring at the décor. "Everything all right?"

"Do you ... live here alone?"

He chuckled. He so rarely had visitors, he'd forgotten this looked like a granny flat rather than some bachelor pad, not that he'd ever been into the whole bachelor pad thing. "My nan lives with me."

She looked at him, clearly surprised, but didn't say anything.

"It's okay, she's fast asleep and on meds – she'll be out for the count. Won't even hear us." He led her into the bathroom, then pulled a face at the hand rail and seat attached to its side, installed there specifically for his grandmother. *Romantic. So nice to look at.*

She didn't say anything about that either. "Feel free to get in and start; use anything you like. I'm going to call your mum, then..." He paused, unsure he should even ask, but he wasn't entirely convinced she wasn't going to collapse in the tub. "May I join you? I don't have to, but—"

"I'd like that," she said, and it was acceptance he saw on her countenance. Of him, or the fact she might need a bit of help right now, he wasn't sure, but he was glad for it either way.

She took her handbag off her shoulder, then placed both it, and the strange jam jar filled with paper down on the laundry basket. He left them there instead of fussing, or taking them anywhere more appropriate. He didn't want to invade her space, or to make her feel pressured about anything.

"I'll see you in a sec." He went to shut the door behind him.

"Jimmy."

He turned back, and momentarily drowned in her stare – such big, dark eyes. His stomach jumped at how beautiful she looked, even now in her state of ... whatever state this was.

She walked towards him, then tentatively pressed herself in to him in a hug, her arms going around him.

He wrapped her up in his embrace, feeling all sorts of wonderful, and confused and terrified all at the same time. He stroked her hair with his fingers, kissed it, then found himself kissing her lips when she turned her face upwards to meet his.

It was a short, tender caress, that said a thousand words, none of which he was sure he was reading correctly. He felt elated. His heart also felt bruised. He didn't know where this was going, but if it was nowhere, it would be pretty much the end of him. *Pack up, move town – your business will go under anyway now, you won't be able to afford your nan's care, and if there's no Pippa, there's nothing to stay for. Nothing to stay for when she realises what you can't offer her.*

He pushed the vile whisper away. What was done, was done. What would be, would be. He cupped her face in his hands. She needed him – he was here. "I'll just be a few minutes, that's all."

She smiled, and it reached her eyes this time. "Okay. Thanks."

He nodded, then left, shutting the door behind him, only realising his legs were trembling when he made his way upstairs to the airing cupboard for the towels. He walked past his nan's room, and pressed his ear to the door.

He could hear her light snoring. *Thank god.*

He went back downstairs, and heard the shower come on in the bathroom. Reaching for his mobile phone, he brought up Helen's number, unsure whether to call the landline, or her mobile phone. He looked at his watch – it was ten o'clock. The kids should be asleep, but it wasn't that late. He opted for the landline, not even sure if Pippa's mum was a mobile phone kind of person, and crossed his fingers that he wouldn't wake everyone up.

~*~

Hot water drummed on her head in such a nice way – so much nicer than the cold of the rain that had done the same earlier.

She didn't really want to be in here on her own; didn't want time to think. She felt suspended in some kind of bubble, part of her not quite believing what had happened earlier with the driver. He'd followed her; he'd spoken to her son. It felt like some kind of violation. She'd felt herself disappearing, fading away, withdrawing from the world because she had no idea how to cope with this new sense of destruction. She'd been doing so well with everything, and she hadn't known it – hadn't known how far she'd come with her kids, with David, with herself – until she'd been standing in front of the man who'd slid into him with his truck.

It had maimed her. What did she do? Where did she go? She'd dealt with so much, come so far; she couldn't go back, and she couldn't go forwards.

And then, she hadn't had to. Jimmy had turned up, and moved her to where she'd needed to go next – in his car, out of the rain, watching the truck driver fade away instead of her. And it had been so bloody wonderful to have someone else make the decision for the first time since the accident. So good to have someone else carry it all for a bit. Her parents had done so much, but it wasn't the same. They helped to carry her burden in a much more physical sense – her kids – and she was endlessly grateful, but *she* still made the choices, thought through the rights and wrongs, worried over every decision in case it was a bad one; menial things like whether Sammy's favourite cereal was too sugary for him *(but he needs it because it was the one his dad had always bought for him)* or whether Becca would miss the toys she never played with anymore if she gave them away *(she might feel abandoned without them – her dad had given her half of those)*. Stupid, stupid, stupid things, but things she'd ask David about without a second thought if he'd been here, and he'd have offered an answer, and by god, she'd taken it for granted – the everyday conversations – how *important* they were.

Tears fell fast, but it didn't matter right now. It didn't matter because this wasn't her shower, or her hot water, and this wasn't her bathroom, so she didn't have to worry, or make choices – these ones weren't hers to make, and it was like the world being lifted off her shoulders, even if it lasted only minutes; only hours...

Jimmy rapped on the door, lightly, before entering.

She didn't say anything – didn't move – not wanting to leave the comfort of the hot spray behind, but waited for him to shed his clothes and step into the bathtub with her.

When he did, he brought solace with him.

Like a child needing her blanket, she reached for him again, nestled in to his chest, his personal aroma combining their present and past for her, cocooning her in a comforting familiarity she trusted.

He held her there, stroking her skin and hair. "Have you washed yet?"

She shook her head.

He reached for the shampoo bottles behind her, then brought them around so she could see them, a smile in his voice. "We have granny scent, and man scent. Which would you prefer?"

She smiled, and kissed him at the curve of his neck. It earned her a small sound of appreciation, but it was enough to warm her up inside. She was now warm through and through. "You choose."

"Let's go for my shampoo. I can't have you smelling like my nan."

She laughed, then sighed when he began to massage the

shampoo through her hair, right where she stood, curved in to his frame.

"I spoke to your mum, and explained everything. She was worried she hadn't heard from you, but she's fine now, and the kids are happy and asleep. Becca missed saying goodnight to you, but accepted she'd see you tomorrow."

"I missed it, too."

"I told your mum about the driver."

She held her breath; felt herself tense against him.

He massaged the top of her neck. "You said he's been following you, so I thought it was important she knew. And then, she told me someone stopped to talk to Liam earlier."

"It was him. He admitted it."

Jimmy's tone hardened. "Let's sleep on it, but in the morning, we should consider going to the police."

"He hasn't done anything illegal."

"He *followed* you. If he wanted to talk to you, he could have written to you, or phoned, or anything else. Maybe it *is* all innocent on his part – misguided, but innocent – but if someone's gone to the trouble of following you, and approaching Liam, I don't think we can take chances he's not messed up."

"He apologised for everything. He asked me to forgive him. Maybe he needs help."

"And going to the police might be the first step towards getting him help – *before* he does anything he regrets because he's not thinking straight."

He was right. "Okay."

He leaned her partway into the spray and began to wash the shampoo off. "Morning's hours away. We don't have to worry about it now. I told your mum to be vigilant of this guy, and I put her mind at rest about you. I told her you were staying with me, and that I'd look after you."

She looked up and met his eyes, then smiled. "Bet she was happy about that."

He returned her smile. "She just sounded relieved."

"She loves you, you know."

"Your mum?"

She nodded.

"I happen to think she's pretty awesome, too." He turned the bar of soap in his hands. "Almost as awesome as her daughter." He soaped her across her shoulders, then dropped a kiss on her cheek. "Is this all right?" he asked, his hands sliding lower.

She returned his kiss on his lips. "It's more than all right."

His blue eyes lit up, but she thought she saw a hint of sadness there, although she wasn't sure why. This *was* what he wanted, wasn't it?

She gasped when his hands slid across her breasts, and closed her eyes, simply relishing in sensation – the joy of mutual touch; allowing it to be; allowing herself the freedom to have it.

A kiss fell onto each breast, and then he knelt and continued with his task, somehow making washing her down seem like a sacred ritual.

She placed her hands on his shoulders and floated away, a semblance of peace humming throughout her being as kisses followed strokes all the way down her length, from top to toe.

When he came back up, he wasn't the *only* thing standing. His cock strained in front of her, hard and inviting. It made her mouth water, and she wondered if she dared to go down on him. She wanted to taste him, but it seemed so personal, which was a little ridiculous considering she'd practically jumped him earlier – took him deep inside her, all the way to orgasm.

He was soaping himself down now, across his armpits and chest, making quick work of it, as he stared at her, eyes glazed with ... more than lust. With care, and want.

Her hands slid down to his hips, before the rest of her slid down to take him into her mouth.

He didn't seem to expect that.

He jumped slightly, as if surprised, then mumbled something she didn't quite catch, and didn't need to. She was consumed by the way he tasted – of hot and heady masculinity.

"Pippa..." His voice was laboured. "You don't have to..."

"I want to." She took all of him into her, sucked hard on his length as she pulled back and released his shaft, then enveloped him again, not wanting to give up the enticing flavour of his desire.

He groaned, and she *delighted* in his momentary lapse, thrusting himself into her mouth, once, twice...

She protested when she found herself being pulled up.

He drove his thumb into her mouth until she opened it for him, then he plunged his tongue into it, meeting hers in a fever-pitched mesh of devotion, drinking his taste on hers.

She felt him lean in to her – over her – and the shower was turned off. "In my bed," was all he managed to sound out, the command (which was probably not supposed to be a command) sending a wave of yearning through her, so strong, she almost stumbled getting out of the tub.

A towel was thrown over her, and he rubbed her hair, patted her down, but it was all now rushed, desire becoming the prominent fuel for their actions.

He led her outside and up the stairs, last door on the right, then closed and locked the door behind him. Only a low, bedside lamp was on, darkening the room, and his eyes looked such a deep blue in the shadows, they were almost ethereal. "Sit down."

She didn't need further instruction. She dropped her towel, and sat on the edge of the bed.

His towel went on the floor, on top of hers, his gaze taking all of her in, in a way he hadn't before – hungry and with intent.

An unexpected self-consciousness swept over her. He'd seen almost none of her in the car, and the water from the shower had felt like a shield over her nudity. Nothing protected her now, and her arms came up across her torso, despite her liking his attention.

"What's the matter?" he frowned. Dropping to his knees in front of her, he slid his palms up her thighs.

"Nothing. I just..." She fought to find words. "I don't look like I did when we were young, you know? I've had three kids." She laughed nervously, and also because she felt a bit stupid feeling so *naked* when they'd already shared so much.

He looked up at her, surprised. "You're worried about that?"

"Nooo," she dismissed, with another small laugh, trying to make light of it. "I just ... you know..." She could feel herself starting to go red.

He leaned forward and kissed her, and she gasped into his mouth when he brushed his thumb against her clit. He pulled back and met her eyes. "You're a mother to three children, and you're the most beautiful woman I've ever seen."

It was hard to find some kind of jokey, sassy come-back when he'd said that so earnestly; so honestly. Her breath caught in her throat and it didn't move when he gently pressed again, between her legs.

"Lie back," he instructed.

She did.

He eased her thighs apart and pressed his lips to her sex, tongue darting out to taste her in a much less savage fashion than she'd treated him.

A whimper escaped her.

He groaned. "I wanted to do this in the car."

"Jimmy..." Her fingers threaded through his hair, then she felt his mouth on her again, more forceful than before, probing, pushing, nipping, licking. *"God..."*

He didn't offer any reprieve in his ministrations, so consistent and rhythmic, it was almost an attack.

Already aroused from his taste in her mouth, he brought her to the edge alarmingly fast. "Wait, wait ... I'm close ... Jimmy..."

His tongue delved inside her, lapped at her; he doubled his efforts, she fisted his hair; hands slid up, found her breasts, fingers clamping her nipples, and her climax was as furious as it had been earlier that night. He left her panting, breathless, and as good as immobile against the shift of the bed as he rose above her, tongue now seeking her mouth – urgent – as his cock nudged the juices he'd coaxed out of her.

One beautiful, fluid stroke, and he was in her to the hilt, her orgasm not yet ended.

"Jesus ... Pippa," he breathed in her ear, but held himself still. "I love the way I fit inside you."

She couldn't speak, her body trying to adjust to his size and his feel as it continued to move in the last throes of bliss.

He started to move with her – small, deep thrusts that sent tiny shockwaves skittering through her sensitised self.

With a sound of defeat, he buried his head in her neck,

his voice as strained as his form. "I can't ... fuck ... I'm gonna just come, okay?"

She made a noise that she hoped sounded like 'yes'.

He didn't hold back, his love-making as expressive as he was in any other way. His entire frame heaved, as he drove himself into her, over and over, harder and harder, until something gave way.

That's how it felt – giving way; giving in; surrendering underneath him – and she came once more, the unexpected orgasm unfurling from her very core, every inch of her delighting in the fullness he provided.

A final thrust, and he all but collapsed on top of her, his hips rocking the last moments of pleasure from them both.

Limbs entwined, they stayed like that; rolled onto their sides.

Held in his arms, sleep crept into the edges of her mind, and as she let every last thought drift into its shroud, she wasn't sure if it was David's, or Jimmy's voice she heard; which had found its way in...

"I love you, Pip."

XIX
Falling

*S*he looked, half in shock, at the ground beneath her feet. She thought she'd fallen; thought it had disappeared.

"Nearly there, Pip."

She lifted her head to see David standing on the other side of the canyon that separated them.

He nodded behind her.

She turned, and there were her kids, beyond the alley, bathed in sunshine and shrieking with laughter as they ran around the field.

"Just a little bit further."

The alley looked ominous – the kind you'd never walk down in a million years. Rubbish bags lay across the gritty ground. Something fluttered past her ankle – the spell.

The paper rolled with the wind down the dark, narrow path. She hesitated. "Is it safe?"

"I don't know. It's not my path to tread, but you made it this far."

"Why does it have to look so ... scary?"

"Because we're not eighteen anymore. We've lived. We've created things that last – things of joy, and things of burden."

She took a few unsteady steps forward, uncertain as she stared at the littered alleyway. An old, empty, coffee cup lay on its side. A bit further up, some documents were torn in *half* – David's care home bills. She stopped in her tracks, then turned back to him, surprised. "This is my litter?"

"Not just yours."

Another laugh travelled down the alley, and she turned to see Becca high up on Jimmy's shoulders. "Jimmy's here."

David heard her whisper. "You can share a path, or you can travel one alone."

She looked at the mess around her feet, then up again at the future it promised. But she found herself turning back with tears in her eyes. "What about you?"

He smiled, his own eyes shimmering. "I can't cross this gap."

"But—"

"Have you read the letter in the jar?"

"No, not yet."

"Why not?"

"I'm afraid."

He shook his head at her, but his smile didn't falter. "What am I going to do with you? You're so stubborn."

"David—"

"You don't need to worry about me, Pip. The only thing I need is for you to be happy. I'll wait right here, until my last breath, for you to be happy."

She was going to choke with grief. A sob caught in her throat. "But I love you; I miss you. If I go, I'll lose so much."

"If you stay, you'll lose more. You know I'm right. I know you know."

Swallowing back her tears, she took another step forward into the alley. She hated everything about it except where it led.

"That's it, honey."

"David..." she whispered, but she kept moving forwards.

"Remember, it's always darkest before the dawn. Good-

bye."

Goodbye? Shit, no. She couldn't do 'goodbye'. Panic stirred. Then, she jumped out of her skin when a horn beeped, the deafening siren not as terrifying as the truck that smashed through the alley, trapping her in its lights, the driver's face the one she'd seen just hours before...

She startled awake, a scream caught in her throat.

Sun streamed through the window, but the bed was empty beside her, and that was almost enough to push her scream out.

The door opened, and Jimmy walked in, a bright smile on his face on seeing her awake. It quickly faded, no doubt because of the expression on her face.

"What is it?" He rushed to her side. "Pip..."

She fought to gather herself. "A dream – bad dream." She hoped Sammy hadn't awoken screaming this morning, with her unable to comfort him.

"Damn it, I wanted to be here when you woke up, but I need to sort stuff out for my nan before *she* wakes up, which is usually 7:30 on the dot." He brought her forwards into his arms.

She resisted for all of two seconds, and then sank in to his embrace, the night's comforts taking precedence in her mind. She hugged him to her, tight.

"It's all okay," he murmured. "And it's going to be a scorching day by the looks of it – not a cloud in sight." He kissed her cheek.

Her eyes fell to something he'd dropped on the floor by his feet when he'd sat down: her bag and the jam jar, and something that looked like a dress.

"I make breakfast for my nan; I can make yours too.

What would you like?"

She met his eyes, finally coming into the present. "I get to meet your nan?"

He laughed. "I guess so. I need to warn you, though, her mind's not what it was. She thinks I'm her husband, and lord knows who you'll be."

She smiled.

"She's nice, though. And harmless. I'd love you to meet her. Oh – I found this." He held up the dress. "It's about three years old, but it's never been worn because it's uneven along the hem. I got a credit for it, so it's sort of just spoiled stock. It might be a size too big, but it'll probably do you until you get home. Your white dress is in the washing machine, and your shoes are stuffed with kitchen roll to dry quicker, but they'll probably still be a little damp."

"Thanks. You're always showering me, and dressing me."

"You say this like it's not my dream come true."

This time, she laughed, a blush creeping up her neck.

He hesitated when he leant in for a kiss, but she reached for him, pressing her lips to his.

He sighed, then deepened the kiss, and she'd be lying if she said she wanted it to end any time soon. Unfortunately, she didn't have much of a choice in the matter.

"Andrew!"

"Ah..." He pulled back. "That's my cue."

"Andrew?"

"I did warn you."

She laughed. "I really would like to meet her."

"Come down when you're ready. Breakfast will be laid out in fifteen minutes or so. I wish I could spend the day with you, but I need to be at the shop all day. I can drive you back to your car though, but we need to leave by eight-thirty."

"You leave you nan here alone all day?"

"No. She's got a daily carer." He tensed a little as he said that, and she wondered why.

He kissed her again, all tension gone. "I'll see you downstairs."

"Okay."

She let him go – heard him wander down the hallway, then have a general conversation with his nan which she couldn't make out for the most part. She wondered how he could afford a carer with his job. Christ, when she'd researched it all for David, she'd almost keeled over at the cost. The only reason she could afford to keep him in a home was because his parents paid for half of it, and because his life insurance policy had paid out for the accident and how it had left him. If she didn't have her job as well (which she wouldn't have been able to keep with him at home) she'd be struggling to stay above water.

Putting him into care had been a heart-wrenching decision – one she had lost sleep over for weeks after she'd made it. She still felt guilty about it occasionally, but this way she could spend more time with her kids, afford things like food and shoes, and he was able to be looked after professionally.

She reached for the dress. Her underwear was folded into it. She put it all on. The dress wasn't noticeably large, even though it was a bit big – it would do.

She stretched as she stood, relishing in how her body felt after the TLC it had received last night.

A sound went off somewhere near her. Her eyes landed on her handbag, and when she picked it up, she saw Jimmy's phone underneath it. He'd obviously forgotten about it. *I'll take it downstairs.*

MESSAGE FROM CAIT
You were right about everything. I'm sorry. I just wanted you to know that. Goodbye, Jimmy. x

She pulled a face, feeling bad for having seen the message, but it was right there at the front of the screen without her even having to touch anything. *And who's Cait?*

None of your business, that's who.

She tempered her twinge of unfounded jealousy, and dropped the phone on the bed next to her handbag so she'd remember to take it down.

Running a hand through her hair for her lack of comb, her eyes landed on the jam jar once more, and on the red envelope in it.

No time like the present, right?

Her heart thudded at what David might have written, but with the sun streaming in through the window, and the warmth of Jimmy's affection, nothing seemed that bad.

She glanced at the clock on the dresser. She had ten minutes, and she could still hear Jimmy in the room across the landing, talking to his nan.

Pippa reached for the jar before she changed her mind. Opening it, however, proved to be something of a challenge: the lid was sealed shut, with time and tree gunge.

She strained with the lid to no avail, then looked around for a towel. There were two hanging at the back of the door – the two they'd used last night.

She got one, brought it over to the bed where she knelt so she could put as much weight as possible behind her task. Wrapping the towel around the lid, she gripped it tight, and then turned it as hard as she could, the towel lessening the rub of the steel against her palm. She thought it gave way a little, so she took a breath in and gave it another go, and ...

POP.

Success!

Part success, anyway. The lid came off, but the force she'd had to use had her dropping the jar, and half of the bits of paper tumbled out around the envelope which was still lodged in there, scattering all over the floor.

She cursed, then got on her hands and knees to pick them all up and shove them back in the jar.

> *Sleep in a tipi under the stars.*
> *Take our future kids to Disney World.*
> *Get a kitten.*
> *Climb Kilimanjaro*

So many things they'd never done. She blinked back tears, the memories so fresh, and the *smell* of the jar. Shit. She hadn't been expecting the nostalgia.

A couple of bits of paper had fallen under the bed.

She reached her arm under to pull them out, bringing a stack of papers sliding out with them. She put her and David's little slips back in the jar, then went to tidy the mess she'd made.

Medical documents about Jimmy's nan – MS, dementia... She tried not to look – this wasn't for her eyes – and she certainly didn't rummage, but certain words jumped out at her. It was like looking at a painting – she couldn't 'unsee' them once she'd seen them.

Jimmy's own medical letter. About his infertility.

She closed her eyes, purposely looked away, and stacked all the papers together, shoving them back under the bed to where she thought they'd been. It was hard to do effectively with her eyes closed though, and a few sheets, stapled together, fell back out.

AGREEMENT
between JAMES DARLING and CAIT BECKLES

**made on the twenty–second (22nd) day of the month
of August in the year Two Thousand and Four (2004)**

**and to be terminated at the request of either party
giving a verbal or written notice of three months.**

Cait?

She looked at the phone on the bed. *The same Cait?* The spelling of the name was certainly unusual. She re-read the date of the 'agreement'. *But this was twelve years ago.*

However, it was the monetary figure that caught her attention, a few paragraphs lower. A *large* figure. And then the word 'services'.

Confusion taking over her guilt at snooping, she turned the page.

And *there* was the description of the 'services'.

~*~

Jimmy was trying very hard – too hard – to *not* see the whole happy family scenario as he laid out the breakfast, his nan already sitting in her seat, not quite realising it was Monday and he'd be going to work soon, but she usually got the idea as soon as Claire (or Barbara) turned up.

Pippa hadn't actually said what she wanted to eat, so he was going the whole hog with cereals, bacon, eggs, and toast, while keeping an eye on the time and trying not to burn himself.

"Goodness," voiced his nan as the plate of bacon went down. "Can we afford all of that?"

"No rations anymore, Nan."

"Oh, yes, of course," she smiled. Calling her 'Nan' never seemed to clue her in on to the fact he was her grandson and not her husband. Her remembering the present was a sporadic thing, and he'd learned to go along with it for everyone's peace of mind. He just hoped Pip would be on board – he suspected she'd find it amusing to some degree, despite the circumstances of her illness. It had been a while since he'd witnessed her sense of humour, but she definitely had one, buried somewhere under the past year.

Her footsteps sounded on the stairs as eggs went straight onto toast. "Hi," he called out on seeing her, then his heart kind of stopped because something was wrong. Definitely wrong, although he had no idea what, but her face had that pinched look that said she wasn't happy and just about holding it together. "What—"

"You left your phone upstairs." She placed it on the table. Her voice was as pinched as her face and ... shit. Her eyes were red. "I have to go."

"Wait."

"Andrew, is this the lady who sells the bacon?"

"Pippa."

"I have to go," she repeated, heading for her shoes in the entrance hall, all her belongings in her hands.

What the fuck just happened?

"Andrew."

"Nan, hang on. Pip." He followed her out.

"It was a mistake, okay? You and I. I'm sorry, I am, but I can't ... it was a mistake."

His stomach dropped. Yeah – this hellish moment felt *exactly* as he always thought it would. Like all his failures crashing down on him in one go. "No, it wasn't."

Her shoes already on, she hugged her items to her chest,

eyes wet and threatening to brim over. "Please. Look, I didn't mean to read it, okay? And I'm sorry about that, but I opened this jar and everything fell out, and when I went to pick it all up, the papers fell out and..."

He shook his head. He had no bloody idea what she was talking about, but he was still trying to think of a way to fix it, because last night had *not* been a mistake – no way. The way they'd been, the way he'd felt ... he'd never had that with anyone before.

"I know about Cait."

He died. Just now. Died on the spot.

"About what she offered you. I read your agreement." Her voice caught. "I'm sorry." She turned and opened the front door.

"Wait." He shut the door again, his demand coming out far more harshly than he'd intended, but he had seconds to put this right or she'd walk away forever. "You *don't* know. It's over. It's ended."

"She sent you a text a few minutes ago."

Of course she fucking did – give me a fucking break! "Then I'll change my damn number – it's *over*."

"When?"

His heart was all he could hear. "What?"

"When was it over?"

He shut his eyes, defeated, because he was going to drag himself to the grave with his next word. "Yesterday. Before you phoned."

Her face crumpled, and he'd quite happily bury himself in that grave for putting that hurt there. "But it's been ending for months. I tried to end it last month,   but—"

"But you need to give three months' notice." She'd seethed that out. Her fire was back. "I *read* it."

Despite it all, he actually felt a measure of relief at her

seething. *This* was Pippa, and it stoked his own fire. He wasn't six foot under yet. "You read something twelve years old, in black and white, and filled in your own colour."

"I'm going now, Jimmy."

She opened the door, and they both stared at Claire's startled face on the other side. "Erm ... hi," she said, looking from Jimmy to Pippa.

Thank god.

"Andrew!"

He grabbed his keys from the top of the rattan box.

Pippa stormed right out.

"Claire, Nan's having breakfast. Could you—"

"I'm on it. Go do whatever you have to do."

"You're a saint." He was pretty sure she actually was.

He heard the door shut behind him as he raced after Pippa. "God damn it, are you going to walk all the way to your car?"

"Yes," she bit out.

"Proving my point that you're too stubborn to even listen to me."

"I don't want to hear what you and your *Sugar Mummy* got up to for twelve fucking years."

"Hey!" He grabbed her arm, and spun her around, feeling sorry for having to, but not willing to give her up – not now. "We've *both* got baggage; we've *both* got pasts that can come back to haunt us. I gave you *everything* I had yesterday in more ways than one – I'll carry anything you give me if it helps you, and I always have. If you want to walk away from that, then fine – walk away – but at least *know* what you're walking away from, Pippa, because until you give me the time of day, you know fuck all."

He appeared to have rendered her speechless. No small feat. He didn't like how it felt – like breaking her down or something, but by god, she was stubborn, and defensive, and last night she'd lowered all shields willingly.

She held her chin up in defiance, even though he saw a hint of regret in her eyes.

Something he'd said had hit home. He wished he knew what it was.

"Fine. Talk."

Talk. Why was it never easy once you were put on the spot?

"I was eighteen, and I was desperate. I've told you the beginning, just not about Cait's part in it. And I was going to, by the way. But last night wasn't exactly the right time, and this morning was all a rush..."

"My dad and brother were scheming to put Nan in a home. She had MS, they were going to claim her mentally incapable, which she wasn't at the time."

Pippa crossed her arms. "I remember you saying."

"Do you remember me telling you at the barbecue how I went to a sperm bank to donate, but couldn't?"

She nodded.

"Well, that's where I met Cait – she worked there. When I went back to the bank for the letter stating why they couldn't take my sperm, she's the one who spoke to me about it. She told me about my sperm count. I was upset, because I needed the money – anything I could make – to get my Nan the fuck out of that house before my dad did."

Pippa frowned, but he had her attention now.

"She asked me why I was so upset; why someone as young as me wanted to donate. I told her about the fuck-up that was my family. She offered me another solution."

"The agreement?"

"Pretty much. At the time ... shit, Pippa. I was *eighteen*. I wasn't thinking about consequences, I was thinking about whether I could live with myself if I went to university and came back to my grandmother in a home and her savings account empty, knowing I could have done something to stop it."

She shuffled on her feet. "I thought you didn't get into university."

"I got in – Sports Sciences. I got the grades."

"You didn't go because of your nan?"

"No one else was going to stop it. No one else was going to look after her, or treat her right. I couldn't think of a single way to help her either, until Cait made it possible: I see her once a month, I..." he chose his words carefully... "give her what she needs, or wants, and I get £5000 a month. And to sweeten the deal, she gave me an advance of—"

"£30,000."

He nodded. "You read it. Money upfront to find a solution for my nan, and six months 'free service' in return to work it off. Then, if I wanted to carry on with the agreement, I'd get paid on a month-by-month basis. The £30,000 was enough for a deposit on my house, and I got a full-time job at Wave Riders – remember that place before it shut down?"

"Yeah."

"I was there for five years, then I found The Boat Shop and bought it. Nan didn't need care at the time, just some help occasionally if her MS was bad, and some trips to the hospital, but it was easy. She was grateful – she knew what my dad was like. I started to pay for care about four years ago when the dementia first began to present itself. Any plans I may have had of ending things with Cait got royally screwed up then.

"Never mind. My nan was getting help. Sure, I missed out on uni, but I made a choice. But, like I said, I was eighteen when it all started. What I didn't factor back then, was that in six months, I'd have started down a path I needed to *keep* affording."

"She made you rely on her money. She completely took advantage of an *eighteen*-year-old."

"Maybe. And there are many times I've wanted to end it over the years, but also many times – when Nan got worse – that I was so grateful for the money. It became messy – complicated."

"What did Cait get out of it?"

"She's twenty years older than me. At the time, she was about to hit forty, and lonely. Her husband's this rich tycoon, always away once a week, and pretty much lets her do whatever she wants when he is. I've never met him – that's part of the agreement – but I'll eat my hat if he doesn't know what she's doing."

"Is it just you? Does she have other guys?"

"There are others. At different times. She saw me at the end of every month – that was our timetable. I've been tested for STDs, partly because of the fertility tests, but you'll have seen in the agreement that wearing a condom was a must – that was *my* stipulation – in case it's a worry you're having. I've never been with a woman without a condom on – not ever. Until last night, with you."

"Not ever?" she asked in disbelief. "Really?"

"Really. I understand your incredulity, but after what my mum did, I just..."

They both fell silent.

"Pippa, I was going to tell you all of this, I swear, but I didn't know yesterday was going to happen until it did, and my three months' notice with Cait wasn't supposed to reach an end for two more months. It's just that after spending the afternoon with you at the beach ... I couldn't be with her again. That's why I ended it yesterday. For good."

"She accepted it?"

"Not at first. But it's not like the agreement's legally binding – it can't be; it's not enforcible. It's just a bunch of terms in black and white to make order out of a situation that so often has none. That's all."

Her shoulders sagged. She looked tired. "What about Emma?"

"What about Emma?"

She met his eyes. "Is that over, too?"

"Yes. Emma was the fun, non-committed relief I've indulged in to counter the intense, not-fun commitment that was Cait. Well, it was fun at first, I suppose. After a few years, the novelty wore off. After ten years, it was only the call of duty that kept me going back."

"Duty?"

"To keep my nan safe. Despite her symptoms, she was only officially diagnosed with dementia a year ago, and I don't think she's got too long left. It's forced me to think about what I really want from my life, because I'm not going to be looking after her forever."

"What happens to her care now you've ended it with Cait?"

"I have enough savings to last six months, so ask me again then. I've got six months to try and make something of the shop, otherwise that goes, Nan's carer goes, the house goes... But hey, I don't have to have sex to keep afloat anymore, so things are looking up." He attempted a laugh. It fell flat, and he should really kick himself for that last comment.

Pippa looked pained. "Jimmy..." She shook her head.

"Sorry. I'm an idiot sometimes." He sighed. "Pippa, I meant every single thing I said and did last night. Last night was the best night of my life. You know it all now; I've laid it out. If you still want me, I am yours – completely yours – there's no one else. Everything to do with Cait and Emma – they were *before* you, and it's all over. I swear it. But I do have other fears – things I need to confess. I'm scared I won't be able to offer you anything, certainly no children. Almost every penny I have, I earned through Cait. The shop's not holding up well right now. And ... while I was always going to tell you about Cait, I've been terrified you'll see me as less of a person because it happened at all; because of the choices I've made. I never wanted to be like my family. I can't help it if you see me that way. But at least, if you walk away now, you know everything. You know what you're walking away from."

"Jimmy..." She wiped at her eyes, although he couldn't see any tears, just exhaustion, and he'd been the one to put it there. He hated himself for that.

"Can you please drive me to my car? I need time to think about everything, okay?"

It wasn't a total rejection; just mostly a rejection. His heart sank, but he'd done everything he could now. "Okay."

As they walked back to his car, he wanted nothing more than to hold her.

The realisation stung that he might never hold her again.

XX
Leap

"Goodbye, Jimmy," she'd said, unable to manage a smile.

No kiss; no hug.

That's how she'd left it as she'd gotten out of his car, and made her way to hers.

She'd crushed him. And the look on his face still got to her. The whole day had gotten to her. First stop had been back to her parents' where she'd been greeted by an ecstatic Becca, and an unusually calm and happy Sammy. Apparently, he'd had a *good* dream about his dad last night.

He and Liam were actually playing *nicely*.

Since she hadn't had any breakfast at Jimmy's, she'd made it there, with her mum throwing her concerned, questioning glances every bloody five minutes.

The driver had left her a note tucked under her windscreen wiper. Although it was half soaked through, she'd had no problem reading it:

If you change your mind...
07743 216742

It felt too close for comfort.

She hadn't been able to face the police – not so soon after everything – so she'd ushered everyone into her car, and they'd been off to see David. Her mum, unusually, had decided to come along, and here they sat, Becca and Sammy both in David's room with a nurse, Liam somewhere down the corridor reading the leaflets on the wall, and her mum and herself seated just outside his room in the waiting area.

She was glad she'd seen David yesterday, because with three half-sized Homo sapiens vying for his attention (however little of it there was), she didn't get a look in edgeways. It didn't matter. All the distraction took her mind off the mess that was last night and this morning. *Last night wasn't a mess – not all of it.*

The heat rose to her face as she remembered the rather spectacular love-making. *'Cause he's had a lot of practice.*

Fuck. She didn't want to think about it.

"So ... you're going to go to the police, yes?" her mum pressed.

She sighed. "I will. I don't know if it's the right thing to do. I don't even know if he's done anything illegal. But he spoke to Liam – that's the bottom line for me. And I don't feel like talking to him; not yet."

"Not *yet*? I'm not sure you should at all given the way he approached you."

"Maybe. But perhaps it's the best way to lay it all to rest."

"I don't know..." She looked anxious.

"Mum, don't worry. Please. I'm *not* going to phone him. I can't give him what he needs anyway. How can I forgive him when I can't even forgive myself?"

That was met with a strange silence, and then she realised what she'd confessed.

Oh, no. She inwardly groaned. She hadn't meant to say that out loud.

What does it matter now anyway – everything's shot to

bits.

"Pippa, what are you talking about?"

She looked at her mum sitting next to her. "It's my fault David's like this." Saying it for the first time, to anyone, after all this time was ... surreal. And heart pounding. Difficult. Yet, surprisingly easy. "He was going to skip his meeting that night. I pushed for him to go – he went because of me. I did this to him."

She looked away, but her mum said nothing, remaining silent. When she looked back, she was just staring at her. "I don't think I need to say anything Pip, because I *know* you know that's not true."

"I made the wrong choice."

"It was *just* a choice – that's all. We don't always know where they'll lead."

"I made the *wrong* choice," she repeated. "It didn't just lead to a scrape on the knee, or ... me puking into the toilet because my boyfriend's a dick. It all but killed my husband – *I* did." She was too tired to cry, but to hear the words aloud... The quiver was there in her voice. "Any choice I make now ... what if it's just as bad? What if it's worse? Liam could've been so badly hurt yesterday—"

"Because of a choice *he* made, not you. Pippa – enough. I understand the pain – I do. But if this is how you're going to live the rest of your life, you're going to live in the shadow of it. You can't run from the future things you want, because you made one choice in the past that led to a hard place."

"Hard?"

"*Really* hard. I know. Really bloody hard. It's only been eight months. A lot of adjustments have had to be made in a short space of time. Maybe you think you've been standing still, but you haven't, Pippa – you've overcome things some would fall at. But you've been doing it for everyone else – for David, for your children, even for his parents in the beginning when you insisted on caring for David at home. It's okay to do it for you, too. It's time to."

She shook her head. "I can't. I know I have choices; I can see my choices, but everywhere they lead... It's all so complicated. Someone could get hurt, and if it's ever Liam, Sammy or Becca, just because I was selfish..."

Her mum sighed.

They sat there in silence.

She heard Becca's laugh from David's room.

"Did you know that when your father and I met, I was with someone else?"

"What?" She didn't think she'd heard that right at first. "No. You were?"

"Yes. But it was your father I fell in love with, and the situation I was in... His name was Colin. I couldn't end it with Colin straight away. It was complicated. He wasn't completely well, and his family were quite involved with my life, but make no mistake, it was your father I wanted, and he ... oh, boy. You have his moral sense of duty, you know that?"

"Dad?"

"Oh, yes. He's always hated injustice of any kind, *and* he had a jealous streak, just like you, and to know he'd fallen head over heels for a woman involved with another man..." She laughed. "It presented quite the challenge for him. There I was ready to throw caution to the wind and see where I ended up, and he wasn't having any of it until I'd cut all ties with Colin – sensible perhaps, honourable for sure, but we almost lost each other because of it."

"You did?"

"We did. Sometimes, the honourable choice is the

'wrong' choice. I was about to get swept away to live in Switzerland. Like I said, Colin wasn't well, and that's where the best doctors could be found for his needs. I begged your father for more. More of himself, more intimacy; for a sign that if I left Colin in his hour of need, I wouldn't be walking into a relationship that didn't really exist. He wouldn't budge. He loved me, but he wouldn't even *make* love to me because I was with Colin. Colin's family was also very well off, and your father was not. He was convinced he'd never be enough for me."

"So, how *did* you end up together?"

"I was at my parents' house having said goodbye to them earlier – they had left for a party – I was dressed and packed for the airport, my car about to turn up, and there was a pounding on the door."

"It was Dad?"

"It was. He didn't say a word. He stepped into the hall and kissed me in a way he never had before, and right there, we made love for the first time." She smiled at Pippa. "And I stayed. He didn't know I would choose to stay, but he knew, at the last minute, he couldn't let me go."

They found themselves sitting in a shadow. It was one of the nurses. "Mrs Fellows, Becca and Samuel are almost done. Would Liam like to see him next?"

"I'll ask him, thanks."

The nurse walked away, and her mum patted her knee as she stood. "I'll go ask him; maybe I'll go in with him."

"Okay." She still felt thrown her mum had been with someone else before Dad, although she wasn't sure why. It was more likely that she would have been, than wouldn't have been, now that she thought about it.

"I still love the grumpy sod," she smiled. "No regrets. Oh, we've had our fair share of arguments for sure, but no one's infallible. You did nothing wrong that day, Pippa. You loved your husband, you did what you felt was best for him, and you kissed him goodbye. The rest was out of your hands. Would you rather have never known him? Would you rather have never had Liam, Sammy and Becca, so their feelings could have been spared after the crash?"

She swallowed back her tears, and blinked. "No."

"No – of course not. There are no wrong choices, Pippa. There are just the choices that feel right at the time."

No charges were pressed, because the driver hadn't technically done anything wrong. Following someone, in itself, was not a crime; talking to Liam was not a crime. But last night's incident was noted. The police told her they would contact Paul Matheson to have a word with him. Other than that, there was nothing else they could do. If he continued to follow or harass her in any way now she'd told him to stop, she could come back again, and they'd be able to take further action.

She felt better in that she'd had to do *something* by her children's safety. She didn't feel better in herself. She wished Jimmy was with her. Telling the police about his part in it... She'd been reminded of his care of her; of his strength last night.

But she couldn't shake it out of her head – the *image* of him with... Okay, so she didn't know what Cait looked like. Instead, her brain had invented an 'older' Emma to take her place, and just as with the car accident, her mind ran wild, her imagined visions probably far more salacious than the reality had been.

Except you know what he's like in bed now. So they're probably pretty accurate.

Her mum was no longer with her. She'd gone straight to the police station after seeing David, but they'd agreed her mum should take her car, and drive the kids home to sort out their lunch. She didn't really want them hanging around the police station anyway, or asking questions about her visit. She'd told her she'd catch the bus back.

Instead, she found herself walking towards the beach – a good half an hour from the town – but her shoes were now dry, and the sun was out.

She bought a sandwich from the corner shop along the way, and finally sat down along the half-busy promenade, and watched the families on the beach. A couple of surfers were paddling further out to sea. Even though she knew he was at his shop and not here, she quickly scanned the beach for Jimmy, and still managed to feel disappointed when she didn't find him.

The Boat Shop was ten minutes to the east, along the beach. *Go and visit. Go and say, hi.*

But she hadn't contacted him, and he hadn't contacted her...

When she'd finished her sandwich, she opened the much larger rucksack she was now carrying – borrowed from her dad – and pulled the jam jar out. The red envelope teased her. Should she read it now?

Her phone rang.

She dove into her bag to grab it, hopeful. The disappointment increased tenfold when Jimmy's name wasn't the one to appear on the screen.

JAMIE

Little brother was still nice to talk to. "Hey, squirt," she answered.

"Hey, crone."

She laughed, and it felt good to hear his voice. They'd spent nowhere near enough time together before he'd sped away to London. "When are you coming home?"

"Soon, I promise. Straight after the funeral."

"How are you both?"

"Merri's doing okay, considering. I'm job hunting in my spare time. How was the barbecue the other day?"

"It was fun. The kids loved it."

"And you – did you love it?"

"Do I sound like I didn't?"

He chuckled. "No, it's just that whenever I ask you how something was, you always reply telling me how your *kids* found it."

"I do?"

"Every time. And I kind of phoned to find out how *you* are."

She smirked, getting the picture. "Mum told you about the truck driver stalking me."

"Got the call from her an hour ago."

"I'm surprised it took this long."

"She's worried about you."

"I know. She was with me all morning, and I'm positive it was to make sure I went to the police station so she could put her mind at rest."

"You told them, then?"

"Yeah, not that they can really do anything – the guy didn't do anything illegal – but I reported it anyway."

"Good. No one should be following you." There was a pause. "She told me Jimmy came to the rescue."

She rolled her eyes. "He did."

Another pause.

She let it linger. No way was she going into any detail

about Jimmy with her brother. But... "Jamie, can I ask you something?"

"Of course."

"Merri's ex-fiancé – he's like, super-rich, or something, right?"

He grunted, not sounding too pleased. "Try millionaire."

"What would you do if you found out she'd *only* been with him for the money?"

"What?" he asked, incredulously. "She's got her own money."

"Jamie, this is hypothetical, just play along. What if you found out he was like some kind of Sugar Daddy to Merri, and she'd been, you know, with him sexually because he paid her for it. Because she'd have no money otherwise. And they've been doing this for years."

"Are you on drugs?"

"*Hypothetical*, Jamie. Jesus, you're really shit at this game."

She heard him let out a breath. "Okay, fine ... well, I dunno. What does she need the money for?"

"What?" she snapped. "She's having all the sex with this guy for cash, and that's seriously the first thought that comes into your head?"

"Well, yeah. I don't think most people do that kind of thing for the fun of it. It's 'cause they need the money. So, what does she need the money for?"

"Maybe ... okay, maybe she had known her mum was ill with the tumour, and she was using it to pay for her medical care."

"And this is happening at the point I meet her again? Like, at that point when she climbed down that tree?"

"Yeah, but when she saw you and realised you were the one she loved and wanted to be with, she ended the whole

Sugar Daddy thing."

"Even if it means she goes broke, and her mum doesn't get the medical care she needs, and might even die because of it?"

Her voice stuck. Hearing it put like that... "Yeah," she forced out, suddenly feeling kinda shitty.

"Wow ... that's some sacrifice. It's sort of like a sacrifice on *top* of a sacrifice."

"What do you mean?"

"I mean that it's got to be a sacrifice in the first place, right? To give yourself, and your body like that? Despite needing the money, she must have had to make sacrifices along the way – a committed relationship with anyone else, for example. No loving boyfriends for her, unless they're *really* understanding, or else she'd be a liar. And does it affect her job? I mean, Merri and her ex worked together. Could be awkward. Anyway, where did I get to? Oh, yeah, okay – she gives it all up because she loves me. To give up the whole arrangement she'd sacrificed those things for – for *me* – knowing what she'd lose if she did, and in this case, what her *mum* might lose if she did ... that's another sacrifice, *on top* of the first. I wouldn't imagine she'd have made any of those decisions lightly. "

Her hand was cramping, she was holding the phone so tight.

"I dunno – maybe I'm over-thinking it... Pip? You there?"

"Yeah," she whispered.

"Am I over-thinking it, or am I getting it? Or am I still just shit at this game?"

"I have to go."

"What?"

"I made a mistake. I need to fix something."

"Wait, I wanted to—"

"I'll call you later. 'Bye." She hung up, flung everything back into her bag, kicked her shoes off, and gathering them in one hand with the rucksack over her shoulder, she rushed down the beach, heading east, as fast as she could.

That wasn't Jimmy behind the till. Where the fuck was Jimmy?

The shop assistant looked up at her, then cocked her head to one side as if trying to figure her out. She probably looked a little manic, but Jimmy wasn't here, and there it was – that pounding sense of urgency that told her she was on the verge of losing something very important. "Hi, is Jimmy in?"

"No, sorry. Can I help?"

Damn it! "He *said* he was going to be in."

"Er ... sorry. He was. He phoned me to cover."

Okay, she was acting kind of crazy. She reined herself in. "Do you know where he went?"

The girl regarded her suspiciously. "He took his surfboard with him, so I'm guessing the beach. I can take a message for you and let him know you stopped by." That was more like an instruction than a question.

"I think I know which beach. It's okay, I'm a friend – I've known him for years."

The girl shrugged, seemingly deciding it didn't matter anymore. "At least you're not that insane witchy woman who stole his poem."

Pippa stopped in her tracks. "The who?" *Don't tell me there are* more *women in his life?*

She waved her comment away. "Never mind. It's my issue. I've lost this favourite poem of his written on some scrap piece of paper, and I'm too chicken to tell him, so I'm trying to remember the words, so I can write it down for him again before I say anything. Ease the trauma, you know? It was only three or four lines, but I'm drawing a blank."

Had she entered the twilight zone? "Jimmy has a favourite poem?" He hardly struck her as the literary type, and that wasn't her being mean – she'd just never seen him with a book in all the years she'd known him. He was more the outdoor 'doing' type.

"Yep. He said he found it in the alleyway outside. I can only remember the first bit: 'Once times thrice, unbind thy heart...' and that's all I got."

No. Way.

No. Fucking. Way.

"So ... did you want me to tell him you stopped by, or are you going to—"

"Thine."

"Pardon?"

"'Thine heart', not 'thy'."

She practically squealed. "Oh, my god! You know it? What is it? Shakespeare? No – it's Byron, isn't it? You have *saved* my *life*. Do you know the rest? Please tell me you know the rest."

She gulped. This was too fucking freaky.

And also ... not. It made perfect sense. Just like finding David's red envelope in the jar. "He found it in the alleyway?"

"That's what he said. It's on this piece of paper that's all burnt or something, and he was all like, *worshipping* it, like it's the holy grail, or something. So ... do you know the rest?" She looked at her, hopefully.

The breeze chimed the bell above the shop door.

"Once times thrice, unbind thine heart from mine..."

The girl wrote it down fast as she spoke.

"...so we may finally..."

The shop assistant did a little dance, and giggled. "This is it – this is it!" She looked up at her when she stopped talking. "Is that the end? Is there a last word? What's the last word?"

She couldn't remember.

She actually *couldn't* remember.

It didn't matter. She said the word that sounded right. "Start."

The shop bell went nuts. The display stand of scarves went over as a gigantic gust of wind caught the free-flowing cotton and silks.

"Oh, *shit*," said the girl, running to grab it.

Pippa looked out the door. "Listen – thanks. If Jimmy comes back, can you tell him Pippa's looking for him; that Pippa's an idiot and she's sorry; that Pippa needs to see him right now."

She raised both eyebrows at her as she eased the stand up. "Oookay ... you know I could just—"

"Thank you!" She ran out the shop, towards the little cove she and Jimmy were at yesterday. She could get to it from this beach if the tide was out, which it was. She just had to walk over the rocks along the shore that formed part of the seabed when the tide was in.

Guess you're getting your shoes wet again.

The bottom of her dress was also wet by the time she

reached the cove. The tide was still going out. She looked out to sea, trying to spot surfers, and had a crushing sense she'd gotten it wrong – this was the wrong beach.

"Theeeere she is."

She spun around, and there *he* was, right behind her. "Jimmy." He was wet out of the water. God, he looked... *Like you're never going to let him go again.* "You knew I was coming?"

He cleared his throat, a twinkle in his eyes, then she spied the mobile phone in his hand. He waved it at her, then read from the screen. "Pippa's looking for you. Pippa's an idiot and she's sorry. Pippa needs to see you right now." He glanced up at her.

She went beetroot. "Right. She texted you. 'Cause ... she can do that."

He grinned. "She can."

There they stood.

He didn't say anything, and words caught in her throat.

She took a step towards him, then another.

He waited, studying her, then finally ... "What are you doing here, Pip?"

Speaking was hard. "Making a choice. I've given you the run-around, and I'm sorry – I really am. But I know what I want now."

"And what's that?" he asked. His tone didn't give much away; his face looked stony. Hell, she hadn't considered he might not take her back until now. She'd already hurt him twice in under twenty-four hours – she couldn't blame him if he turned her down. Jamie was right, he'd be losing so much to be with her – a free lifestyle, and a hell of a monthly wage, no matter how he earned it; the care his grandmother needed; potentially his job...

She was bringing 'baggage' into this, too. But she

couldn't do 'open', no matter how complicated her own history. She almost turned around and ran right back the way she'd come. *Run again, and you'll keep running – then what?* "I want to do this. With you. I want an 'us' – at least to try at 'us', because I like you a hell of a lot. Because you look damn good both in and out of Speedos," she smiled.

He didn't. Didn't even blink.

Shit. Her smile faded. She could no longer hold his gaze. She looked down, but took a breath in and another step forward so she was right in front of him, no more than an inch between them, then forced herself to meet his eyes once more.

Last time – third time lucky. "Because yesterday, you put Liam first when you didn't have to. Because being with you last night..." She ignored the heat rising to her face. "I didn't think I'd get to feel that way again with anyone. I can't promise where it will lead, and it might not be easy – you said it yourself: we've both got pasts that can come back to haunt us. But maybe ... if we face it together, we can scare the ghosts away. *Just* us, though – no Emmas and no Caits. If..."

His expression was completely unreadable.

It's too difficult; you're too late. "If you still want me, that is."

He stared at her. And stared. His eyes didn't leave her face, until he blinked, and a sneaky tear fell from under his lashes. "*If* I still want you? *If?*"

One step, and his hands were in her hair, his lips against hers.

For a moment, she was stunned, caught off-guard; then, she let herself fall in to him, sighing into his kiss, and the promise of a new start. *Just* a promise – that was all either of them had – but it was enough. Every question, every trace of doubt, faded from her mind. There was only his kiss.

And the right choice.

XXI
Legacy

11th June, 2005

Dear Pippa,

I know, I know ... you didn't want me to write this,
but I had to. I did. I don't know about you, but the
new life you're carrying – this baby that's ours – it's
done something to me. We were immortal, did you
know that? Did you feel it like me? We had the
world at our feet and we were going to live forever.
Then came life – growing inside you – and I became
mortal.

The world is still at our feet, but we're now
passing it on. Our children will be the immortal ones
– no longer I.

I speak for myself, of course. You might always
be the goddess you are.

I had to write this, because I now feel ... transi-
ent. I won't last forever, but our legacy will.
Everything we teach will last well beyond the confines of time. So, I wanted to say, in black and
white, so there is no doubt, that if anything were to
ever happen to me – if I am buried under the ground

at the time of you reading this, or otherwise indis-
posed – if I cannot be with you, please be free.
Please be happy. Please follow love into the future
because the past is done. Because what we do now –
right now – is what we leave behind, so always be
happy NOW. Be free NOW. Love NOW.

That's what I'd like to leave behind for our kids
– more than climbing great mountains, more than all
our goals and wishes – I want to teach that immortality exists, but only in a single second. So, the key
to immortality, is to BE in each single second.

Have I discovered the meaning of life? Haha! If
so, please pass it on.

I love you, Pip. And I'm going to love you more
when our new baby is born.

And more after that,
and more after that,
and more after that.

Don't be mad I left this in our jar. It's because I love
you, and us, and all the future kids we're going to
have.

Big Daddy hugs,

David xxxx

Epilogue

Candy hadn't felt this content in a while. At least, it was as content as she could be sitting in a hospital ward, waiting for her girlfriend to be discharged.

Tim had been wonderful last night, and while they hadn't quite *made* love, they'd *shared* love – all night – and that was more than they'd done in a while, and he showed no signs of backing out, or withdrawing as he had previously. He was *with* her.

She found herself smiling as she waited for him to finish his conversation with the doctor. She should be listening to it too, but she wanted to see Lauren the minute she woke up, she'd missed her so much, and they'd said a few minutes ago she was stirring, so here she was, parked outside her ward – waiting.

She looked at the window at the end of the corridor. Its blinds were down, and what a shame, because it was such a sunny day. Surely everyone in here could do with some sunshine.

Reaching into her bag for her bottle of water, her fingers grazed something soft. She pulled a face. It was that organza bag with those tumblestones in. With everything that had happened, she hadn't had a chance to take it out yet. She looked around the waiting area for a bin, but couldn't see one.

She took a sip from the bottle, then put it back in her bag and pulled out the spell instead, only she pulled it out with the back facing her, and ... *Oh, crap!* There was a name and number on it, belonging to some accountant. Jimmy's accountant?

Shit, this was bad. She'd *stolen* the spell, and Jimmy probably needed this number. Damn. She shoved it back in her bag, feeling guilty. *Typical – see? This is what happens if you take stuff that isn't yours.* Although, technically, it was Merri's.

The nurse approached her, and she stood, thinking she was coming to tell her about Lauren, but nope – she walked right on by, and Candy sat back down trying not to look stupid.

"Hi, again." Ice machine woman approached her instead, and sat in the spare seat next to her. "We must stop bumping into each other like this."

"Indeed, we must."

She laughed. "Don't worry – you're safe. We've just been dismissed, so hopefully, that's that. At least for a while."

"Congratulations. We're still hoping to hear."

"The waiting is horrible, isn't it? Do what I do – bring your work."

"No, thanks!"

She smiled.

"What's your job?"

"Boring stuff – book keeping – but it's a damn sight better than *waiting.*"

Candy laughed. "By the way, I'm Candace. Thought it was about time I introduced myself."

She took her hand, shaking it. "I'm Rachel, pleased to meet you."

Then, the nurse *did* approach them, but not for her.

"Miss Collins? Everything's signed – you're all set to go."

"Great, thank you." She turned back to Candy. "That's me done. I'm gonna help my ex get our son home, then I think a large glass of wine is called for."

"I don't blame you – have a great night."

"Thanks, you too." She patted her on the thigh as she rose, and left.

Candy gulped – didn't *mean* to think of how warm her hand felt through her jeans, but couldn't help it.

And then, she frowned. Something pressed on her mind, but she couldn't put her finger on what. She watched Rachel talking to a woman she assumed was her ex, and that must be their son with them.

Her eyes widened. An internal bell went off.

Opening her bag, she pulled the spell back out, and turned it around.

Rachel Collins
accountant
07957 234890

She looked back up, wondering if she should ask if this was her...

Too late.

She'd gone.

Author's Note

This was a hard book to write. Pippa's pain was prominent in me throughout, as was Candy's, and even as I wrote, I knew that – despite the thread of 'magic' running through this series – her story couldn't be solved overnight. A 'quick' fix doesn't exist for her. There's history there that can't just be wiped. But there is hope – there is always hope.

With *Once Times Thrice* I wanted to create a series that was very, very real, even with the magic spells present – no magical "happy ever afters", but the hope of new beginnings; of promises; of abundance yet to come. The same kind of hope you feel when looking out to the horizon across the sea on a sunny day. The same kind of promise a dawn or a sunset brings over the expanse of the ocean.

If I were to have one wish for this series, it's that every book in it, when read by readers, leaves one feeling that sense of hope in their own lives, and about their own lives. At any moment, we have the power to make a choice and change tomorrow. That's the seat of true magic.

Dianna
June, 2016

A list of my other books and series, including buy links, can be found on my website, here:
http://www.diannahardy.com/books.html

Also by Dianna Hardy

Broken Lights

A gritty and suspenseful contemporary romance.

Norman Smithson is at the end of the line. His wife left him, women don't look at him, he was made redundant, and at forty, he could be just that little bit slimmer. He would be a has-been if he'd ever been a 'was' in the first place. He's not the Alpha male of the 21st century – or of any century. He was the chubby oddball who used to sit silently at the back of the class so he wouldn't get picked on.

Rosa is a dreadlocked, tattooed and pierced twenty-some-thing, who uses her image as armour to keep everyone away from every broken thing about her. But her past is about to catch up with her ... at the exact moment Norman finds himself in completely the wrong place, at the worst possible time.

One gunshot, one scramble for life, one unlikely couple, one very long night ... can one damaged woman and one ordin-ary man, find the extraordinary in the very last second they're given?

Broken Lights is a standalone story of what's really worth fighting for when one second is all you have left.

Please enjoy an excerpt from *Broken Lights:*

CHAPTER ONE

"If there was anything we could do to change the circumstances, then of course we would, but as it stands, we need to move forward and up. Especially up. The world has altered so much in the twenty years since you've been here, and the internet has been nothing short of a revolution. Dynamism is the new keyword. Or should I say, 'hashtag'."

Mr Bill Christead – or Mr Craphead, as Norman liked to think of him – laughed out loud at his own joke, tossing his head so far back in his chair that his two mercury fillings could easily be seen.

Norman gripped the black, plastic arms of his office chair, wishing his palms weren't sweaty, and prayed there wouldn't be two wet print marks left behind when he removed them. Like now. He placed his hands on his thighs instead and wiped them on his trousers in what he hoped was a discreet fashion. He could do with not being so shit at this whole confrontation thing, but the reason he worked behind a damn desk was *because* he was awful at the whole confrontation thing.

His heart hammered a mile a minute. "Mr ... erm..." *Craphead, Craphead, Craphead...* "Christead – I'm not sure I understand correctly. I'm proficient at using most aspects of various computer software, as well as the internet, and my knowledge of the company's database is ... well, I was here before it was set up so I know all the—"

"Dynamism, Norman." And then Craphead stared at him as if waiting for him to say something.

Norman blinked, pursed his lips in compliance with the expectation that he *should* say something, although he had no idea what, and then darted his eyes around the large office he'd never made it into despite twenty years of excellent productivity, not a single day in late, with almost no sick days at all. It had never bothered him before. He liked his work safe and constant so he could guarantee an income for his family. If that meant predictable, then so be it. Predictable wasn't a bad word if it put quality food on the table, paid for five star, luxury holidays and gave his two daughters the upbringing they deserved. His wife deserved all the pampering he could afford, too, considering the hours he put in, keeping them apart at times. They'd met in high school. They'd been each other's firsts – first and *only* – and she'd seen him at his worst. She was everything to him.

Norman's eyes landed back on his superior—*what is he? Twenty-five?*—his lips still shaped into the unknown word that never left them. He must have looked as confused as he felt.

Craphead let out a long, heavy, slow sigh. The kind that demonstrated he was talking to an idiot. "You don't have it."

"Oh. Have ... you mean ... er – have what?"

Craphead frowned, but spoke patiently. "Dynamism."

"Oh."

Pause.

Now, Craphead's eyebrows rose as if he'd just had his point proven.

Norman's mouth felt dry, even though his hands were still clammy. What a strange physiological function that meant water could drain from where you needed it the most – leaving you parched – and travel, instead, to a most inconvenient part of your body.

How dynamic did he have to be behind a desk?

His gaze fell on his feet, encased in polished black shoes, which turned inwards, just a little, towards each other.

"Since the takeover two months ago, we've been asked to make sure all staff are competent in all areas of communication – with people; face to face and all that – essential for a company that will be moving more into the PR side of things. We've also been asked to reduce the number of employees and double up some of the job descriptions. With regards to databases, our new computers can deal with all the inputting and outputting, and … whatever else is done, after all, they're just numbers. They follow a formula."

Just numbers.

"But someone's got to input all the numbers and commands in the first place," said Norman, his tone rising as if in surprise, but really, he was just trying not to go to where his brain wanted to take him – to that deflating word no one in their forties wanted to hear.

"And you *have* input them, Norman."

Longer pause.

Craphead sighed again. "*Aallh*righty, I've been trying to ease you into this gently, but I'm just going to say it now: we're letting you go."

Redundancy.

He'd known it. He'd turned forty just five days ago. He'd known it was some kind of cursed number for him, because his father had died of a heart attack at the age of forty. 'Forty' had always been stuck in his mind like a leech, draining life, ever since he was eleven years old.

"You'll receive a statutory redundancy payment of course."

Only statutory?

"At twenty full years of service, we've calculated it to be the full amount, I think…" He rummaged through a couple of papers. "Thirteen thousand, nine hundred and twenty pounds."

Under fifteen thousand pounds? Jesus Christ, that didn't cover a year's wage – it barely covered three months! Three months to find another job? Who the fuck was going to hire him at forty?

"So," continued his superior, rising from his chair.

"Oh..." Norman stood. His seat creaked at the loss of his weight.

Craphead held out his hand.

Norman stared at it, blankly. Now? *Holy shit! He means NOW.* "Now?"

Mr Christead regarded him with what was obviously faked sympathy. "Well, yes, Norman – may I call you Norman?"

The first tremor of irritation made itself known. He'd been calling him Norman ever since he'd fucking got here eight weeks ago.

"Your redundancy is to commence immediately. Of course, you can take your time cleaning out your desk."

Oh, thank you very bloody much.

"I'm very sorry."

Say something! Stand your ground, demand to speak to the Board of Directors, refuse to leave, state your case, convince them they need to keep you!

Norman took his hand, numbly. "Thank you."

Pussy.

'Thank you?' Did you really just thank him for making you redundant?

Even Craphead seemed to wince at that as he shook his hand. "Oh, wait..."

His eyes widened, and he felt his breath hitch with hope for just half a second. Another fault of the human condition, 'cause he already knew, logically, there was no hope left with regards to his employment.

"Here." Mr Christead shoved an empty cardboard box

towards him that he'd picked up off the floor behind his desk.

Had all this prepared, did you?

Viewing his hand as if it weren't his own, Norman reached out and took the box, and then, like one of those robotic systems that would take his place, he turned and walked out of the room, one foot in front of the other, until, somehow, he'd made it all the way to his desk – the one that had been his work-home for five years. Before that, he'd been at another desk down the hall, and before that, two floors down.

Twenty years.

He'd known his wife for twenty-two.

Still detached, he began to place his belongings into the box, one by one. It should have taken longer. It didn't even take ten minutes.

He looked around at his peers. Most avoided his gaze; some threw him 'I know how you feel' and 'I'm so sorry, but I'm glad it didn't happen to me' looks.

His colleague, Simon, was the one who knew him the best even though he was only twenty-eight – he had been here three years. Those Norman used to work with, way back when he'd started, had all left; sought out new and better positions years ago. Riskier positions.

But Norman had had a baby on the way at the age of twenty-five. He hadn't been willing to risk anything, and it was a decision he'd been happy with. His eldest, Lindsey, was fifteen now, a top student, and about to start her GCSEs at school – a really damn good, independent school.

How the hell are you going to pay for that now?

Simon wasn't in today. He was at a job interview, but Norman was the only one who knew that.

Donning his scarf, coat and gloves to keep the October chill out, he picked up his box and shook away the nonsensical visual of a red carpet rolled across the floor as *My Way* played in his mind on repeat, and walked towards the lift that would take him to the exit.

Six months, he calculated as he pulled into his street. Six months was how long he could afford to keep things going with the money he had in his current account, instant access savings, and his redundancy package.

Even if he were able to go a bit longer, the clincher would come next June when the school fees needed to be paid for the start of the new school year – that would wipe him out. But maybe he'd have found some other form of work by then.

Yes. There are an indefinite number of toilets that need cleaning, my old mate.

Fuck.

He killed the engine right there, where he'd stopped by the side of the road, not wanting to pull into his driveway for some reason. Maybe shame; maybe guilt. *How could you let this happen to your family?*

He exhaled. Tina would understand – of course she would. She was his rock. It wasn't the first time he'd had problems at work, and although those had been minor – nothing like this – she would help him piece everything back together. They'd get through this, after all, they'd gotten through everything else.

He glanced at his box on the passenger seat, then grabbed his wallet from his pocket and opened it to see the photo in the clear window inside. It was one of their two girls at age twelve and nine, both of them smaller, blonde versions of Tina, taken on holiday three years ago. That had been a good holiday; the often talked about two weeks of sunshine, heat and fun, visiting Disneyworld in Florida.

Good job they'd done it already, 'cause it wouldn't be happening again any time soon.

Swallowing all his worry, he grabbed the box, opened his door, and clumsily stumbled out of the driver's side. Placing the box on the roof of the car, he reached in behind his seat to pull out his coat and scarf, and stuck them on the box, not bothering with putting them on since he was thirty steps from home.

One ... two ... three...

He wasn't sure if Tina would be back yet from her part-time job at the opticians. God ... maybe he needed more time to prepare before relaying this kind of bad news.

No. It would be better if she were already home, then he wouldn't have to think about it.

Anxiety swirled in his gut.

Tucking the box under an arm, he got his house key out of his pocket and let himself in. This had been their home for over ten years now – big and wonderful and detached. A four-bedroomed beauty in Richmond, London. As he wiped his feet on the welcome mat, he tried to estimate how much they would save by selling it and downgrading to a three-bed. No way would the girls share a room – they bickered enough as it was.

And it's not like they used the one-hundred-foot garden that much. If they went for a flat, they could get something nearly as spacious in lieu of a garden...

Jesus, Norman, stop thinking of the worst case scenario. You might find another job that pays just as well.

Because everyone was clambering all over each other to hire non-dynamic forty-year-olds.

The muffled sound of something falling came from upstairs.

So, Tina was home after all.

Norman let out a shuddering breath and made his way

up, his still-numb brain trying to piece together the start of the conversation, but nothing came to mind.

Stupid, non-dynamic mind.

"Oooooohhhh."

Norman stopped two steps from the top and glanced up. Had she hurt herself when she'd dropped something?

He was just about to shout her name, when someone else got there first. "Tina! God..."

Someone ... else.

~*~

Poor Norman! But it's all right – he's got one hell of a night in store for him that's going to change everything.

Broken Lights is available in eBook and paperback from all good book retailers.

More Titles by Dianna Hardy

Dark Paranormal Fantasy Romances:

The Witching Pen series
Plus the companion short novel Saving Eve and the bonus short story prequel, Wilted.

Witches, angels, demons, Heaven and Hell all come together in a dizzying story of friendship, love and forgiveness. A titillating mix of paranormal romance and urban fantasy brings you a sensational series you won't forget.

Eye of the Storm series
An international bestselling fantasy series.
Werewolves living in the Surrey Hills come face to face with family secrets, ancient mythology, and monsters – both human and created – that want them extinct. Humorous and highly erotic in places, this is dark paranormal fantasy, not for the faint of heart.

This series is followed by:

After the Storm novelettes
Blood Never Lies (duet novels)

Also, this dark, enchanting novelette:

'Til Death Do Us Part
An Adult Retelling of The Little Mermaid

The day you get married, is supposed to be the happiest day of your life. Dreams are made of such things. But I forgot. I could blame the witch if I wanted to – in fact I did, for quite a while after – but the fault can only lie with me. Being with him made me so happy – so very, very happy – that I chose to forget. I chose amnesia. If I had had any foresight into how my flippant choice would ruin him, I would have saved him the heartbreak. I would have forfeited my knowing him, my own selfishness, lived forever in the pain of unfulfillment, if it meant he could be spared...

When you love someone so much that your heart aches without them in your life, would you give up everything you've ever known to be with them? Would you give up your identity?

This is exactly what Aria did. But her sacrifice comes at a great cost, with startling consequences. With no memory of her previous life, she's forgotten what she really is, and who she's left behind: a jealous, possessive God, who's finally found her and will stop at nothing to keep her heart from ever straying again.

In this dark and erotically passionate retelling of *The Little Mermaid*, can a love founded on humanity stand the passing of time, an angry sea-God, and even death itself?

Poetry:
A Silver Kiss (Vampire Poetry)

About The Author

Dianna Hardy is an international bestselling author of (cross-genre) fantasy fiction, most notable for her dark paranormal fantasy and the raw, intense *Eye of the Storm* series. But her heart-warming *Once Times Thrice* series proves she thrives in the light as much as the dark. Whatever your poison, what she loves most is to bring you stories that are action-packed, fast-paced and not short of heat, with the focus on character development, relationship dynamics, and the plot. She writes full-length novels and short fiction.

She currently lives in South Hampshire, UK with her partner and their daughter, where she writes full-time.

Official site:
www.diannahardy.com

Facebook:
www.facebook.com/authordiannahardy

Twitter:
www.twitter.com/thewitchingpen

www.ingramcontent.com/pod-product-compliance
Lightning Source LLC
Chambersburg PA
CBHW030414180626
46812CB00005B/2002